Root Magic

Eden Royce

WALDEN POND PRESS

An Imprint of HarperCollinsPublishers

Walden Pond Press is an imprint of HarperCollins Publishers.
Walden Pond Press and the skipping stone logo are trademarks
and registered trademarks of Walden Media, LLC.

Library of Congress Control Number: 2020947638
ISBN 978-0-06-289959-0

Typography by Carla Weise
22 23 24 25 26   PC/BRR   10 9 8 7 6 5 4 3 2 1
❖
First paperback edition, 2022

To my ancestors,
including those whose names
I'll never know

When Gullah people die, babies in the family get passed over the coffin so the dead person won't come back from the beyond to take them away.

No one did that today with me and my twin brother, Jay, of course. We were about to turn eleven years old, and that was too old to get passed over the coffin. Instead, me and Jay stood next to Mama and my uncle, Doc Buzzard, in that graveyard, listening to the pastor say lots of good things about Gran. The noonday sun beat down on the back of my neck and beads of sweat dotted my forehead. Heat pressed in on me like an aunt I didn't want to hug. Every so often, a rush of breeze blew in off the ocean and across the marsh. I closed my eyes and let it wash over me, cooling my hot skin.

A huge, deep rectangle was dug into the moist, black dirt, and we all stood around it in a circle. Me, Jay, Mama, and Doc were in the front, and behind us stood other people from the island. Over my shoulder, I saw many of the people who weren't family but came to pay their last respects to Gran standing nearer the shade of the huge evergreen trees lining the cemetery's edges.

Everyone was sad and crying, even those people who weren't related to us. Gran had been the best rootworker for miles around, and she had helped all of them at some point. She could make potions to give folks luck to win a court case or to make their boss less angry. She could create compresses to draw out the poison in snake bites. Some people thought rootwork was from the old school, or even fake, but everyone who knew Gran and Doc knew better. Even the pastor said it was a great loss to the community that Gran was gone. He said it must have given her some peace to hear President Kennedy's speech earlier this summer, on the radio. It called for all people in America, including Negroes, to have equal access to jobs and public school education. While Gran wouldn't be here to see it, she'd left this world knowing that better days were coming.

I looked at all the people here to celebrate Gran's life. But my life felt like a puzzle I didn't know how to put together. On one hand, I missed Gran so much, I wished she would come back and things would return to the way they were before she died. But on the other, I wanted better days. And I knew Mama wanted something better for all of us, something better than . . . well, just about everything that had happened since Daddy left.

Early that morning, Mama wove palmetto leaves into roses for us to wear at the funeral. She tried to show me how to do it, bend and twist and pull the long, flat leaves into the spiral flower shape, but my fingers were too clumsy and I couldn't get the leaves to do what I wanted. She had to take mine away and weave the rose herself. Then she pinned it onto the front of my dress like a piece of jewelry.

Mama was in her best Sunday outfit: a black short-sleeved dress, white gloves, and black patent-leather heels. A wide-brimmed hat covered her black hair, which she had pressed straight with a hot comb off the stove that morning. She was patting the tears off her smooth brown cheeks with a starched white handkerchief. Doc, however, wasn't doing any of that. He just held his good hat in his hand and let the tears run down his face and into his bushy salt-and-pepper beard.

I couldn't cry. I felt so much hurt inside, but it wouldn't come out. Like the time I fell out of the big live oak tree near our house and couldn't breathe. Mama said I just had the wind knocked out of me, and I would feel better soon. I hoped I'd feel better soon about losing Gran. Emptiness opened up in my heart, and I wondered if it would ever be full again. Her stories of Br'er Rabbit's tricks on the other animals always made me laugh. She even told good scary stories, about haints and spirits, creatures that she said roamed around the South Carolina marshes where we lived. Some of those creatures used to be people; others were things that no one understood but everyone knew to stay away from. I loved her stories about boo-hags best. They were night creatures with blue skin that they could remove before slipping under doors and through keyholes. When I trembled, she would hug me tight and tell me she would always keep me safe from them. I hugged her back and told her that I knew they were only stories and not really real.

After the pastor finally finished talking, the pallbearers lowered the wooden coffin with my gran in it into the huge rectangle in the ground. Each one of the family members in turn threw a handful of dirt into the grave after saying goodbye. First Doc, then Mama, then Jay.

"Your turn, Jezebel," Mama whispered, smoothing her hand over and down one of my pigtails. In the heat of late summer, the scent of her bergamot hair pomade was like sweet, sun-hot oranges.

I walked up to the great big hole in the earth and looked inside. Sunlight reflected off the polished wood, almost blinding me. It wasn't only a hole; it was Gran's final resting place. The place I would have to come back to if I wanted to visit her.

In the pocket of my good Sunday dress, the black-and-gray-striped cotton one, I felt for the doll Gran gave me and squeezed it. She'd made it out of crocus, a gunnysack fabric, and used scraps of bright cloth to make a dress and headwrap for her. Then, just before she died, she breathed into the doll and pressed it into my hand. She was too tired to do any more than that before she fell back on the bed. Later, Doc told me that Gran's breathing into the doll gave it some of her spirit, and it would be a way she could be with me even after she was gone.

I named the doll Dinah.

Everyone was waiting for me now, so I crouched down and grabbed a big handful of dirt and sprinkled it onto the coffin. The dirt hitting the box sounded like heavy raindrops falling on the roof of our house. It sounded like an ending.

"Goodbye, Gran," I whispered, sobs clogging my throat. "I miss you already."

Only then did I finally cry. Tears hotter than the air around us ran down my face and neck, wetting the collar of my dress. But I didn't care. These tears were the last things I'd ever be able to give my grandmother, and I wanted her to have all I had.

Once the grave was filled in, we left small gifts on top of it. Jay brought Gran's favorite cup, the one with a tiny chip in the rim from when he dropped it on the floor. I tied a strip of fabric from her apron around the handle, and we set it on the mounded dirt. Mama left a shell, polished smooth from the ocean water running over it. Doc kissed a tiny bottle of some liquid he pulled from his pocket and pressed it into the dirt.

After the repast lunch the people at church made for us, we walked home along the hard-packed dirt path that led from the cemetery all the way to our house. We lived on a Sea Island called Wadmalaw, about twenty miles from Charleston, the biggest city in South Carolina, and our house was right on the water, next to the salt marsh. Our family had a part of those marshlands that was just ours and nobody else's. We'd catch food there, like fish and shrimp and blue crabs. It was also a place for me and Jay to run and play. Our neighbors around us had their own parts of the saltwater inlet too, where they would also go fishing. We all respected each other and would always ask permission before going onto someone else's land to catch food.

I could taste the salty breeze from the ocean on my tongue as we got closer to home. Me and Jay walked side by side, a respectable distance behind Mama and Doc.

"I don't wanna start school again tomorrow," Jay said. "I miss Gran, and I ain't ready for summer to be over—"

"Shh," I replied, pointing at Mama and Doc. We were close enough to hear what they were talking about.

Rootwork.

I knew a little about rootwork from all the time I spent with Gran and Doc after school. Mama was always getting home late ever since she opened her roadside market stall. And on Saturdays, when Mama sold the sweetgrass baskets she made along with our extra vegetables at the stall, me and Jay spent all day with Gran. We helped her pick flowers and roots that she would mix with water and rum to make perfume. Once my hands got steady enough, she even let me help pour the sweet, flowery perfume into little clear glass bottles that Mama would sell at her stall the next day.

Once, last year, I had asked Gran to teach me and Jay some root magic. "You already doing it by helping to make the perfume!" she said. But then she added that we would learn more when the time was right. I pouted while Jay sucked his teeth. But Gran laughed and said she would show us her biscuit recipe instead. Gran made the best biscuits: warm, fluffy dough with a fine layer of crisp butteriness along the edges. All my pouting was gone at the thought of getting to eat those perfect little circles, and Jay's stomach rumbled. Me and Jay raced to get all the ingredients she said she needed while she added wood to our cast-iron stove in the kitchen.

Now, Jay nudged me with his scrawny elbow, bringing me out of the memory. We were almost home.

We turned onto the path that led out to the marsh. Dust still clung to his black shoes as he shuffled his feet along the path. "Don't get your dust on me!" I told him. Most of the time I didn't mind getting dirty. I loved running and playing outside, even sinking my feet into the marsh's pluff mud, which was warm and soft as cake batter. But this was my best dress, and if it got too dirtied up, Mama would tell my head a mess.

"You hear Doc and Mama say root?" he asked.

I nodded. "I couldn't tell what all they were discussing, though."

"Me neither," Jay said.

"*Hice tail*, y'all," Mama called back over her shoulder as she and Doc picked up the pace.

I knew what that meant. It was Gullah for "hurry up." Gullah was a language of English mixed with different West African languages. It's what the people who were forced to be slaves—my foremothers and forefathers—ended up speaking after they were first brought here to the Carolinas hundreds of years ago. It belonged to us. My family still spoke it sometimes, to each other and to other people on the island who knew the language. Mama wanted me and Jay to speak English; she felt it gave us a better chance to do well in school and get a good job later on in life. Gran spoke Gullah a lot. Hearing it just then made me feel closer to her.

Still, Mama's words were sharp. It was her I-mean-business voice, and so me and Jay ran to catch up. We were close enough to home now that I could see Gran and Doc's rootwork shop—now just Doc's shop, I supposed—and our little shotgun house in the distance, and we came alongside the start of our farm and our full, late-summer crops. Our vegetables were ripe and I could smell the scent of tomato leaves. Bees buzzed all around us, bobbing in the thick, steamy air. A few wide-winged butterflies soared over our heads, and I knew they could smell the fresh, green scent of the vines too.

Rows and rows of fat red and orange tomatoes hung on our vines. There were lots of green snap beans, stalks of yellow sweet corn, Sea Island red peas, crookneck squash, benne seeds, and purple okra that looked like fingers reaching for the sky. Just last week we helped Mama plant collard and mustard green seeds and sweet potatoes to harvest later in the fall and into winter. We had eggs from our many chickens all year round. There was even a fig tree—sometimes, Mama had me and Jay pick figs for her to make into jam and sell. Along with rice and seafood from the marsh and ocean around us, the crops we grew and the eggs we collected were what we ate, and also what Mama sold to support us at her stand.

"It's too hot out here to argue," Mama was saying to Doc. "We'll finish this discussion once we get home."

Getting home wouldn't take much longer. As we passed the crops, we came to the rootworking shop. It was a small cabin, with wooden clapboards blasted by the sun and sea salt air until they'd turned grayish brown. The cabin stood all alone by itself on the road to our house, and it was the place Doc did all of his business. Everywhere you looked inside were rows and rows of wooden shelves, and on every shelf was some kind of bottle or jar or basket filled with a liquid or a powder or even whole dried flowers or curls of shaved tree bark. The cabin smelled like a flower shop inside a forest: fresh-turned dirt, sweet spices and pine, surrounded by new blossoms. The customers loved that smell. They would come to buy a potion but would usually end up talking to Doc for a while. Doc gave good advice to the people of our community, and not just about magic or medicine. He had what Gran used to call "good common sense," and people came from all around to ask what he thought about a certain brand of fertilizer, or what he'd heard about a company that was hiring workers.

Doc's advice made me think of Gran, and tears burned my eyes again. Before Gran got sick, she used to be the one everyone in town went to for her opinion. And she was always happy to give it to people in need. She didn't like to take money for it either. But a lot of the local people—called *binyas* in Gullah—were so grateful they brought things anyway. People would come up the path to the house with bags of fresh-caught shrimp or a bushel of snapping blue crabs or a few whiting just off the fishing pole. Gran would give the bag to me and Jay and sit down with her guest at the kitchen table. At the sink, me and Jay would clean the guts out of the fish and take the heads off the shrimp while Gran listened. Once the person was done explaining, Gran then told them what she thought they should do about their problem. Her visitors would always get up and leave happier than when they came. I wanted to be able to do that for people one day.

I was so caught up with what was in my own head that I wasn't looking where I was going, and I ran right smack into the back of Mama. Since Jay was right beside me, he bumped into the back of Doc, and our uncle reached down and placed a hand on Jay's shoulder to stop him from moving around and running up to the house.

"What's going—" I started to ask.

"Hush now," Mama said.

That's when I saw why both Mama and Doc had frozen all of a sudden. A police car was parked right in front of our porch. The red and blue lights on top of the car weren't on, but it still made me nervous. The black-and-white car stood smack-dab in the middle of the path, between us and our house. And on our porch, up the rickety front steps Gran had made Doc fix a few months ago, was a policeman.

Deputy Collins was standing there like he owned the place, hands on his hips, one of them near the gun strapped to his right leg. He had a rail-thin body, but with loose, floppy cheeks like a bloodhound. Sweat stains showed under his arms as he looked down at us. The porch overhang threw deep shadows on his pale face.

Mama's whole body was stiff next to me. Her hand shook as it grabbed mine a little too hard and pulled me behind her. When I looked over at Jay, Doc had a hand on his head, doing the same. Doc's usually sunny, smiling face was blank as a chalkboard. A bead of sweat rolled off my forehead, stinging my eyes, but I didn't dare move to wipe it away. I clutched at Mama's hand and she squeezed it before letting go. She stood up real straight—putting iron in her back, Gran used to call it—and then she stepped forward.

2

"Can we help you with something, Collins?" Mama asked. She was keeping her voice calm, quiet. When she really wanted to yell, me and Jay could hear her across the fields even if she was still inside the house.

"You will show me respect and call me Deputy Collins, Janey Turner." The policeman took his time and looked over each one of us as we stood out in the hot sun and he stood on our porch in the cool shade. "Or you know what'll happen."

I could hear Mama gritting her teeth, but when her voice came out, it sounded polite. I might have been ten years old, but I knew Negroes could get arrested or beaten up for talking back to a white person or for saying a white person lied. Even if it wasn't against the law for a white person to hurt a Negro.

"What can we do for you, Deputy Collins?"

He folded his arms over his bird chest. "You can get over here and open this here door so's I can search this house."

Mama didn't move an inch. "For what reason?" she asked.

Deputy Collins sneered at us. "I don't need no reason, Janey."

He was right. I knew about police barging into local rootworkers' homes. Whispers at church and from the people who came to Mama's stall or Doc's cabin said that Deputy Collins was the worst one of them, that he was looking for reasons to bother rootworkers, even take them away. The Daniels, another rootworking family on the island, got dragged out of their house and away to jail. Nobody had seen them since. Now, people said, it was best to let Collins search. Refusing or asking why would just make the deputy angrier than he already was. And if he got really angry, he might drag Mama and Doc off to jail, leaving me and Jay alone.

Deputy Collins wiped sweat off his face with the back of his hand. "Now come on and open this door before I force it open like I did that junk-filled cabin."

We all turned as one and looked behind us. The

padlock Doc kept on the door of the cabin when he wasn't in his shop had been pried off.

My heart was pounding so hard I could hear the beat in my head. I wanted to tell him to go away, that we weren't bad people, and that we just wanted to be left alone. But I couldn't. I was so scared I just stood there. Stood there in our front yard with the sun burning down on my neck, sweat running down my forehead, my whole body tight as a drum. My skin felt too snug for me and I wanted to jump out of it.

Mama bit her lip, probably to keep her words inside. She marched up to our porch and opened the screen door, then unlocked the front door, then swung it wide to allow Deputy Collins to walk in first, the rest of us behind him.

A blast of hot, sticky air hit me as soon as I walked inside. The house had been closed up since early this morning when we left for the funeral. On an ordinary day, we would open the windows first thing to let the hot air out of the house and let the sweet summer breeze in. We all waited while the deputy went through each one of our rooms in order: our front room, Doc's bedroom, Mama's room, the room I shared with Jay, the washroom, and the kitchen. He looked through everything, opening drawers and dumping the contents on the floor, ignoring Mama's and Doc's pleas for him to not destroy what we had.

"Mama?" I whispered.

"Shhh, Jezebel. It'll be over soon enough."

As Deputy Collins tumbled and fumbled around, he knocked into a small bud vase I had forgotten to take and place on Gran's grave. I wanted to run forward to catch it, but Mama held on to me. I nearly jumped out of my skin when it shattered against the floor. Jay's face was like a rock, but tears were shining in his eyes. And not like the tears we had for Gran. These were tears that came because we couldn't do anything to stop what was happening to us. Not without taking the chance that one of us might get hurt.

Finally, as Mama said it would be, it was over. Deputy Collins came out of the room I shared with Jay. He was breathing hard, but the look in his eyes was even harder.

"People round these parts say you all are some kinda magic witches or something. I don't believe in no witchcraft myself, but I do believe you people are up to no good." Deputy Collins pointed his sweaty finger in Doc's face, and I could see, even under his thick beard, how my uncle's jaw clutch up tight. "I got my eye on you Turners. And I will catch you one of these days."

"Catch us doing what?" Jay muttered under his breath so only I could hear. "Living?"

I pressed my lips together to keep from answering him. No one else said anything either, and the quiet stretched like a rubber band, long and quivering. Finally, it was Mama who broke it.

"I need to clean my house now. Good day, Deputy Collins."

The deputy looked like he wanted to say something else, but he didn't. Instead, he stomped toward the front door, shoving over one of the kitchen chairs around our table as he went. Then he pushed the screen door open with his shoulder, letting it slam shut behind him. A moment later, we heard the engine of the police car scream to life and tires skidding in the dirt, scaring our chickens into a bunch of squawking.

When all was quiet, Mama collapsed into a chair. Her breathing was fast, like she'd been running. I picked up the chair Deputy Collins had pushed over, brought it next to her, and sat down. Doc took a pitcher out of the icebox and splashed some cold sweet tea in a juice glass for her.

"You okay, Mama?" I asked. She looked tired and her hand shook as she drank the tea.

Doc poured some for me and Jay too, then for himself. He eased himself into a chair across from Mama with a serious look on his face.

"Janey," Doc said. "What happened with Collins is even more reason for you to let me teach the kids some root. We need to get them started on helping to protect ourselves and this place."

"I thought rootwork was just, you know, luck potions and healing medicine." I held Mama's hand but looked at

Doc. "Like that stuff you make when my tummy hurts."

"Healing is part of it." Doc took a long drink from his glass and wiped the sweat from his forehead with a clean, white fingertip towel. "It's a service we provide because Negroes can't go to hospitals around here. They won't let us in, even if we're sick or hurt. So healing is an important part of rootwork."

"But it isn't the only part?" I asked.

"It sure isn't!" Mama snapped. Her black patent-leather clutch bag lay on the table, and she was smacking it, in quick motions, with the cardboard church fan she got earlier. It sounded like a tree branch hitting the house in a storm.

"Janey," Doc sighed while Mama grumbled to herself.

"What are you talking about?" I whispered, wondering if root was secret and I shouldn't talk about it too loud.

"The sort of things you've seen me and your gran doing since you were young, that's only part of what working the roots is about," Doc said. "But your gran always said that as soon as she was gone, it was time for you both to learn about the rest. About protection. About making the lives of people you love better." Doc rubbed Jay's head with the palm of his hand.

My socks were slipping down into my buckled Mary Jane shoes. They were dusty from the road, and the dirt made my skin itch. I pulled them up anyway. "Protection from what?"

Doc thought a moment. "Bad people and angry spirits."

Jay said, "White people?"

"Well, sometimes, yes," Doc answered with a small nod. Mama shot him a look, but he didn't notice and kept on talking. "But there are plenty of Negroes who believe what we do ain't right either. That it ain't godly. So we get a hard time from both sides."

"Then why do it at all?" I wondered out loud.

This time, Doc did look to Mama. "Go on, then," she said after a moment. "You started this; it's not like I can keep you from finishing."

Doc nodded. "It's part of our history," he said. "If someone doesn't teach it, if someone doesn't learn it, the magic will eventually disappear. You know those trickster stories of Br'er Rabbit and Br'er Bear your gran used to tell? They connect us to our roots in Africa. And working the roots, our ways to protect ourselves and to get rid of spirits, they do the same thing. Even what we did today, to say goodbye to your gran." Doc rubbed his hand against his beard. "All of that is what makes us Gullah Geechee people who we are. If no one tells the stories anymore, if no one learns the magic anymore, our ways will disappear from the world. Then all we'll have is what other people think of us." He bent his head to look both me and Jay in the eyes. "And how important is what other people think of us?"

Me and Jay answered together: "Not as important as

what *we* think of us."

"You're both going to have to remember that when we start learning root magic."

"But you talking about mixing potions and powders and stuff, right?" Jay asked. "It ain't *real* magic, is it?"

Doc leaned back in his chair, rocking it on two legs. "It's real as you believe it is."

Me and Jay shared a look. That sounded like the sort of thing grown-ups said in the storybooks we read when we were little. Folks called rootwork "magic," but all I ever saw Gran and Doc do was sell medicines to people who came to our farm for help: powders wrapped in waxed paper for headaches; a yellow cream for mosquito bites and bee stings that smelled like fresh-cut grass; a clear, thin liquid to mix with warm water for tummy aches. The tummy medicine tasted like liquid candy canes without sugar, but it worked. I guess making people feel better was a kind of magic, but the way Doc was talking about it . . . I wasn't so sure.

Maybe Doc knew what we were thinking, because he said, "We're getting ahead of ourselves. As I was saying, your gran really wanted you to learn rootwork, and now that she's gone, I'll need more help to protect our land and all of you." He straightened up again. "That is, if I can get my sister's permission."

With that, he looked at Mama. Mama, though, chewed at her lip and didn't speak. She was thinking, considering her brother's words.

"Janey," Doc said to Mama, "you know things are happening around these kids. They need to be able to protect themselves."

"I know no such thing. They're ten years old!"

I piped up. "We're almost eleven."

"Yeah, day after tomorrow," Jay said. He found a loose string on his shirt and pulled at it. Mama gave him *the look* and he wrapped his hands around his glass instead.

She sighed. "They shouldn't even have to think about this business yet. They should be busy being kids! I don't like it one little bit."

Doc pushed his fingers through his coily hair. "I know that's how you feel. But this is the world we live in. And these kids were born into it. That's a fact we all had to deal with—you, me, even Danny when he was here."

Jay nudged me in the ribs again. I managed to hide my grunt from his sharp elbow. I'd heard Daddy's name as well as he did, but I wanted to make sure I didn't miss a word of their conversation.

"I know that!" Mama said. She fanned herself now, and lifted her damp hair off her neck. Then, quieter, she said, "I know. Before Danny disappeared . . . oh, forget it. They're my children and I want them safe."

Doc nodded, then got up from the table and opened the window. A cool afternoon wind blew in, cutting through the oven-hot kitchen. "Then let me teach them."

Even though the sun had moved from overhead, sweat still beaded on my forehead, then rolled down my face on the same path my tears did earlier. Even Jay, who usually fooled around, running and ripping, only shuffled his feet along the floor, waiting.

Finally when Mama did talk, she took a deep, shaky breath first. "Lynchings, beatings, and more than half the time, the police are right there when it happens. Or they're the ones doing it. How are we supposed to live in this world and be safe?" Her eyes were wet and shiny. "Is root gonna protect Jez and Jay from what's out there? Brick powder and goofer dust don't stop the police. I'd rather deal with haints and hags."

While we waited for Doc's response, the sounds of summer drifted in through the window and the front door. Wind rustled the trees and the chickens clucked for their afternoon meal. Jay hated being quiet, so of course he found something to say.

"We'll be careful, Mama."

"I know you will." She gave Jay a sideways look over her shoulder. "Well, as much as you can be."

"You're never careful," I said, laughing. Jay stuck his tongue out at me. My brother ran headlong into everything, and I usually had to be the one to get him out again.

"Go change out of your good clothes, you two."

I suspected Mama and Doc needed to talk among themselves anyway, so me and Jay ran back to our room. I grabbed my soft blue denim dress and headed for the bathroom. I ran water in the sink and washed my hands, face, and neck. I took off my white ankle socks and placed my feet on the side of the cold metal tub while I washed them too. Once I buttoned up my play dress, I left my good one in the laundry basket.

When I came out, Jay was coming out of our room. We headed back to the kitchen, where Mama was cleaning up the mess Collins had made

"I don't want my kids in danger," Mama was still saying. "With Collins sniffing around . . . I don't want to lose anyone else. My heart can't take it."

"They're living in this world, ain't they? So they're already in danger." Doc put his hand gently over Mama's. "I'm just trying to give them a fighting chance. Our mama taught me how to protect this family. Let me teach them. Rootwork is part of who we are."

"Of course it is! But I want them to have better chances in life." Mama glanced over at me and Jay. "Go to school, get good jobs, have a bright future."

Doc nodded. "No reason they can't do both." He gave me and Jay a solid look as we sat across the table from him, where he'd refilled our glasses. "That is, if you think you can keep up with your schoolwork *and* learn to work root."

"Yes!" me and Jay yelled at the same time. I bounced in my seat. The more I thought about it, the more excited I was. If Gran wanted me to learn how to be a healer and make medicines and potions, then now that she was gone, that's exactly what I was going to do. I wanted to learn to be just like her and help our family and our community stay safe and healthy and happy. The thought of doing something Gran had wanted made the empty place inside me fill up a little.

"Now remember, Jezebel. Jay won't be in your class anymore." Mama tapped her first finger against her lips like she did when she was thinking. The school had spoken with her last year about moving me straight to sixth grade after Jay and I both finished fourth, and she thought it was a good idea. "Are you sure you can keep up with all of that on your own?"

"Yes, Mama. I'm sure I can."

"Jez is a smarty-pants," Jay said. It was my turn to stick my tongue out at him. Part of me was excited for the first day of school. But a big part of me didn't want to go at all. I never made any friends there. The local girls whispered when I walked past, and once or twice I heard the word "root." They said it like it was a bad thing, even though I knew some of their families came to buy medicines from Doc. They weren't mean out in the open; they just didn't include me at lunch or in games at recess. It never used to bother me too much, because Gran was always there for me when I got home. When I told her about those kids, she'd say, "Study your schoolwork, Jezebel, not chirren that don't know what they're talking about. People tend to be scared of what they don't understand, even if they need your help from time to time." She said I'd have to get used to it if I was going to learn to work the roots.

But now, she was gone. She was my best friend as well as my gran, and I'd lost both.

"I'll be fine," I told Mama now, twisting the end of one of my pigtails. "It'll help me feel closer to Gran. I miss her."

She kissed my forehead. "I know. I do too."

"So what do you say, Janey?" Doc asked. He was smiling like he already knew the answer.

Mama looked at Doc long and hard, like she was searching inside him for answers. Then she took a deep breath and blew it out. She put two huge pots on the stove, then tumbled a big bag of plump figs into one and ripe tomatoes into the other. She filled both pots with water, and I knew we would be helping her pack jars of her fig preserves and tomato jam for the market tomorrow.

Jay never had any patience. "So is that a yes, Mama?"

"It's a yes."

Me and Jay whooped and threw our hands in the air.

Doc smiled but said, "When we start lessons, no more playing around. You'll have to listen close to what I tell you. There's a lot to learn."

"Hopefully you'll be as excited about doing your schoolwork," Mama said. "Now hand me that sugar dish,

Jez. And Jay, get me a lemon."

As I got up to get the sugar, I saw Mama fix Doc with a serious, hard look. She poked him with her wooden spoon. "Take care of my kids, you hear?"

I went over and hugged her, laying my head against her tummy. She hugged me back, really tight, but I didn't mind at all.

"Be careful, Jezebel," she whispered into my hair. Her breath was warm and soft, and she smelled like baby powder and sunshine.

She let me go, kissed me on the head. Then she yanked her apron with the pink and red roses on it off the nail on the kitchen wall, put it on over her head, and tied it around her waist.

Doc rubbed his beard thoughtfully. "Plenty of light left today. How long before dinner?"

"Couple hours. I need to make jam for the market tomorrow first." Mama pooched her lips out. "You fixin' to start lessons now?"

"No time is better." When Doc scraped his chair back from the table, I gulped the rest of my tea.

"Jezebel!" Mama scolded. "Drink slowly or you'll choke."

"I'm fine, Mama! Come on, Jay!"

Before we did anything else, I ran to our room and grabbed one of my composition notebooks. When Jay and I got outside, Doc was stacking heavy boxes of empty jam jars as well as the crates he and Mama would fill with fresh-picked vegetables and fruit in the morning.

"What's the notebook for, Jez?" he asked.

"For root lessons."

Doc stacked the last box and wiped his forehead. "Ah, I see. That's smart. Rootwork is usually passed along by word of mouth, so writing it down while you learn is a good idea. You'll have it to study on later."

"So what sort of magic are we gonna learn first?" Jay asked, impatient as ever.

"Something simple." Doc motioned for me and Jay to follow him out to his cabin. "I'll show you how to make root bags. These bags can be used to help with almost anything. You can hide them inside the house to give you a peaceful home, or carry one around with you to make you feel safe. You can even use them to wish for something you want or need."

What I wanted most of all was to have Gran back, but I knew nothing could bring people back after they've passed. But maybe I could wish for a new best friend. Someone who didn't care that I was learning rootwork. Someone who liked me anyway.

Doc placed some felt material in a bunch of different colors on his worktable, then gave us each a needle and thread. We cut out rectangles of felt and sewed up the left and right sides. He also gave us string to tie the top closed when we were finished.

"I'm doing green, for money," Jay said.

I chose orange as my bag's color because it stood for change, and it would be a big change for me to have friends my own age. Even one friend would be good.

Then came the fun part. Doc said we could fill the bags with anything we wanted, as long as there was an odd number of things in the bag.

Jay filled his bag with a piece of dried snakeskin he found, a rock polished smooth, and a handful of sunflower seeds. I filled my bag with a dried bay leaf, a shiny new penny, a piece of pecan tree bark, and a handful of salt.

"That's four things," Jay told me, pointing at my bag.

"I know, I can count." Lastly, I wrote the word "friend" on a piece of paper, folded it up tight, and put it in my bag. "Now that's five." I stuck my tongue out at him.

Doc shook his head at us and took his pipe from a drawer in the worktable. "Now, breathe into your bag. This wakes it up and gives it a purpose."

"Purpose?" I asked.

"Yes, Jez. Everything in root needs *intent*. That's a clear idea of what it is you want to get before you even start. Think hard and focus on what you want to happen." Doc filled his pipe with dried peach skin and tobacco leaves.

Jay huffed and puffed into his bag. I took a huge deep breath and blew all the air in my lungs into my bag.

"Which one of us did it right?" Jay asked.

"Both of you. Now tie them up," Doc said. After we

did, Doc gave us a little cologne to drizzle on the root bags. "To feed them," he said.

"Why we gotta feed them?" Jay asked.

"Because they have part of you, your breath, inside them."

"So . . . they're alive?" I said.

I could tell Doc was impressed. "Exactly."

"Gran breathed into Dinah. Does that mean she's alive too?"

"Now you're getting it, Jez," Doc said. "Go on—you have to hide the bags somewhere until they complete their purpose."

Jay poked at his bag. "What purpose?"

Doc put his pipe between his teeth. "Whatever you wanted when you sealed up the bag. Go on and hide them now."

I ran off to our room while Jay ran toward the woods. Part of me was sad to know that we would have to start keeping secrets from each other. But a bigger part of me was excited to know I might finally get a friend. I looked around for anywhere I could hide my root bag so no one would see it. The sun was going down, making long shadows on the floor of the room. They stretched out, reaching into the hallway, toward the front of the house. I imagined that shadow could pass over the whole kitchen, even drift under the floor.

That's it!

I jumped up from the bed and ran outside. After I looked around to make sure nobody saw me, I wriggled under the house toward the tiny hole in the floor me and Jay used to use when we wanted to listen to the grown people talk after they'd told us to go play.

On my side of the hole, there was a crack I usually traced with my fingers while Jay had his turn looking up into the kitchen. I found the crack again, wiggling my first finger inside to see if it would hold the root bag. Then I held the bag in my hands, this little bundle of cloth and bits of things. *A friend, please.* I thought it hard as I could. *Someone to talk to and play with, like Gran.* At that, I thought I might cry again, but I held back.

Even though Doc didn't tell me to, I kissed the bag. With a bit of pushing, I wedged my very first bit of root-work inside the crack tight. I patted the bag, safe from discovery, and crawled out from under the house.

No one was around to see me. I brushed the dirt off and walked inside, my heart beating fast, wondering what would happen next.

3

When the sun broke through the curtains at the window in the room I shared with Jay I was already awake, excited and nervous all at once for the first day of school. We'd be at the same school we always went to, but a new year meant different teachers, different subjects, lots of new things.

Jay didn't care too much about the learning part of it, but he liked school because he got to play ball and dominoes with the other boys at lunchtime. I was the opposite. I loved to learn all the new things and read the books, but that was it.

Mama had let me sleep in rag rollers the night before,

so I had big corkscrew curls instead of my usual pigtails, and she put bobby pins in my hair, crisscrossing two on each side. She also surprised me with a plaid dress she'd made from one of Gran's old ones. It wasn't brand-new, but it was new for me. Wearing something made from one of Gran's dresses was special. I could almost smell the lemon and pine of her favorite soap still on the dress.

"Oh, thank you, thank you!" I hugged her and she squeezed me back.

"You're welcome," she said with a hitch in her voice. "Don't you go getting yourself dirty, now."

"I promise," I replied.

"You know, there will be more new children at your school this year," Mama said.

"Really?" If there would be new kids at school, I figured I'd have a better chance to find a friend. Maybe the root bag was working already.

Mama fluffed my curls. "Remember what Pastor said yesterday, about the new education laws?"

I was so busy saying goodbye to Gran, I only half remembered. But I nodded anyway.

"Well, I heard that a few of the well-off Negro families who used to pay to send their kids to private school will be sending them to yours in support of the new laws. Some good private school teachers are starting to work at your school this year too."

Mama and I went to the kitchen and found Jay was already dressed and waiting at the table. His navy-blue school pants weren't new either, but he wore one of his newest shirts. He'd already gathered eggs from the chicken coop. Mama thanked him—it was then that I realized Gran wasn't here to cook for us in the mornings like she would before school. The radio played the morning news, and we all listened to the announcer man as Mama whipped up breakfast:

Eleven Negro students will integrate Charleston County's white schools today—the third of September, 1963. South Carolina was the only state in the union that had yet to desegregate its schools. White parents are outraged, threatening to remove their children from public schools and place them in private education. Plans to open private schools exclusively for white students have been submitted to the county, and it's believed many will open their doors next year.

In 1954, the US Supreme Court ruled that segregation was unconstitutional in the landmark decision Brown v. Board of Education. This decision made a path for Negro children to be taught alongside white children in the same classrooms. But for nine years, South Carolina has operated as if this law did not exist.

The newsman went on to say that police were being called out to protect the Negro students going to white schools for the first time.

Me and Jay must have looked nervous, because Mama tried to make us feel better.

"Don't worry," she said, stirring a bubbling pot of grits on the stove. "That's going on in Charleston first, not out here where we are."

"Will we get to take a bus to school instead of walking?" Jay asked. He scooped spoonfuls of ambrosia, Mama's fruit salad, into his mouth.

Mama nodded. "It'll be a good thing when it finally does happen, because you kids will get better schooling. Newer books. Teachers with more training. But I swear, I'll worry myself sick."

"Why are they so"—I searched for the word the newsman used—"outraged?"

"A lot of whites think we're lower than they are. Not good enough to share space with them." She sighed. "Since they're planning to open up more private schools, you may not have to deal with the outrage."

Jay scraped the bottom of his bowl of fruit and I squinched my face up at the sound. "Why do they have police there, though?" he asked.

"To protect those children, just in case. Not all police are out to hurt us—some are good people wanting to do what's right. Others will do exactly what they want to, whether it's against the law or not." She let out another heavy breath. "The trick is to figure out which one is which fast enough."

I wanted to get a better education, but the thought of getting on a bus to go even farther away to school was scary. I was glad I didn't have to think about it yet. This year already had plenty of things for me to focus on.

"All right, both of you. Hurry and eat. You can't be late on your first day."

I sat Dinah against the sugar dish and had a hot bowl of grits for breakfast. The thought of what would happen on the first day of school made my stomach wobble. This was the first time I was ever leaving for school without hugging Gran goodbye. Already I missed the feel of her mushy kiss on my forehead. So when I finished, I hugged Dinah tight. It was the closest thing to hugging Gran.

"Wish me luck," I whispered to her, swallowing back the lump in my throat. Dinah's little gunnysack hand was soft against my cheek, and her mouth was in a twisty, wavy line. "I'll be home soon," I told her. Then me and Jay kissed Mama, took our lunches and our books and pencils, and headed out for the walk to school.

A group of fancy-looking girls were watching us as me and Jay came up the long walkway that led to the school. They were wearing pretty dresses and sitting together on one of the low brick walls that ran all around the property. A few of them I recognized from last year; others I didn't know. I smiled at them, but they didn't look at me.

A couple of boys Jay knew called to him. "See you in class!" he said, and made to run off.

"You mean after school," I said. "We're in different grades now."

"Oh, right. Well, after school, then."

I watched him join his friends, watched them slapping each other on the back and laughing. Another lonely place opened up inside me, right alongside the empty space Gran used to fill. Remembering I was supposed to be brave and make a change this year, though, I decided to try talking to the girls. I hugged my notebooks to my chest.

Before I could take more than a few steps, a hard shove from behind sent me stumbling. I caught myself from falling but scraped both my palms and my knee on the brick wall. My notebooks toppled down around me in a scattered pile. The girls laughed, and I felt my face burn.

"Clumsy!"

I looked up to see another girl standing over me. Her eyes flicked over my clothes and face and hair. Then she went and stood with the others. I didn't recognize her; her dress looked brand-new and crisp, and her shoes shone in the sunlight. She must be one of the new girls from the private school Mama talked about.

"You pushed me," I said, brushing the dirt off my hands and ignoring the sting in my palms from where the skin was raw.

"Oh, really? I didn't see you," she said, her two long black braids scraping her chest. "Old-fashioned things bore me."

The other girls laughed again. One of them said, "Nice, Lettie."

I was frozen. Kids at school had called me a teacher's pet before, but I'd never had anyone say anything about my clothes being old-fashioned.

"This isn't old. My mama—mom made it for me."

Why did I say that? It just made them laugh harder. Classes hadn't even started, and this was already a disaster.

Lettie leaned over and sniffed me before I could move away. "It smells like old lady. Did she make that for you out of an old-lady dress?" When I didn't respond, she made a sound like a bird chirping. "Oh my, she did! Was it your grandmother's dress?"

Gran. I had to blink to hold back tears—Lettie would think I was crying because of her, and no way was I going to let that happen.

One of the girls I remembered from last school year whispered in Lettie's ear, and her eyes grew big before they all broke out into giggles. Before I could say anything else, though, the bell rang for class to start. I ran up the stairs and inside, thankful that the clanging drowned out their laughter.

I found my classroom and chose a seat on the end of a row, so I would only have people on three sides of me instead of four. That way, I wouldn't feel so surrounded.

Of course, Lettie and her friends came in not long after I did; I knew I wouldn't be lucky enough to be in a different class from her. As everyone around me talked to their friends about what they did over the summer, I took out my composition book and wrote: *September 3, 1963.*

That's when I felt eyes on me.

I scanned the rest of the room again. Kids were dropping books onto the floor, scraping desk chairs back, but I couldn't figure where this feeling was coming from. Until, finally, I did.

A girl sat in the back of the class, staring at me. She looked a little older than me; the front of her striped dress already showed signs of her growing up. She gave me a tiny smile, so small I wasn't even sure I saw it at first, but it was there. The smile seemed real, so I returned it.

The door to the class opened once more, and a tall, thin, brown-skinned woman walked in. She wore a yellow knit suit with matching buttons and short white cotton gloves. The woman headed straight for the big desk at the front, the heels of her shoes clicking on the tiled floor. She stood there with her hands folded in front of her, and the class got quiet. Even the smiling girl turned her head toward the movement.

"Good morning, class," the woman said, taking off her gloves. Her voice was clear and strong. It rang out, and I was sure even the kids in the back could hear her. "I'm your new teacher, Miss Watson. Let's get started by taking attendance."

Miss Watson started calling our names, and while I knew most of the kids from around the island, I tried to keep up with the new ones as she said them. Lettie's last name was Anderson, so she was one of the first ones called. The smiling girl was Susie Goins. Sooner than I expected, she got to me.

"Jezebel Turner?"

Before I could speak, I heard Lettie's voice sing out. "Cheep, cheep, cheep." Lots of the girls laughed.

The first school day of the year was about three minutes old, and already I wanted to be away from here. Back home with Jay and Doc, learning to work root. Maybe Doc had some sort of potion to keep away the kind of high-post girls who make you feel bad, just for being you. If such a spell existed, I'd learn it.

Raising my hand, I answered, "I'm here."

Miss Watson made a mark in her book.

After we finished taking attendance, Miss Watson talked for a while about what we'd be learning this year in mathematics and language arts, and we had our first lessons in those subjects. I took lots of notes because I didn't want to forget a thing.

Then she moved on to history. That's when she told us about the eleven Negro kids who were going to study with white kids at the white schools for the first time today.

"This is important, class," she said. "One day, this thing happening now will be history. Other children will learn about it in their schools all over the country. You must remember your history. Write it down. Tell it in your own words."

A boy whose name I couldn't remember raised his hand. "Why do we need to write it down? I don't even like history."

A couple of his friends forced out laughs, but they didn't last long.

Miss Watson sat on the edge of her desk and smoothed down her skirt. She answered not like a teacher talking to a student, but like she was talking to another grown-up. "History, Thomas, is the story of who we are. And sometimes, Negro history is told by people who don't think we're important. People who don't think we make a difference in the world." She gazed around the class then, like she was making a point to look at each one of us. "But we do matter. What we think matters. Our voices matter. And our stories matter too much to let someone else tell them. People need to know that."

Miss Watson stood up and opened a drawer in her desk. "Let me share something with you. This is a poem by Langston Hughes, a Negro poet," she said, pulling out a small book. "It's called 'I, Too.' Does anyone know about poetry?"

We all shook our heads. Last year, we learned about novels and short stories and plays. But no poetry. And nothing written by any Negroes.

When Miss Watson read, the whole room was silent. Her voice was soothing, but smooth and strong too. It filled our classroom. I imagined her voice dancing on the air and drifting out of the opened windows to help anyone who needed to hear her. I wondered if her voice was her magic. If it was, she was powerful.

The bell rang, breaking her spell. Miss Watson closed her book. "That's all for now. Time for lunch, everyone."

I put my books in my desk. It was strange not having Jay in class with me. He would have already had lunch by now, and would be outside with his friends having recess. For not the first time that day, I felt really alone. I took my paper bag and headed for the cafeteria. Since I brought my lunch, I didn't have to wait in line for food like some of the other kids.

The tables were mostly empty, and I chose a seat by one of the windows looking out onto the playground. Maybe I could see Jay from where I was sitting. Warm sunlight streamed in the window, and after a moment I closed my eyes to let it fall on my face.

I got that feeling again. Of someone watching me. Heaviness sat on my shoulders and I opened my eyes.

That girl from the back of the classroom—Susie—stood in front of me holding a tray of cafeteria food. She blinked at me twice, really fast, like something was in her eye. Her night-black hair was twisted back in two braids that she had pinned up around her head to look like a crown. She smiled carefully, like she wasn't used to it.

"May I sit here?"

I blinked. "Why?"

Susie tilted her head. "Why what?"

"Sorry, I meant, well . . . why do you want to sit here?" I looked around the cafeteria, which was filling up now. Lettie and her group were sitting in the center of the room, and most of the other kids were sitting closer to her. She was practically the most popular person at school and she hadn't even been here a full day yet.

"I don't like bunches of people." Susie shrugged. "And it's cooler over here by the open window."

That's when I realized I was being rude to someone who hadn't given me a reason to be rude back. "Okay," I said.

"Thanks." Susie sat down in front of me and unfolded her napkin. "We don't have to talk if you don't want to."

"No, um. We can." I had some of Mama's Hoppin'

John, a dish of peas and rice cooked together. It was one of my favorite things to eat. We usually only ate it at New Year's, but Mama had made some special for our first day back at school. "You're new, right?"

Susie nodded.

"So you just moved here?"

She nodded again.

"Sounds like you're the one who doesn't want to talk."

Susie laughed. "Sorry. I don't have lots of friends, so I forget how to act around people sometimes."

This time I nodded. I never knew how to act around people. I took a drink from my thermos of lemonade.

Susie did her strange double blink again. "My family used to live here a long time ago—up by Robinson farm. But we moved away."

I didn't know any Robinsons, but then I didn't know all the people on the island. Some of the farms were really large. "When did you come back?"

"About a week ago."

Another double blink. She placed her sandwich on her napkin and removed the top slice of bread. With her butter knife, she scraped off some of the peanut butter and licked it.

I giggled and Susie's eyes went round, like she'd been caught doing something wrong. "What?"

"Nothing," I said. "I have strange ways of eating things too."

"You do?"

"I eat all the tiny seeds inside the string beans first."

"That *is* weird!" Now she was giggling too. Then she leaned forward and whispered, "You wanna see what I can do?" Before I could answer, Susie ripped her apple in half with her bare hands.

I gasped. "How did you do that?"

She laughed and spread peanut butter on half the apple. "I'll show you if you show me how to write really pretty like that." She pointed to my composition book.

"It's a deal," I told her.

4

After school, me and Jay raced home, ignoring the wall of breath-stealing heat outside. Usually we would be running along the cooler marsh bank, climbing the branches of the big live oak trees, smelling the scent of pluff mud, and getting in all the fun we could before we had to go in for dinner and do homework. But not today. Today we ran down the dirt road toward home for our first real rootwork lesson.

Doc wasn't in his room when we got home, so we headed to the cabin. The lock Deputy Collins had broken was fixed, so Doc had to be around somewhere. If he'd left his cabin door open, he couldn't be far away. We went back in the house to change out of our school clothes. For the first time ever, Gran wasn't home to greet us when we got home from school. My throat tightened up looking at the empty kitchen. It was so quiet in here. No pots banging around, no visitors chatting away at the table, no cold drinks or treats waiting for us. Next to me, Jay sighed. He put his arm around my shoulder and squeezed.

"I miss her too," he said, reaching up to raise a window.

"That's why we have to learn. So her memory isn't gone forever." I took a deep breath in and held it until my head felt light as a balloon. Then I finally let it out in a big huff. "Even if it means I have to deal with those snotty new girls at school. Lettie's never going to quit when she finds out I'm learning to work root."

Jay frowned. "Somebody bothering you, Jez? Need me to—"

"No, it's okay." I gave him a squeeze back. "Let's get changed and find Doc."

Seconds later, we were sitting in the yard watching the chickens peck for corn and bugs. Doc wasn't anywhere to be found.

"Do you think he forgot?" I asked my brother.

Before Jay could answer, the door to the cabin swung open and Doc stomped out. He brushed dust off his clothes and placed a huge rock in front of the cabin door to keep it open.

"Where'd he come from? We just looked in there," Jay said, pointing.

When Doc saw us there in the front yard looking at him, he jumped like he'd seen a ghost from one of Gran's stories. "What're y'all doing out here?"

"Waiting on you," I said.

"Me?"

"Yeah," Jay piped up. "You know . . . lessons?"

"Oh! I got busy and clean forgot we were going to do that today."

I was about to be disappointed when I noticed his eyes sparkle. He was teasing us.

"First things first. Y'all two need to look out for each other when you're working roots. Don't let Jezebel go off by herself, Jay." When Jay agreed, Doc pointed a finger at me. "And you know better than to leave your brother anywhere."

"Yessir," I said, saluting him.

"Now that's clear, c'mon in here with me."

Doc's cabin was where he stored everything he and Gran used in their potions and powders. While they had sometimes let me and Jay write out labels and such, Doc had never let us spend much time in the cabin. My heart beat faster just thinking about all the secrets and mysteries waiting for us inside.

"Wow," Jay said.

Doc's supplies had started running low when Gran got

sick, but he must have been busy restocking his products. The pine shelves smelled sweet and clean, like they were fresh cut, and were filled with bottles and jars of roots and dried flowers. A table, covered in carved wooden bowls and handfuls of branches, stood in the middle of the room. Bundles of herbs tied with tan string hung from the ceiling. Mixed up with the scents of Doc's and Gran's handmade potions, the whole place smelled like spice-filled woods after a hard rain.

I could see dust-covered jars pushed toward the back of the top shelf. I stood on tiptoe and my fingers were barely able to reach the shelf at all. I jumped and got a quick look at them, but it was difficult to see in the sunlight filtering through the cabin's windows. Were they hidden back there by accident or on purpose?

"I've never let you two in here much before because I didn't want you getting into anything." Doc took a deep breath. "Just because we're going to start working in here doesn't mean I want you coming in on your own, that clear? I usually leave the door unlocked during the day because I'm going in and out all the time, but the last thing I need is y'all fooling around in here by yourselves."

"Fooling around doing what?" I asked.

"Anything," he said, running his finger along the row of shelves. "Twins in this world got more to worry about than normal people."

I put my hands on my hips. "You saying we ain't normal?"

"*You* ain't," Jay said, his nose squinched up.

I hit him in his scrawny arm. He yelped, then pushed me. Since he put all his weight behind it, I stumbled and banged my shoulder on Doc's worktable.

"Stop it, y'all." Doc's voice cut through our fighting. "See? This is what I'm talking about. You need to work together."

A carved wooden box stood on a shelf pushed back behind a round basket woven from black and green telephone wires. Doc took down the box and showed it to us. When I peeked close, the carvings were of water and ocean waves. But I couldn't see any way to open it – there were no hinges or locks or anything. Doc held the box close to his chest and opened the lid, almost as if by magic. He showed me and Jay the inside. Lots of long, twisty vines lay on a checkered handkerchief.

"These are called Devil's Shoestrings. They're one of the most important ingredients for protection spells."

I reached out and touched on the strings. They felt dry, but when I pressed one, the Shoestrings bent easy as a honeysuckle vine.

"Ugh," Jay said, peeking into the basket. "They're all dark and ugly."

Doc set the box down on his worktable. "One thing I

need you kids to understand. And I want you to listen real close now." He tilted his head and looked at us through one eye like a bird. The air in the cabin felt like it was vibrating, moving around me. "Dark is not ugly. Get that out of your minds right now." His voice was stern, but the look on his face was gentle. "You are both Black, and your mama taught you to hold your heads up and be proud. You're Turners, and that comes with a legacy."

"What's a legacy?" Jay asked.

"Something from your parents and grandparents," I said.

"And even further back than that," Doc said. "Rootworking and magic has been in this family for over three hundred years. Maybe longer, in some way or another." Doc rubbed his palms together, the sound of his rough skin like sandpaper. "So that was your first lesson in rootwork."

"That's it?" Jay stuck out his lower lip. He looked so funny when he pouted and I couldn't hold in my laugh. "I thought we were gonna actually *do* something."

"We can't always just do fun stuff." I crossed my arms over my chest and glared at Jay. "It's like math. We have to learn the *principles* first. I'm up to it. Are you?"

Jay threw his hands up in the air. "I'm here, ain't I?"

"All right, all right, you two." Doc looked at us thoughtfully. "There is something I need help with if you think you're up to it, something very important. We're gonna lay down some protection for the house."

"Didn't Gran use to do that?" Jay said.

"She did, but some of her magic is fading now that she's gone." Doc went clink-clunking around in some boxes stacked in the corner of the cabin. "Since we have a lot more to worry about right now, I think it's best we set some protection that will last a long time and only need touching up once in a while."

Doc removed something that looked like a big metal key from a basket and handed it to Jay. He then pointed to a new can of paint on the bottom shelf. "Jay, open that up there."

Jay lifted the can of paint with both hands and dragged it to the floor. He wedged off the lid with the metal key and then peeled off the thick, dried skin covering the white liquid underneath.

"Now, Jez, you pour this, drop by drop, into that can of paint there." Doc pressed a small bottle of blue liquid into my hands. "Keep adding drops until it gets to be haint blue."

"Haint" was the word Gran had used in her stories to mean ghosts, or spirits of people and things that hadn't moved on from our world to the next. Even though it was an old word, Mama and Doc used it sometimes too.

"Haint blue is the color ghosts and spirits hate most," Doc continued. "It reminds them of *the big salt*—that's the ocean. Since ghosts can't cross water, they stay away from the color."

"Okay." I tugged on one of my pigtails. I had a hair ribbon that was haint blue, but Mama only let me wear it on the Sundays we went to church. I knew the color was special, but not like this. "Then what do we do with it?" I asked.

"You paint the house." When we just stared at him, Doc laughed. "I never said rootwork wasn't real work." He lit his pipe, and the scent of tobacco and dried peaches started to cover the smell of spice and wood from the cabin. He pulled Devil's Shoestrings out of the basket one by one, then started to braid them in a circle. "Now get that paint mixed."

I carefully added in the liquid Doc had given me. Jay brought a new paint stick over and went to stir it all up.

"We're supposed to do that together," I told him. "Let me hold part of it."

"Ain't long enough for you to hold it and pour in those drops at the same time. I'll go first; then you can stir when there's enough liquid in." He sank the stick into the paint and blue rose to the top.

"No, you'll do it all and not leave anything for me." Stirring paint was one of my favorite things to do. I loved it when the separate colors would come together all smooth into a brand-new shade.

"I will so! You need to wait, Jezzie."

He yanked back on the stick at the same moment I

decided he was right and I should trust him and wait. The stick flew up, catching against the lip of the paint can, flinging huge blobs of light-blue paint all over the inside of Doc's cabin, and all over me and Jay, too.

My favorite denim dress—with pockets big enough to hold my doll, a peach, and anything I found out in the marsh while I was running around—was ruined. A line of paint slid down Jay's dark cheek, headed toward his chin. He wiped at it with the back of his hand, and it smeared into a chalky, ashy smudge that ran along his arm as well.

Mama was going to kill us dead.

Doc slammed his fist down on his worktable, making the roots and herbs inside the jars rattle. "That's enough out of both of you! Look at my ceiling. Blue paint is no good inside a place. If something gets in here with one of us, it's already too late."

"You mean hags?" I joked, grinning. I picked at a dark spot on my dress until I realized it was a small hole. "We're gonna paint the house now, so they won't be able to sneak in after today!"

"I'm glad to hear you both remember those stories." Our uncle returned his attention to his table, brushing aside stubborn gnats as he scraped bark from a twisted, blackened branch and put it in a jar. "They were a warning to keep you safe. There's worse things than hags out there."

"Like what?" Jay asked.

"Deputy Collins," I whispered.

Doc got a faraway look on his face like he did when he was listening. Soon, I heard it too.

Footsteps.

Someone was coming up to the cabin. A knock sounded on the door. We looked up as a light-skinned man with a pencil-thin mustache and tired eyes stuck his head in. He held a beat-up fishing hat in his hands, crushing it in his trembling fingers.

"Begging your pardon, Doc. You got time to *krak teet* some? To ease my heart a bit?"

Doc smiled at the man. "Mr. Benjamin, always got time to talk with you. Sit yourself down in here."

I didn't think Mr. Benjamin was that old, but he looked weary. "Sorry I didn't make it to your ma's service, Doc. I just . . . couldn't take no more."

Doc pulled a stool from under the table and sat next to the man. He placed a comforting hand on the man's shoulder. "Don't you apologize, no sir. Your own loss is still fresh on your heart."

"What happened, mister?" I asked.

Doc gave me a sharp look. "Jezebel—"

But Mr. Benjamin held out a hand. "That's all right. Gotta speak on it sometime." The man turned to me and said, "I lost my daughter a month back. She got real, real sick, then she died."

"I'm sorry," Jay said.

"I'm sorry too," I told him. "I wish we could help."

The man's light-brown eyes looked watery and sad, but he smiled at us. "You two learning from your uncle how to work the roots?"

We both nodded.

"Then maybe one day you will."

"That's all a part of what we rootworkers do." Doc pushed aside the ingredients littering his table to make room for the man to lean on. "Not everyone needs a potion or a spell. Sometimes they need someone to listen. And since Mr. Benjamin wants to talk grown people's business, you scoot on out of here. Better get on with the painting. I already scraped off the old, flaking paint from the wood. You do the bottom of the house up as high as you can reach, and I'll be there after I finish talking with Mr. Benjamin to do the rest."

We hurried back to the house and greeted Mama where she stood at the kitchen sink. She was up to her wrists in soapsuds and called out to us to be careful as we whizzed back outside. We picked out a spot around the back of the house and dipped our brushes.

"Sorry I got angry about the paint," I said as I pushed the brush back and forth over the cracking wood slats of the house.

Jay was quiet for a moment, slapping the paint-swollen brush messily. "Yeah, me too. I guess I didn't figure we'd be painting the house as a root lesson."

"Me either." With my bare fingers, I wiped off a drop of paint from my arm. "Remember when Daddy used to do things like this? Painting, mending stairs, patching the roof."

Jay nodded. Somewhere way far back in my mind I remembered Daddy being around to do those things. Then, one day, he went out to work and never came home. We didn't even know why he left us. When we thought we might be forgetting him, me and Jay built him in our minds. From scratch. I would remember how tall he was, and Jay would remember his deep, rumbly voice. He could even imitate him telling some of his jokes, while I remembered his eyes were turned down at the outside corners and deep brown like springtime mud. At first, we thought it would be enough to keep us going until he came back. Back then, we wanted it—expected it—to happen every day of the year. Then it slowed down to only special days, like Christmas or our birthday. Now we didn't expect it at all, but we wondered all the time where he was and if he missed us too.

I thought about all of this as I painted, and since Jay was quiet, I figured he was thinking of Daddy too. We painted and painted as the sun dipped lower in the sky. Too soon, Mama stuck her head out of the front door.

"Kids, time for dinner!"

"Aw, Mama, we're almost finished," Jay whined.

"Don't you 'aw, Mama' me. You were nowhere near finished." She swatted away some gnats with a dishcloth. "And just look at the paint on your clothes!"

"We were getting there," I said, hoping the paint would come out with a little turpentine. We put the lid on the paint, dumped our brushes into a jar of paint thinner Doc had set out, then marched up to the porch. "And we didn't even get the chance to play today."

"Well, that's what happens when you have school, homework, and root lessons." Mama smiled like she knew we would complain. "You sure you still want to keep up with these lessons of Doc's?"

I pushed my lips out so Mama would see I knew what she was doing. "Yes, ma'am," I said. "I'm sure."

"Okay, then. Get in here and get cleaned up for dinner." She tugged one of my curls. "How was your first day in the new class?"

"Good and bad things happened today," I said. "But mostly good."

"I'm so glad to hear that, Jezzie."

"Me too." Then I smelled the chicken roasting and I ran off to get washed up. If I didn't hurry, Jay'd grab both of the chicken wings for himself.

The sun was finally starting to set by the time we ate dinner, did homework, gathered eggs, and got our clothes ready for school the next day. Mama sent Doc off to find her some saw palmetto to make tea. I washed the empty glass jars Mama's customers brought back, and Jay dried them. Mama had just made wild strawberry jam. The big metal pots sat on the counter covered with muslin cloth to keep the bugs off while it cooled. She had a basket of okra on the counter waiting to be pickled next.

"Mama, when you make teas with plants, isn't that rootwork?" I asked.

"No, missy, it isn't." Mama lifted the corner of one muslin cloth and stuck a spoon into the jam.

I didn't want to make her angry, but I wanted to know the difference. I leaned against the two big boxes on the counter, sticking my finger in the diamond-shaped spaces between the rows and rows of empty jars inside.

"How come?" I asked.

"Yeah," Jay asked, mashing his fingers into the soft beeswax Mama used to seal her jars. "Doc boils teas too."

"Because rootwork takes intent. And all I'm intending to do is make myself a drink, not throw hexes or fix somebody's condition." Mama put the back of the spoon, covered with jam, against her bottom lip. "Now those jams are cool enough. You both get to filling up those jars."

I was about to do exactly that when the hard sound of gravel under moving tires cut through the quiet evening. I rose up on tiptoe to look out of the kitchen window, but I couldn't see the car. Chickens squawked and scrambled, but the driver was careful to move the car slowly, to give anything a chance to move.

"Somebody's coming to the house!" I hissed.

We all waited like statues while the car pulled to a stop outside our front window. Mama twitched back a corner of the curtain and peeped out. Me and Jay huddled up behind her so we could see too.

I gasped when I saw it was a police car.

Mama cursed and let the curtain drop. "You two stay right there. Don't you move a muscle."

My hands were shaking so much that I had to put down the jar I was holding. "Jay, look!" I whispered.

We both watched as the door to the police car opened and the tallest white man I'd ever seen stepped out. He practically had to unfold himself from the car. His beige uniform was clean and pressed sharp. He reached in the car to get something and my breath caught in my throat like a fish bone. Once I saw it was only his hat, though, I could breathe again. The tall man gave a quick look over to Doc's cabin, then loped up our front steps.

Mama grasped the scissors from her sewing kit on the table in one hand. We waited, listening for the sound of the man's footsteps on our porch. He opened the screen door and knocked, a gentle one-two-three rhythm.

"Don't answer it," Jay said.

"Hush now," Mama said, opening the door.

The man was so tall that he was taller than Mama,

even though he was on the porch and there was a big step up into the house where Mama stood.

"Mrs. Turner?" He looked at the scissors in Mama's hand, then raised his dark eyebrows. "Were you expecting someone?"

The man didn't sound like he was from around here. His tone was smooth and calm, not like any of the other police officers I'd heard before with sharp-edged voices.

Mama ignored his question. "Can I help you?"

"My name is Nate Edwards, and I'm the new sheriff. I want to extend my sympathies for the loss of your mother."

Mama had a tiny frown between her eyebrows now, but she was still polite when she spoke. "Thank you, Sheriff Edwards."

The man saw me and gave a tiny smile. Then he was all seriousness again when he talked to Mama. "I'm sorry to bring you more news at such a difficult time, but I want to inform you of a development."

"What sort of development?"

He took off his hat and held it in his big hands. "It's my understanding that people in this area have had . . . run-ins. With some of the local deputies."

"They were more than run-ins."

The sheriff nodded. "I imagine they were."

"And this development?" Mama asked again.

"Some talk I overheard around the station. Something

about searches of Negro people's homes without cause. I thought I'd warn you in case—"

Jay peeked over my shoulder. "Collins was here already."

"Is that true, Mrs. Turner?" He watched Mama's face real close, like he was trying to memorize it. I could tell from the shock on his face that he didn't know. "Are you okay? Did he hurt you or the kids?"

"We're all right. Only my mother's flower vase was hurt. He broke it when he went crashing through my house."

The sheriff's jaw worked back and forth. "He came *inside?*" When Mama confirmed it, Sheriff Edwards didn't say anything for a minute. Then he slapped his hat into the palm of his hand a couple of times. "What was he looking for?"

Mama snorted. "How would I know? Police come to the houses and farms out here a few times a year to tumble through what little we've got and leave the place a mess. They never say what they're looking for. And those who question them are always worse off."

Sheriff rocked back on his heels, looking thoughtful, like he was trying to figure something out. "Collins shouldn't have done any of that."

Mama sniffed. "Well, get him to stop then. Arrest him." When the sheriff didn't reply, she said, "Oh, I see. He's only a danger to us, not to white folk."

"Mrs. Turner—"

"You delivered your message and I thank you for the notice." Mama sucked her teeth, a sure sign she was mad.

"If you need anything—" He started to say more, then stopped. He looked sad when he finally talked again. "For what it's worth, I am sorry. I'll be checking in from time to time."

"Mmm-hmm." Mama frowned, then gave a short laugh. "You do that, Sheriff."

He looked like he was going to say something more but then just put his hat on his head and stepped back from the door, nodding at Mama, then us. "G'night, Mrs. Turner. Kids."

The police car's engine started up, and dust clouds followed the car as it left our farm. After the dust settled, I asked Mama, "Do you think he would help us?"

"I don't know, Jez." Mama placed her scissors back in her sewing box. "Only time will tell."

Doc returned from gathering right as we were screwing on the lids for the last of the jars. He was whistling a song I didn't know, and he had a sweetgrass basket over his arm. When he placed it on the kitchen table, me and Jay rushed over to look inside.

There were bunches of herbs that I knew and some I didn't. The ones Mama cooked with, like sage and thyme, I recognized by the shape of their leaves. When I rubbed those leaves, they left a fresh smell on my fingers that I loved. Mama's saw palmetto was in there, along with cat-grass and mint leaves. I handed the stuff for tea to Jay, and he placed it all in a clean cloth for Mama to sort through to make the blend she liked.

"The new sheriff stopped by," Mama said.

Doc's mouth dropped open. Then he dropped his whole self into a chair.

"Close your mouth before flies get in." Mama stacked the full boxes of jam jars by the front door. "Finally, something I found out before you."

"You always find out bad news before me," Doc replied. "At least we know and we can prepare."

Jay pooched his lip out. "That new sheriff don't sound nothing like Collins."

I tapped Doc on the back of his hand. "The man was trying to help us."

"Hmm," Doc said.

I knew then that this was exactly why we needed to learn more root. I hoped Mama didn't get scared about the policemen and change her mind about letting us learn. But when I saw her put on another pot with vinegar and spices to pickle the okra, I knew there was no time to worry about it. We had work to do. And we were so tired when we finished, Mama didn't even have to ask us to go to bed.

As I lay down on my clean sheets, I looked out of the window at the stars filling the sky. At that moment, I missed Gran so much. Things didn't feel as solid anymore without her. Doc was a great rootworker, but if Deputy Collins arrested him, we would be without any protection at all.

I prayed that wherever Gran was, she was content, and that when the time came, I'd be able to help protect us. I cuddled Dinah close and listened to the sound of Jay's soft snores for a long, long time before I finally fell asleep.

5

When I came into the kitchen the next morning, Doc and Mama were both moving slower than usual, like they didn't get enough sleep. I understood, because I didn't sleep last night either. The encounters with Deputy Collins and Sheriff Edwards had us all shaken up. I thought again of Gran too. When she was living, Mama would sit with me and Jay and eat breakfast Gran cooked, then get up and head right for her food stall when she was finished. Now, she and Doc had to get up earlier and cook, then clean up the kitchen before going off to work. Gran had left such a big hole in our lives to fill that I wondered if I could even be a drop in the bucket.

Mama looked at me strange as I sat down at the table. "You changed your hair?" she asked.

I nodded before digging into my bowl of buttered grits. At sunrise, I had gotten up and tugged a comb through my hair, then my best to part it down the middle. I put my hair up in the two pigtails I usually wore it in. Finally, I tied a white ribbon around each pigtail before twisting my hair and snapping a barrette on each end. No way was I going to wear my hair out in curls again, not after Lettie said I looked like some old lady. It was enough that I had to wear my old clothes to school. So I was going to stop trying to look pretty. There were more important things for me to worry about anyway.

"I thought the curls looked nice on you, Jezzie."

"Thank you," I said. "But I like my pigtails."

Mama frowned, but she only said, "Okay. As long as you're happy." She sipped her coffee. "But tomorrow, let me part it for you so it will be a straight line."

"Glad I don't have hair to fool around with," Jay said, rubbing a hand over his head.

"You don't have brains up there either."

"Hush up, Jez."

"Both of you, stop it." Mama put down her cup. "I want to talk about what happened last night."

"Janey," Doc started to say.

"No, let me finish." She put her hands down flat on the table. "What happened last night and the day before doesn't change anything. You two still need to go to school, and do chores, and everything else. This is not something for you to be worried about."

"Just be extra careful when you're outside playing or going to and from school." Doc tapped his unlit pipe against his lip. "We'll still have lessons, but stay alert. Like I always tell you, don't leave the other alone."

Me and Jay agreed. It was the second time in two days we had police at the house. I hoped there was something in that haint-blue paint that would work on people.

"Finish up—it's time for school." Mama stood and refilled her cup with water from the kettle. "Go on. I got to get you two outta my hair this morning."

We drank the rest of our tea, grabbed our books, and after a quick kiss on the cheek from Mama and a hug from Doc, headed out the door.

"Hey," I said as we ran down the steps. "Do the boys at school tease you about root?"

"No, they think it's cool. But we don't talk a lot, except about ball and stuff." He gazed over at me, his wide eyes narrowed into little slits. "Them girls bothering you?"

"One of the new girls is."

"If she's new, then she don't know nothing about it." Jay rolled his eyes. "Maybe Doc can teach us some kind of a hex to put on her."

He laughed, and I tried to force a smile. Lettie might have been new to our school and to the island, but that didn't make what she said any easier to take. The other kids laughed when she'd made fun of me, which meant they agreed with her. Or it meant they weren't going to stick up for me, which amounted to the same thing.

We took our normal path to school, but before we even got to the front gate, a group of boys called to Jay. One of them had a magazine with a plane on it, waving it in the air. Jay whooped and followed behind his friends, leaving me to walk through the gate on my own. Lettie and the other girls were already gathered on the lawn. I looked around for Susie, hoping for someone, anyone, who I could walk with. But if she was there, I didn't see her. I held my books tight, determined to ignore the girls as I walked past.

As I got closer, Lettie looked me up and down. She checked the watch on her wrist. "Hey, it's the Wicked Witch of the South! You were almost late!" Her sneer wasn't as bad as the one I got from Deputy Collins, but it was still pretty impressive. "What happened? Did your broom break down?"

Everyone started giggling. I had no idea how Lettie found out that my family worked root—probably that local girl who whispered in Lettie's ear told her my uncle was a witch doctor. Doc didn't mind the name, so I didn't either. I couldn't understand why that word made people so uncomfortable. Maybe it had to do with that song "Witch Doctor" that came on the radio sometimes. The last time I heard it, I listened to all the words, even the nonsense ones, and whoever wrote that song didn't know *anything at all* about witch doctors. And neither did Lettie.

My face felt hot, and the words came out of me before I could stop them. "You don't know anything about root magic! That's not how it works!"

"Oooh!" Lettie waggled her fingers in front of my face. "Shows us how it works, then. We want to see some of this magic, don't we?" She looked back at the other girls and they laughed again.

"Shut up, Lettie," I told her.

She placed her hands on her hips. "Is that all you can do? Tell me to shut up? You're still a witch baby." Her laugh was loud, like our chickens squawking over the last bits of corn. "I bet that stupid magic doesn't even work. It's stuff only backwards country people believe."

"If I could, I'd make you disappear!" I shouted in her face before stomping inside the school. More chicken-squawk laughter followed me.

The bell hadn't rung yet, and so the hallways were almost deserted. Only a few teachers hurried by, barely glancing at me as they went into a room marked Teachers Only. I stood in the stuffy hall that smelled a little like bleach, closed my eyes, and breathed deep, calming myself down. I wanted to be able to work a spell on Lettie to make her go away. Maybe I should ask to go back to fifth grade with Jay. But then, I thought, Miss Watson wouldn't be my teacher anymore. I sighed and opened my eyes.

Somehow, Susie had found me. She came up to me, grinning. She was pretty and tidy looking with her crown of braids, just like yesterday.

"Hi, Jezebel. You okay?"

"Hi." I shifted my books to one hip. "I'm fine. Just . . . Lettie being a pain."

"Yeah," Susie replied, rocking back on the heels of her Mary Jane shoes. "She's a nasty so-and-so. I heard her parents talking to Miss Watson. They're all mean."

I shrugged, not wanting to let Lettie ruin my day again. "I wondered if I was going to see you walking to school today."

Her eyes opened wider. They were shiny and reminded me of the black patent leather of Mama's pocketbook. "Which way do you come? From by the marshes? We could walk together! I mean, if you want."

"That would be great! I usually walk with my brother, Jay; but he won't care if you come."

"I'd like that." She smiled warmly. "Can I ask you a question? What Lettie was saying out there, about magic—what did she mean?"

The bell to start school clattered. Susie and I started walking down the hallway to class. Would she make fun of me too? I didn't think so. But even if I could trust her, what was okay to tell her about rootwork, and what wasn't okay? I should ask Doc what he thought. "I'll . . . tell you later."

I waited all through the morning subjects, hoping Miss Watson might read us another of her favorite poems. The day was hot, like the sun was breathing on us, but the windows of the school were open and a light breeze ruffled the papers on our desks.

Finally, she opened that desk drawer again. "This poem is by Gwendolyn Brooks, another Negro poet," she said, sitting on the edge of her desk again. I got the feeling it was her favorite reading position.

"A *girl*?" Thomas said loudly.

"Gwendolyn is a woman, yes. Women can be poets too. In fact, in 1950, she became the first Negro to win the Pulitzer Prize." Miss Watson opened the book. "That's pretty much the biggest award they give for poetry. And she continues writing to this day. Isn't that something?"

Murmurs went through the entire class.

"I taught you about Shakespeare and his sonnets this morning," she continued, clearing her throat. "Well, now I'm going to read you one by Mrs. Brooks. This one is called 'the sonnet-ballad,' and it's one I read to myself over and over again."

I settled into my seat and waited for Miss Watson to begin her magic. Reading aloud sounds like something more for younger kids, babies almost, but it wasn't. That she chose one of her favorite poems to read to us made me feel like she was showing us something no other teacher had before. She was sharing a part of herself, knowing that we might not like the same things she liked, but doing it anyway. Her voice changed when she got to certain parts of the poem. It swelled up to fill the whole room with sound, then it whispered softer than the wind through trees. Our whole class hushed and listened, but I pretended she was reading only to me. I closed my eyes and let the sound of her voice wash over me, forgetting about the girls calling me names this morning.

When me and Jay were almost home from school, we found Doc waiting for us at the top of our road. He wore a straw hat with a wide brim to keep off the sun, and the tail of his white shirt flapped in the wind. He was twisting something around in his hands. He nodded at us as we approached, then shoved the twisty thing in a bag he had thrown over his shoulder.

"How was school?" Doc asked us.

"Fun, but not as good as this is gonna be," Jay said.

Doc walked with us down the road to our farm. "How about you, Jez? Everything okay?"

"Are those new girls still bothering you?" Jay stuck his chin out.

"Yeah, but what can I do? They think root is stupid

and ignorant." My load of books felt heavier than usual, and I shifted the weight of them to my other arm.

Doc sighed, long and deep. "I'm afraid there will always be people—even other Negroes—who feel that way about rootwork, Jez. In fact, they would rather forget it."

"Why?" me and Jay asked at the same time.

"Well, maybe they think rootwork and other magics like it are old-fashioned and only for uneducated people." Doc pushed his hat back on his head. "Or maybe they don't want to remember our history because some of it's painful."

Jay nodded. I could tell he remembered the other stories Gran told us about how white people treated her when she used to work in the city. They would shout at her and shove her as she walked to her job, and sometimes they even threw their drinks on her.

"But that's not all people, right?" I thought of Susie, the question she asked this morning, like she was curious about rootwork.

"No, not all people," Doc said as we got up near the house. Crisp blue-and-white-striped sheets were drying on the clothesline, snapping in the wind. Fat bees buzzed in around us, dipping to sample flowers. "But you need to be careful about who you tell, like your mama's told you. For your own protection."

"I'll try," I promised.

"Good." Doc smiled. "And speaking of protection, that's what we're going to be continuing with for today's lesson." He handed me and Jay a small cloth pouch each. They had reddish-brown dirt inside. "Pour a little of it behind you as we walk. Make sure you have about half of it left when we get to the cabin."

We did as he said, sprinkling the dirt in our footsteps.

"Pour the rest of it in a circle around the cabin," Doc told us when we got there. "One of you go right and the other left. Come back to me when you're done."

We placed our books on the ground and ran around the cabin, using up the rest of the dust.

"Good." Doc nodded. "You both did that real well."

Jay frowned. "Throwing dirt ain't that interesting."

"Yeah," I said. "I was hoping we'd do something more exciting than painting this time."

"That wasn't any old dirt." Doc fixed us with a sly look. "That was brick dust mixed with something special: graveyard dirt."

That caught our attention. "Now *that* sounds interesting," Jay said.

Doc laughed at him. "It can protect anything, big or small. Best to always keep some of this made and close by."

He opened his cabin door, and we followed him inside. Then he showed us how to grind the brick pieces, then how much graveyard dirt to mix with it. "Last, but most important: make sure you always leave a gift for the person whose grave you get the dirt from, as payment. Otherwise, it's stealing."

Doc let us fill up our bags again from his supply, but he promised he would take us out to the cemetery one day so we could gather dirt to make our own protection powder. "Now, I know you want to be doing more than painting houses and spreading dirt. You two grew up around me and your gran picking plants and herbs, making medicines and such. Yes, there's more to it. More than I've ever shared with you before. Some of it will be fun, some of it will make you nervous, some of it you won't like at all. But before we can get into those things, you need to learn the basics. Protect yourself." He looked at both of us in turn. "And always take care of each other. Understand?"

Jay scowled his face up like he did when we had green beans for dinner. He hated them, but they were my favorite vegetable. "Just show us how to curse somebody with a spell."

Doc smacked him on the head with his rolled-up newspaper. I laughed because I knew it didn't hurt.

"That's what I want both of you to hear me on," Doc said. "If there's anything I learned in this life, it's that problems are going to find *you*. Problems I won't be able to prepare you for, no matter how many spells I teach you. And the only thing that's going to get you through is your belief. Your faith in yourselves, and your trust in each other. Nothing works without that."

We both nodded, even though I'm pretty sure we didn't understand his full meaning.

"What else are we learning today, Doc?" I was hoping to learn something, anything, that might protect me from Lettie. I was pretty sure Miss Watson wouldn't be happy if I poured graveyard dirt around my desk.

Jay rolled his eyes. "Probably gonna have us scrubbing floors or something."

Doc took a jar full of cloudy water out of his bag and placed it high up on a shelf. "One day, you might have to do exactly that."

"Really?" I asked, my hands on my hips. "Is cleaning house really part of root? Because it sounds like a way to get us to clean for you."

Doc chuckled. "I wouldn't lead you wrong, Jezzie."

"Oh yeah?" I lifted my eyebrows. "What else are we going to do then?"

"First, change your clothes. I already painted most of the house while y'all were at school, but there's still a bit left, and you're going to finish that up. . . ." Jay was already groaning. "*But* if you finish quick and do a good job, you can have the rest of the afternoon to play."

I wanted to learn more spells, but getting most of the afternoon to play wasn't bad. We ran off, dodging the chickens milling around in the yard, tuck-tuck-tucking a food call to each other. We put on our playclothes, still splattered with paint from yesterday, then grabbed the brushes and went around the house to the places we hadn't finished the day before. Most of it was done, except for under each window of the house. Hopefully we'd be done in time to play down in the marsh.

I tried to keep the paint from dripping on me today, but it was no use. Jay soon had smears of paint on his overalls and down his arms, so at least I wasn't alone. Mama could be mad at both of us.

We worked together quietly, until I remembered something and nearly dropped my brush. With Gran's passing, school starting, and starting our root training, I almost forgot. "It's our birthday today!"

"I know," Jay said. "How we gonna celebrate without Gran making our cake?"

I shrugged. "Do you think Mama and Doc got us anything?" Mama and Doc had so much more to do now that Gran was gone, I wasn't sure if they even remembered.

"I don't believe they'd forget our birthday." Jay shoved his brush all the way down into the can of paint, getting blue all over his fingers. "But we ain't got much money, especially with Gran's funeral and all."

"Yeah." Already tired, I rubbed sweat off my forehead with my arm. It didn't do any good. Heat surrounded us, hanging in the still air and coming up from the earth. I put the brush down and wiped my face on the hem of my skirt. The fabric darkened with my sweat and the dirt and dust clinging to my skin. "But I bet she'll have something."

When Doc came out of his cabin and up to the house, he stared at what we'd done.

"If you had turned like this when you first started painting, this whole house could've been finished."

We stood there side by side, silent, but proud that he saw the work we put in.

"Go on and play some now. Don't go too far out though; it's almost dinnertime."

We whooped and ran off, past the plump, squawking chickens roaming the yard, away from the house, and down the soft slope of farmland that ran along the woods. Doc's words were a memory as we found trees to climb and ran off the aches in our backs from the work.

Soon we got to the edge of the salt marsh that separated us from the ocean, tall sea grasses bending and blowing in wind hot as bathwater, forcing the bubbling scent of pluff mud into our noses.

"I'm gonna get a hidin' man," Jay announced, kicking off his shoes on the grass and rolling up the ends of his overalls to his knobby knees. We loved playing with baby fiddler crabs. They liked to hide inside old spiral snail shells, but we knew how to get them to come peeking out of their hidey-holes. And that's exactly what Jay, already ankle deep in the sucking mud, was doing. He bent down and plucked a shell from the grass, then put the open end of the shell to his throat and hummed low and long. When he pulled it away, he grinned, and I knew the crab's curiosity had made its wobbly eyes peer out.

"Can you get me one? I don't want to take my shoes off."

"Then you don't want a crab."

"Dog bite it, Jay." I cursed in the only way Mama said was all right for a lady, and took my shoes off. I cursed for real when I saw drops of blue paint on each of them. A quick glance at Jay's showed he had paint on his left one, but not the other. Hopefully turpentine got paint off leather.

I placed one foot on the brown-black mud. The layer of muck had small holes all over it, where marsh gas breathed out. Larger holes showed where frogs and crabs and crawling things made their homes, protected from the burning heat of the sun.

Jealous of Jay's catches—he had two now—I took another step. For a moment, I stood there, looking out at the marsh and listening to all of her sounds: insects buzzing, crickets singing, bubbles popping on the surface. I smiled and stepped forward, Mother Marsh pulling at my ankles.

"Time."

It was a voice, as loud and clear to me as my own thoughts. I glanced around, expecting one of our neighbors from a nearby farm to be fishing on the water's edge.

But no one was out here except for my brother, comparing his two pets and choosing a winner to take home.

"Did you hear that?" I asked. Jay wasn't listening and I had to ask him again.

"Hear what?"

"That voice," I said, annoyed.

He looked back over his shoulder toward the house. "Could it be Mama calling us? I don't think we can hear her way out here."

If Mama wanted us, I was pretty sure we'd be able to hear her yelling if we were in the bottom of a pyramid way out in Africa. "No, it was something else."

"Well, I didn't hear nothing."

"For true?" I said. I was sure I'd heard something. It was getting late; I didn't know how long we'd been out here, but the sun was dipping lower and Mama would want us home for dinner before sunfall. "We should probably be getting back soon anyway."

Jay looked up into the sky, now stained with faded purples and pinks and hot orange. "Yeah . . . ," he said, drawing the word out like he didn't want to go. Finally, he put the hidin' men in his pocket. He stepped toward me, lifting his feet high to get them free of the thick mud. As he passed me, I lifted my foot to follow him, but it didn't come up. I yanked it up again, with no results.

"Jay?" I said. "I think I'm stuck."

"Shut up, Jezzie, and come—" He stopped talking

when he saw my face. I was pulling my legs up as hard as I could, but they weren't moving. "Stop playing and pick up your feet."

"I can't!"

Jay grabbed me under the arms and yanked hard as he could, making me think my arms would come out of the sockets. I squinched my eyes tight but let him keep on. I was scared; at that moment, I wished I had Dinah with me.

It's time.

That voice came again, like the wind herself whispering to me. I didn't know what it meant, but it scared me even more. "Did you hear that? That voice just now?"

Jay was still yanking on me. "I don't hear nothing but your breathing and your hollering." But he had an idea. "I'm gonna hold on to you and you lift your right leg up, okay?"

I nodded, my throat tight. The marsh felt different somehow. Early September was always hot, but there was now a chill surrounding it, one that hadn't been there when we stepped out a few minutes ago. My head felt light, like it was trying to remember everything at once, then gave up.

Jay grabbed me around my middle and held me straight while I tried to lift my leg. I pulled up hard, twisting as I did, but my foot wouldn't leave the ground. A frog croaked near me and my heart jumped.

"Go get Mama!"

"No! I'm gonna get Doc." He let me go, then turned and squelched out of the marsh to the edge.

I turned as best I could to watch him go. He picked up his shoes from the marsh bank. A smear of light mud shaped like a handprint had dried on the side of the black leather, stopping where the wide splash of blue paint covered the top.

"Jay! Let me see your shoe."

He brought it over and handed it to me. I saw that the muddy fingerprints stopped before they reached the blue.

"It's the blue," I whispered. "It really does work." A gust of warm wind blew over the marsh, tickling my neck. "Do we have anything with a lot of haint blue on it?"

Jay still had the stick he'd used to stir the paint in his back pocket, and he took it out.

"That might work," I said. "Shove it in the ground near my foot."

"Okay," he said. "Ready?"

I took a deep breath, then nodded.

Jay jammed the stick down into the mud next to my heel. Mud closed around the stick for a moment, then shrank away, leaving a small gap. I pulled up and my foot came out with a loud, sucking pop. With one foot free I pushed myself back and sat my bottom on the edge of the grass. Jay wedged the paint-coated stick under my other foot, and the grip loosened enough for me to scoot all the way back to safe ground.

I lay down on the bank, breathing hard, looking up at the raw-bacon sky, streaked with color. The sun was low now, making the shades richer and deeper, but the hot, moist wind was still heavy on my chest. My back was getting damp as I lay there, and it was only after a little while that I realized my brother was calling my name.

"Yeah?" I was free, but inside me I felt strange, like I'd lost something but couldn't remember what it was.

He sat silent for a moment, not looking at me, thinking. "You okay?"

I wasn't sure. When Jay finally pulled my foot away from the marsh's embrace, I'd heard the voice again. It had said my name. *Jezebel*. Close to my ear, deep in my chest I'd heard it, whispery and slight.

"I'm okay."

He stood up and brushed off his pants. "Then we better get on home."

6

When we walked in the door, Mama looked at us like we were wild children living out in the forests who'd come into her house asking for food.

"What in seven holy bells happened to you two? You are a level mess."

Mama, for her part, looked so pretty. She had on a clean, starched dress, not new but nice, and her hair was twisted up in one of those knots she liked to wear when it was too hot to hold a decent curl. Her beige apron with the green palmetto trees was around her waist.

"Nothing," I said.

"You don't look like nothing happened," she said, hands on her hips.

"We was playing, Mama, that's all. Picking up crabs and stuff." Jay moved a hand toward his pocket, but the look on Mama's face stopped him.

"I wish you would leave those things alone. Not like you can eat them. Go on and wash up for dinner. Your hands and face and those alligator-looking feet. Use the basin outside, not the one in the bathroom."

We both mumbled a "yes, ma'am" and rushed back outside.

Jay and I dragged the tub over to the water pump in the back and filled it. The sun had heated the pipe so the water was warm when we soaked our washcloths. We scrubbed our faces and hands, then took turns sitting on the edge of the tub scrubbing our feet. Back in our room, I rubbed Vaseline on the bottoms of my feet before I put on my house slippers, but Jay stuck his feet in his slippers dry.

"Feel better now?" he asked.

I nodded. "I think so. But . . . something is out there, Jay. I don't feel right about it at all." Jay was quiet; I could see he maybe didn't really believe me about what happened. But he helped when I needed him to. That was good enough. I patted his arm and said, "Let's go."

He followed me out of our room and into the kitchen, where Mama and Doc were sitting at the table. Bowls of stewed butter beans with bits of crispy salt pork sprinkled on top were at each place on the table. In the middle sat a big pot of white rice. A bottle of vinegar hot sauce sat in the middle of four glasses of iced tea, the edges of each one sporting a wedge of shiny-skinned lemon. We fell on the food, spooning the peppery bean soup ladled over fluffy rice into our mouths. It was warm and comforting, even in the heat of the kitchen, and when Mama placed leftover biscuits on the table, we didn't complain about not having fresh ones as we usually did. We dipped them in the creamy soup, thick with onions and bits of roasted meat, and jammed them between our lips. Jay went back for more soup, but all I wanted was more rice. I reached for the pot and refilled my bowl.

"Easy, easy," Doc said, laughing at our eagerness. "Where's the fire, y'all? No one is going to take the plate out from under you. Take your time. Enjoy it."

We slowed down as instructed but still finished our dinner way before Mama and Doc. Jay and me sat, wiggling in our seats, waiting to see what we might be getting for our birthday.

"Looks like you better handle business, Janey," Doc said, reaching for another biscuit. "Or you'll get holes worn in the bottom of those chairs."

Mama agreed and got up from the table. "I don't know what's got into you two today. Frantic as bats outta torment."

"*Eleven*," Doc said. "That's what's got into them."

Mama went into her bedroom, shutting the door behind her. When she came out a few moments later, she had two packages wrapped up in the brightly colored comic section of the newspaper. Me and Jay gasped. Then we clapped our hands. I was just as happy to see Mama smiling as I was to get my gift.

"Thank you!" we said at the same time. We hugged them—me with Mama first, then Doc after. Jay went the opposite way, Doc before Mama.

"Lordy, I swear. Never seen you kids act so grateful in all my born days. You haven't even opened the things yet." Doc chuckled. "Oh, and you can add this to your gifts." He reached into his pocket and held something out to us.

I took the circle of what looked like braided branches from his hand, while Jay stared at his. I elbowed him in the side.

"Ow!" he yelled. Then he took the circle and looked at it like it was a nasty thing on his shoe.

"What is it?" I asked.

"Remember the roots I showed you yesterday?"

I did. "The Devil's Shoestrings?"

"Yes, these are bracelets I made from eleven of them woven together." Doc smiled. "What do you think it's for?"

"Protection?" I guessed. I rubbed the bracelet made of twisty vines.

"That's right." Doc nodded. I could tell he was pleased

with my answer. "My grandmother used to say if you tie up Devil's Shoestrings, it'll trip up any evil that's after you."

"Wow," I said, sticking my hand through. It fit perfectly. I twisted my arm back and forth to see the bracelet from all sides. It looked like a tree had wrapped its roots around my wrist. I put my hand in my pocket, where Dinah was, to show her my new jewelry as I thanked Doc for the gift. "Is that story true?"

"Sure is." Doc finished off his dinner and took his plate to the sink. "You wear that on your ankle or your wrist, and one of these days, I'm sure you'll find it helpful."

"I will," I said.

"Boys don't wear bracelets." Jay pouted.

"Some boys and some men do," Mama said. "Remember, these are gifts, and we could take them back real easy. So what do you say?"

"Thank you," he muttered, but he didn't put his on.

Red hot in the face that we had to be reminded of our manners, me and Jay both sat in our chairs and carefully peeled off the sticky tape from the colorful sheets of newspaper, making sure we didn't rip or tear any of the word bubbles in the process. I folded mine as close to the way it had come as I could and sat it next to me, for reading later. Jay's was crumpled but still carefully set aside. He got his package open first.

"Oh yeah!" His excitement was plain on his face as he held up the balsa-wood airplane model kit. It included a tiny paintbrush and pots of paint to make the plane look like it was from the war.

"Hope you ain't too sick of painting to want to get that done and ready for flying."

"No, sir." He was already looking at the instructions on how to put it together while I opened my gift.

I got a new dress for Dinah, a tiny scrap of yellow trimmed in red polka dots. There was also a little package of hair barrettes with the same polka-dot ribbon wound through them, which were for me.

"They're so pretty!"

"Do you want to wear them to school?" Mama asked. "I can put them in for you."

"Um, maybe." I didn't want to wear anything that was going to call more attention to me. "Maybe I can save them for special times." Mama nodded, even though she looked a bit disappointed. My heart sank into my tummy. I squeezed her tight.

"Lord, they grow up fast, don't they?" Doc was setting out his pipe and tobacco. "Come on, Janey, serve that cake before I go light this up. Cake and pipe smoke don't go together."

"There's cake?" Jay put the airplane box down on the table and looked around for it, his eyes bright as noontime.

We hadn't seen Mama's cake tray, the metal one with the matching covered lid, when we came in. Now that we were looking, we still didn't see any cake, but the scent of it was on the air—brown sugar and warm butter. Mama went to the stove and took out her big iron skillet with a folded-up kitchen towel and her oven glove. She sat the pan on the top of the stove and placed a platter on top of it. Then she turned the whole thing upside down and lifted the skillet, revealing our birthday cake. She brought the platter to the table, and we oohed and aahed, bringing a bigger smile to her face. Rings of pineapple lay on top of a yellow cake, with rivers of brown-sugar syrup running down the toasty-looking sides. A plump red cherry lay in the middle of each pineapple ring.

Mama and Doc sang "Happy Birthday" to us and Doc cut one huge slice and put it on a plate between me and Jay. We always shared one piece of birthday cake. It was good luck to get the first piece on your birthday, so that was the fairest way to do it. I took one big triangle of cake on my fork and ate it real slow, but Jay ate his half of the slice like it was going out of style. All of the moist, sweet treat was gone before we sat back in our chairs. His finger traced the syrupy puddles on the plate to get the last bits.

"Thanks, Mama," I said. "Can we be excused now?"

"We?" Jay asked, eyeing up the bits of Doc's slice that he hadn't finished.

I tried to give my brother the same stare that Mama used on us when she expected us to fall in line, but it didn't work. He kicked me under the table. Mama poured cups of coffee for her and for Doc and told us we could both go. "Both," she said again when Jay didn't move.

He got up, trailing behind me. I could feel his eyes jabbing into my back. When we got to our room, he asked, "What you do that for?"

I laid Dinah's dress and my hair barrettes on the bed. "Because we need to talk about what happened."

"You getting stuck in the mud?"

"I wasn't stuck and you know it. Something was holding me there."

Jay poked out his bottom lip. "Wasn't nothing pulling you down."

"I didn't say it was pulling me. I said it was holding me there. So I couldn't get loose. Not until we shoved that stick covered in haint blue in the mud. And I heard a voice."

"You fool up, huh?"

"I did hear it. I swear. I'll swear it on a stack of Bibles." My mouth tightened up into a line.

He looked at me sideways, then went to the milk crate by his bed that served as a night table. Jay plucked out a small book, and I recognized it as the one Jehovah's Witnesses gave out.

"That's only half a Bible. Jesus's part."

"This the only one I got. You gonna swear on it or not?"

I put my right hand on the Bible and held my left hand up. "I swear."

Jay stood back from me in case God struck me down for lying. Then he said, "Okay." He sat on his bed, flipping the book around and around in his hands.

"Well, what do you think?"

Jay shrugged. "I dunno. What the voice say?"

I sat on my bed across from him. "That it was time? Like this." I made my voice all whispery and light. "*It's time.*"

"But did it sound like, you know . . ." He fought for the right words. "Scary?"

"I . . . I think so. Should I tell Mama? Or Doc?"

Jay put the book down and crossed his feet over each other so he could pick at a bit of dead skin on his heel. "You know Mama don't really want us learning root. If she thinks something bad happened, or that you're scared, she'll make both of us stop."

"Yeah." I picked Dinah up and held her close. I knew what Jay said was true. But I also knew that Gran and all the other witch doctors and rootworkers and healers before her put up with a lot more than voices in a marsh, or some silly girl's jokes. They faced real danger to help others. I remembered about a year ago, when the police got it in their minds to investigate all the witch doctors and rootworkers in the area. They were going around and knocking on everyone's doors—whether they did magic or not. If the person didn't let them in, they busted down the door and went in anyway. Sometimes, they dragged people out of their houses. Sometimes people got shot. And sometimes, they just disappeared.

That was the first time Deputy Collins came to our farm. Gran told me and Jay to stay inside while she spoke to him. I remembered the look he gave her—like she was a nasty bug he wanted to step on. His voice got louder and angrier with each word he spoke, and his fingers did a little tap dance on the gun hanging around his waist. Most of all, I think, he hated that Gran didn't act scared of him.

Truth was, I was scared. But I did my best to hide it. Gran had told us when we were really little that some people would hate us on sight because of our color and some would hate us because we were a rootworking family. She said we must never run from either one, because Turners don't run from nobody.

No matter what happened at school, or in the marsh, I wasn't going to let her down.

"If I can't tell Mama, I can't tell Doc either. He's gonna tell her whatever I say."

"True," Jay agreed. "But if you don't go back out to the marsh, Doc will ask why you ain't going—then you gonna have to tell him. And he'll be mad you ain't said nothing before." Jay paused like he was going to say something more, but changed his mind. Then he straightened up his back and words rushed out from him like an untied balloon. "If something's wrong, you got to say so. The longer you hide it, the harder it is to . . . you know. Besides, when did Doc ever not know something he needed to know?"

I screwed up my face. Dinah lay on the bed and I turned to dress her in her new outfit. Her red stitched smile had flattened out, like she was judging me. I shook my head and whispered, "I can't tell him, Dinah." I put her on the windowsill, where I could see her but wouldn't have to look directly into her face.

Before, I could ask Gran for her help. She always knew what to do. But I couldn't ask her anymore.

The crack of wood breaking startled me, but I let out a breath of relief when I saw it was only Jay punching out the pieces of his model airplane kit. He spread them out on the bed. The cover of the box showed a picture of a plane with gray and blue and white coloring. "Tomorrow I'm going to ask Doc for some red paint. Know why?"

I shook my head.

"Because the only Negros allowed to fly in World War II had planes with red tails."

"How do you know that?" I'd never heard Jay talking about planes and flying before.

"My friend Larry at school told me. His uncle was one of them pilots. He has a picture of him in a uniform and everything." Jay carefully laid out all the pieces of his model airplane like they would break if he was rough with them. "They called the Negro pilots Red Tails or Red Tail Angels. But the stores don't sell these planes with red paint."

"Why not?" I asked.

"I don't know. Probably because they don't think it's important. It's like they don't want us to know we have heroes too. Negroes who were brave, and not scared."

"They fought in a war," I said. "I bet they were scared."

Jay sighed and touched the set of paints. "Yeah, but they did it anyway."

7

It was black-dark outside, but I was still awake.

Even though me and Jay had gone to bed, I couldn't sleep, so I stared out of the window. The moon shone round and full in the deep night sky. I could hear Jay's raggedy breathing—not snoring, he said—coming from his side of the room. To me, it was still our birthday until the sun came up. And that's what I was thinking about.

I thought something amazing was going to happen when we started to learn about our family magic. That I would find some special magic inside me. Instead, it seemed like root had only stirred a bunch of bad things up.

Deputy Collins continuing to creep round, Lettie getting everyone in class to laugh at me, whatever had happened in the marsh . . . It seemed like things would be a lot easier if I just gave it up.

And at that moment, I really wanted *something* to be easy.

I sighed and turned on my back, my long cotton night-dress twisting around my knees. That's when something moved near the window. It must have been a cloud over the moon . . . but I could have sworn I'd seen Dinah move. I rubbed my eyes, then looked at her again. She was as still as ever, sitting on the windowsill where I placed her.

Another shadow flicked across the window. I squinted, looking at Dinah really close. When I leaned her against the windowsill earlier, I had arranged her new dress so the little pleats lay flat in neat rows, the way Mama had pressed them. Now those pleats were spread wide, like Dinah had swung her gunnysack legs.

I gasped, then pressed my lips together to keep the sound in. My heart beat faster. Maybe it was the wind? Me and Jay left the window cracked at night so cool air could creep in.

I stared at Dinah in the darkness, unblinking, until my eyes got dry and itchy. There was no more movement, and soon I let my eyes close, once, then twice. I was about to close them again when I heard the brush of stiff cotton.

I held myself still but limp, a slit in my eyelids just wide enough to see through.

Dinah was moving.

It was a small movement at first. She sat up. Then, a minute later, she turned her head one way, then the other, then she looked *right at me* before she pushed her little round cloth arms under her stuffed body and stood up. She looked at the dress, and her red stitched mouth wiggled back and forth, as if she couldn't decide whether she liked her new outfit.

I froze where I lay. The sheet on top of me felt heavy as a winter blanket, holding me in place on the bed. I fought the need to run, breathed slow and deep to stay calm. Did this have something to do with whatever had grabbed me in the marsh? Had a real, honest-to-goodness haint gotten inside my doll?

Carefully, Dinah lowered herself down onto the thin bedspread. Her weight didn't make a dent in the material until both feet were planted and firm. Then she made her way, foot over foot, swaying like a drunk squirrel, to the edge of the bed.

Part of me was scared to move, because she would know I was pretending, but the other part of me had to watch. I made a light snoring sound and turned over in the bed like I was getting settled.

Dinah's steps halted for a moment, then she hice-tailed it out of the room.

I couldn't believe it. I shook my head and rubbed my eyes, thinking I might be dreaming, so I pinched myself and looked at the windowsill. It was still empty.

A squeak from the front of the house told me the screen door had opened and closed.

"Jay, wake up," I said in a loud whisper.

He continued to breathe deep.

I got up, my bare feet soft on the wood floor, and shook him. "Wake up!" When he didn't move, I pinched him, then covered his mouth with my hand when he yelped.

"Shhh!" I told him, pulling on his arm. "Listen: we need to go outside."

His eyes were slits of white in the darkened room. He was mad at me for waking him up. "Huh? Why?"

"Dinah's gone."

He scratched at his belly under his white T-shirt. "Somebody tief her?"

"No, nobody stole her. She got up and left." Before he could call me crazy, I jumped back on my bed and pointed out of the window. "Look!"

Jay cut his eyes at me, but he got up. He crawled out of his bed, tiptoed across the room, and kneeled down on mine. "I can't get why— Lord afire!"

Dinah was making her way down the dusty path from the house, waddling along like one of our chickens.

His mouth dropped open. He must have truly been shocked, because he didn't even come back with a smart-mouthed comment. It was one of the only times I'd ever seen him with nothing to say. He pointed outside.

"I told you!" I hissed as we pressed our faces up against the window.

Where was she headed? The marsh?

Finally, my brother found his voice. "What kinda mess is that? Did you make her walk?"

His voice was too loud and I shushed him before I answered. "No! How could I?"

"Do you think it's a haint?"

"I don't know."

"But they ain't real, are they, Jez?"

"I don't know!" I said again. I was scared when I first saw Dinah move, but now I was curious. Gran had breathed into that doll, for *me*. I wasn't about to let some haint run away with her, whether they were real or not. "We have to follow her."

"What?" He shook his head while he waved his hands in front of his face. "Not me. Dolls walking in the middle of the night? Leave me outta this."

I tugged at his arm. "We have to. What if she's off to tell Doc about today?"

"Then that'll be good. He can deal with whatever it is. I don't want to get mixed up with no walking dolls." He got up and scrambled back over to his bed. "I'm gonna stay nice and safe right here."

"Suppose she gets torn up by dogs or something."

Jay groaned and put his pillow over his head.

"Well, *I'm* going out there," I said, putting my socks and shoes on. "You better come too, because if I get hurt, first thing Mama and Doc are gonna ask is why you didn't go with me."

He pulled the pillow down from his face. "Fine!" He yanked his overalls on over his nightclothes and stuck his feet in his shoes. Then he grabbed a flashlight from his milk crate. "You gonna need something to see with. You ain't no cat."

I took the small hurricane lamp off my bed table, went to the kitchen, and lit it with a match. Then we eased the door open and crept outside.

Jay turned on his flashlight. He muttered, "Looking for daggone doll footprints in the moonlight. No sense in that."

"We're gonna check the cabin, then check at the marsh," I told him.

With that, we snuck to Doc's cabin, quiet as we could. He wasn't there. He had been working, because there were bowls of root cuttings and such on the table, but there was no sign of him now. There was no sign of Dinah, either. So from there, we headed toward the marsh.

"You sure you wanna do this?" Jay asked. "Considering . . . ?"

I swallowed hard. "Yeah. I'm okay."

A gust of wind came through the dark and brought the night to life. It rustled the leaves on the trees. The stalks of corn and benne made a shushing sound. Crickets, frogs, and other night creatures chirped. Clouds covered the moon and stars. I couldn't see anything beyond the single line of light from Jay's flashlight. My lamp flickered.

My heartbeat felt like it was pounding in my head. I could hear my blood rushing through my body. An owl hooted. Long grasses rustled, tickling our ankles. We marched quietly toward the marsh, the evening air steamy, making sure we stayed on the path. We were past our crops when Jay went still next to me.

"What?" I asked, leaning to look over his shoulder.

"Thought I felt something brush past me. Like a spiderweb. A leaf, maybe."

He tilted his head to listen, and a puff of air blew my flame out, like somebody had made a wish. Now Jay's dim flashlight was the only light we had.

Side by side, we turned, letting the beam of light cut through the darkness and the thin shadows. We saw nothing except grass, trees, crops, and the hard-packed dirt path as we moved. Doc's cabin seemed miles away. From where we stood, our house looked tiny and impossible to reach.

A moment before we completed the circle, the flashlight hit something. It was as if there was a patch of night it couldn't get through. Jay froze, then, inch by inch, he moved the flashlight back the way we had come. I was hoping it had been a mistake. That he had taken his finger off the switch for a minute. But the thick darkness ate up the beam again.

Then, darkness spoke.

Happy birthday.

And it reached for us.

We screamed, not caring that anyone heard, and turned to run back to the house and to Mama. As we sprinted, a crackling sound came from behind us, like someone stepping on dry leaves. The flashlight showed how far we were away from safety.

"Not gonna make it home," I panted.

"Doc's," Jay huffed, and turned off the path. A heartbeat later, and he wrenched open the door to Doc's cabin. We both fell inside, slammed the door behind us, and lowered the bolt.

The door thudded like someone was pounding on it from the outside, but it didn't give.

Jay and I huddled together, listening to the banging and the rattling of the lock. I set the lamp down, then we broke apart to search for something to protect us.

"Gotta be some potion here to get rid of that thing," I said, searching through drawers and on shelves. The shelves were lined with bottles and jars, maybe hundreds of them in all different sizes. Some brown, some blue, all glass. I wished I knew more about what they all did.

"But what is it?" Jay's voice was strained tight with fear, and it cracked on the last word.

"I don't know." I kept scrabbling through the items in Doc's cabin, searching for . . . "The dirt! The brick dust and graveyard dirt! Do you see any?"

Jay held up jar after jar to his flashlight, dropping them all back into the baskets he plucked them from. "Nothing. What do we do?" He had a smudge of dust on his dark-brown cheek, and his lower lips trembled. I expect I looked the same.

I squeezed his arm. "We need to find something. We can't let that thing get us!"

"It ain't gonna get us, Jezzie. I'm gonna give it a good licking with this." He hit his palm with the flashlight, testing its weight.

A wooden walking cane lay in a corner. When I picked it up, I saw the tip of it had been whittled sharp. I didn't know why Doc would sharpen a cane, but it would make a good weapon. I tested it by making little jabs at the air. When I saw my arm, I realized I wasn't wearing the Devil's Shoestrings bracelet Doc made for me. I'd taken it off before I went to sleep. I wanted to kick myself.

"Let's go get it," Jay said, moving toward the door.

I pulled him away. "Don't get too close!"

That's when the banging fell silent. We pressed ourselves against the back of the cabin and waited, both of us with our heads cocked, listening. There was nothing.

Then, just when our breathing was getting back to normal, we heard something under our feet. Scraping.

The floor rattled back and forth as if someone was shaking it. Jay raised his flashlight above his head to use like a hammer. I braced my feet apart, shoving the point of the walking stick outward. I told myself that I'd use it. I was sure I could. Maybe.

Me and Jay looked at each other, then back down to the shaking floor.

I heard a crack like the bolt on a door sliding open. The floor shifted again. Then a part of it slowly began to rise up.

My arm was shaking like a leaf in a storm, but I held the cane fast and pulled my arm back. My only thought was: *You can do this, Jezebel. You have to protect yourself.*

The trapdoor in the floor opened all the way, and Doc's head rose up from its depths.

"Kids?"

I was so relieved to see it was our uncle that my whole body sagged. I had to lean against the wall for support. To my right, I heard Jay's breath come out in a long, low whistle. Then I realized I was still holding the cane out, and Jay still had the flashlight.

Doc stared at both of us and said, "Looks like we might need to have a talk, huh? Pretty sure you have something important to tell me."

Slowly, we lowered the weapons, and Doc eased himself

out of the cellar. He let the flap fall back down, and the hatch disappeared into the rest of the dusty, gritty floor. I didn't know his cabin had any space underneath it, and from the look on Jay's face, he didn't either.

Doc sat at his worktable and emptied his pockets. A few clear bottles with cloudy liquid in them, some dried branches, and a balled-up brown paper bag. He laid the things out in a pattern particular to him and hummed a soft, light tune I hadn't heard before. After a while, he said, "Well? I'm waiting."

"Dinah jumped up and ran off—"

"We was following Jezzie's doll—"

Doc waved his hands to stop us from speaking at once. "Wait . . . wait . . . easy now. One at a time. I can't hear myself think when y'all are chattering like magpies."

Jay looked at me, then started talking. "When me and Jezzie was at the marsh earlier today, she said something talked to her, then she got stuck in the mud and couldn't get out, then after we went to bed she woke me up and said we had to follow her crazy doll down the path and something in the marsh ate the light from the flashlight and then chased us into here." He took a deep breath like he was going to say more, then he clamped his lips shut.

Doc sat there, hands still, looking at Jay while he talked. He always liked to give a person's story his full attention. Then he turned to me, his eyes all serious, but calm. "Is that right?"

I nodded. "And it talked to us. It wished us a happy birthday."

"What about getting stuck in the marsh?"

For a minute I didn't say anything, even though I knew I had to. "Well . . . I got stuck in the mud. It was like the marsh held me still and wouldn't let me loose. But I figured it out, Doc! We used one of the blue paint sticks to get me out." I took a deep breath. "So there's really nothing to worry about—you can still keep teaching us rootwork."

If Doc was angry with us about what happened, he didn't show it. He just asked, "What about then? Did you hear anything when you were stuck?"

Jay and I shared a look. "I heard a voice. Clear as day, saying it was time."

"Time? Hm." He stroked his graying beard. "Did it *hurt* you?"

From the way he said the word 'hurt,' I knew the answer was important. I had been scared, but . . . "No, it didn't hurt me."

"Okay," Doc said. "Did it *feel* like it wanted to hurt you? This is important for both of you." He glanced at Jay. "But womenfolk mostly trust what they feel more than menfolk. It's called intuition. Think hard now, Jezebel.

Did you feel, somewhere deep inside, that it was going to hurt you?"

Intuition? I'd never heard the word before, but I knew what Doc meant. Oftentimes, I heard Mama and even Gran say they could feel things. Mama could feel when rain was coming on, when something was wrong with me or Jay, when someone was trying to fake her out at the market charging a higher price than was right. And Gran knew—she always said she *knew*, not that she felt—when someone was guilty or innocent. One time, we heard on the radio that Mr. Mackie from the garage got arrested for stealing, and she said the police had the wrong man. Turned out she was right.

I closed my eyes and tried to remember. Remember through my fear. In my mind I pulled away the layer of strangeness that had covered everything. Was it bad? Did I feel it being hateful? *Time*, it had said. *It's time.* The voice was one I didn't know, and it sounded like speaking was hard for it, like trying to walk through the knee-high mud in the marsh. Whatever it was hadn't hurt me and I felt—no, I *knew*—that if it had wanted to, it could have easily done so. But instead, it had kept me still and made me listen. I thought of the words to the song we sang in church. *Peace, be still.*

"No, it didn't mean me harm. I—we—were running around so much, hollering and everything. I wasn't paying attention." I looked over at Jay, who was giving me a strange look, like he'd never seen me before. "It wanted me to listen."

"Have you been listening lately?"

"I . . . I've been trying," I said, and pulled a loose string on the hem of my dress.

"I know you have." Doc gathered both of us together in a hug then.

I'd been so scared I was going to get in trouble. That Doc was gonna say he couldn't teach us anymore because it was too dangerous. I slumped into his hug with relief.

Jay squirmed to get free. "Doc, what was it out there? You must know." My brother crossed his arms in front of his chest and stuck his lower lip out.

Doc reached for his pipe. "I know you grew up seeing me and Gran make potions and such all your lives, but there are things in this world that you've never experienced before." Doc let out a heavy breath. "Your mother didn't want me doing spirit work around you two and I never did. Never talked about most of the other parts of rootwork. Hexes, spirits, and creatures from the next. She wanted you to go to school and get real jobs rather than feeling like you had no choice but this life." He smiled, but it seemed sad. "Looks like even though I hadn't introduced you to this aspect of rootwork, things got outside of my control. My mother was right. I needed to prepare you kids for this world, and I didn't do that properly. Anyone can learn recipes and rituals, but not everyone has a natural connection to the earth and the creatures that share our world." He nudged us at the same time. "That's something both of you have, in different ways. You're new, so it's delicate, but it's strong."

Doc turned up the wick on his hurricane lamp, an old oil one with a tall glass cover to protect the light when it was windy. The cabin got brighter and my worry faded some in the warm light. "I wanted to wait to tell you both about the true world of rootwork, but seems like an expert thinks it's time you both know."

The only person I knew who had more root understanding than Doc was Gran. Everyone on the island knew that. I didn't know what expert he was talking about, but at that moment, I wished so much that Gran could have been here to teach me alongside Doc.

Before Gran died, I used to climb onto her big bed and tell her my dreams. Once, after she heard one of my dreams about a crow and a crab, she got quiet. She took a deep breath and told me I'd do great things one day, but before I did, I was going to have troubles. I don't know if all this is what she meant, but this was definitely trouble.

I crossed my arms in front of me. "Who is this expert?" I asked, suspicious.

Doc said, "You two need to talk with your grandmother."

Our mouths dropped open. "What?"

"It's a lot to introduce you to in one day," Doc said.

"But sometimes, we can speak to those who've passed on, just like we're all speaking to each other now. Other times, ancestors come to us in dreams. Or we have to seek them out to ask for their advice." He smiled. "This is a very special thing, your gran crossing to speak to you. It's an honor."

"Jez?" Jay was looking at me, scared. I knew he was scared because I was too.

I bit my lip. Rocked back and forth on my heels. "It must be hard to cross over."

Doc nodded. "Takes a lot of energy for a spirit to communicate."

"Then . . . then it would be rude not to talk to her if she came all this way." I took Jay's trembling hand and squeezed it. "Right?"

"Right." He squeezed my hand back. "And Gran always made time to spend with us. We can spend time with her."

"Proud of y'all," Doc said as he stood up and walked over to the cabin's front door. He lifted the wooden bolt and opened it. We held our breath.

The dark shape from the woods lay flat on the ground outside. It rose, hovering at the doorframe, before carefully folding itself inside. It touched my hands, then my head and shoulders. I wasn't so scared this time, but I stayed still, unsure of what would happen next. The shadow didn't feel cold or evil; it felt curious and somehow—pleased. It did the same with Jay, and while he scrunched away from it at first, he eventually relaxed and let go.

Once he did, everything changed.

The dark shape fluttered and flapped, then it folded itself again and again until it was a rectangle as small as the palm of my hand. Then it fell to the floor.

From within the dark rectangle, another shape rose up. This one was a shadow shaped like a person. As it floated up and out of the shape on the floor, I smelled the scent of lemon and pine. Then came gardenias and benne candy, all bubbling sugar and toasty seeds.

It was Gran's smell.

The shadow stood there unmoving. Stars twinkled within the dark shape. Without thinking, I raced over and hugged the shadow. It felt like her too: warm and solid with a little softness under a long, starched-crisp skirt.

I couldn't believe it.

All of a sudden, I felt her, intensely. Smart, and wise, and how she knew—she always knew—the right thing to say. No matter what. She protected us, loved us, gave us everything she had, everything she loved: stories and songs and recipes and magic. And I missed her so much.

I mumbled into her skirt, "Ah muss moo."

Her chuckle was a soft and gentle puff against the top of my head. It was comforting, like a fire when you come in from a walk in the cold.

Then she spoke. "I miss you too, my Jezzie Belle." Her voice was exactly the same, and I would know it anywhere.

Jay came up beside me. "Hi, Gran," he said, and reached out to her.

"Hi, Jay Bird."

Gran's arms wrapped around us, and she hugged us both. When her shadowy self lifted, she raised us up too. We clung onto her while she swung us in midair. It was flying and getting hugged at the same time and it was perfect.

When she set us back down on the ground, we were full of questions.

"How did you get here?"

"Is this real magic?"

"Can we do it?"

"How long can you stay?"

It didn't matter that me and Jay talked at the same time and talked over each other. Gran just sparkled even more. Maybe because we weren't scared anymore.

"I done walk, swim, and fly to get here. But I wouldn't miss this birthday. You's eleven now, and that's momentous." I could feel her smile and her happiness. "And yes, it's real magic. And you can do it, if you work hard." I couldn't see Gran's face clear within the shadow. Instead, she looked as though she was in front of candlelight in a dark room when she thanked us in Gullah. "*Tenki*," she said. "*Fuh la'an disya ruht.*"

"How long can you stay?" I asked again.

"Jezebel." Doc's voice had a warning in it.

"It's all right," Gran said to Doc. "These chirren gotta know."

Gran bent down in front of me and Jay. She was still in shadow, but her eyes and her smile sparkled with love. "I must go," she said. Gran kissed me on the forehead, then Jay.

"But remember this: *Hice da famblee.*"

Raise the family.

"How do we do that? I don't understand." Gran was usually patient with us and explained things when we asked her. Her words now made me confused, like I should know something I didn't.

"You will," she said. "When the time come. Know I love y'all, hear?"

Once more, she hugged us tight. Then she stepped back, onto that black rectangle. As the dark shape began to fade, we heard her voice one more time.

"We gonna see each other again, you know. One day. Oh, and Jezebel, better leave your window open for Dinah."

After that, she was gone. But I could still feel her kiss on my forehead. Still smell her scent like perfume on the air. My heart felt like it was growing inside me, it was so full of love and joy. I wanted to spin around and around until I was dizzy.

She told us being eleven was special. Momentous. And

it already was. I wanted to hold this moment inside me forever.

But it was time for us to go back to bed. Doc ushered us out of his cabin and we headed back inside, quiet as we could. Jay yawned and climbed under the bedspread. I sat on my pillow, remembering.

Something had opened up in me: a huge deep well that wanted to be filled. I knew now why learning my family's magic was so important. There was more to rootwork than I ever imagined. More than the kids at school could understand. More than Deputy Collins could scare out of us. And I was ready to learn it all.

I was tired, but I felt better than I had since Gran passed away. I raised the window a little more, like Gran asked, for Dinah to get in. Then I climbed under the covers.

"I think I can do this," I whispered to the night. "It's scary, but exciting too. And I love knowing that I'm doing things the people in my family even a hundred years ago used to do."

I lay back on my bed and said my prayers for the health and happiness of everyone in the family, making sure to still include Gran. When I looked over at Jay, he had his face smashed into the pillow, already asleep.

Soft light from the moon and stars came through the sheer curtains into our room, making patterns on my bedspread that I traced with my finger. Sounds of the marsh filtered in through the cracked-open window: frogs croaking, cicadas singing, and the call of screech owls.

My eyelids got heavy. "This is going to be a big, important year," I whispered to myself before I fell asleep too.

8

When I woke up, I felt Dinah's little gunnysack body under the covers. I rolled over onto my tummy and hugged her tight, not caring that the girls at school would make fun of me even more if they knew I played with dolls. She had a little bit of Gran inside her, just like me.

Dinah had been out in the woods all night, but her clothes weren't dirty at all. I checked, and her dress was still clean and crisp and her hair trailing from under her headwrap was fluffy and soft. She smelled like pine trees and cinnamon. It made me think of Gran all over again, and so I pretended to talk with Dinah like she was my grandmother.

"Where were you all night?" I asked.

I moved her head with my first finger as though she was answering my question. "Dis my new frock, *enny*? Had to go have me a little fun."

I laughed at the voice I used for Dinah's, high and whiny. "That's true, I guess." I sat up in bed and lifted her up with me. "Tell me, how come I didn't know you could walk by yourself?"

Her little red stitched mouth smiled. "You don't know erryting 'bout the world. Least not yet."

I smoothed Dinah's crepe wool hair and placed her on the bed, then shoved my hand through my Devil's Shoestrings bracelet and got up to get ready for school. On the way to the washroom, I shook Jay awake. He groaned and threw his pillow at me, but I was too fast. I made it out of the room, laughing all the way.

I was hungry thanks to my adventure the night before, and all I wanted was rice for some reason, but Mama was already dishing up our breakfast of steaming grits. As we ate, a car pulled up the dirt road that led to our place. I rushed to the window to peek out, elbowing Jay so we could both see.

It was a police car.

Mama craned her neck to see as well. "Lord, I don't need today to start off with no foolishness."

"You gonna be all right?" Doc asked. When Mama

nodded, he took his opportunity to leave out of the back door.

It was Sheriff Edwards again. He parked by the chicken coop and got out, unfolding his height like a sheet. He took his hat off the seat next to him, but he didn't put it on. Instead he tucked it under his arm and made his way up to the house.

We ran back to the table and sat like we'd been there all along. Before he could knock, Mama smoothed her dress, then pulled the screen door open. The sheriff's brown hair was damp around the edges, and his shirt was still pressed straight with sharp creases in it.

"Mighty early for a visit, Sheriff," Mama said, blocking the door with her whole body. She looked about half his size, but the sheriff stayed a respectful distance away from the open door.

"Sorry about that, Mrs. Turner, but I was hoping I might get some eggs."

"Eggs?" Mama repeated, surprised.

Me and Jay looked at each other, just as confused as Mama.

"There's plenty eggs in the market. Why he want our eggs?" Jay whispered to me.

"I don't know," I told him, tracing the vines in my bracelet.

When Mama didn't answer, Sheriff Edwards said,

"Oh, and some corn too, if you have any." Mama stood there staring at him, and he added, "Please."

That little word somehow put her into action. She put six eggs into a cardboard container and placed it in a peach basket. Then she added four ears of corn from the box she was planning to take to the roadside stand to sell once we left for school.

"And would you add a jar of your fig jam? I'd be grateful." He pulled out his wallet to pay for it all.

Mama handed him the basket of food, and he placed a few bills in her hand.

"This is too much," she said with a frown. "I don't take charity."

"I didn't think you did. But I got first pick of everything today, and I expect that costs a bit more."

Mama still frowned, but she didn't say anything. She slid the bills in her apron pocket. "Anything else, Sheriff?"

He looked over at me and Jay where we sat at the table. Then he took a big, deep breath. "I spoke to him yesterday. Deputy Collins. About harassing folks without cause. He didn't take it too well, but I wanted you to know."

Mama balled her hands up into fists at her side. "I don't know if you made things better or worse for us, Sheriff."

"I hope better. Now he knows I won't stand for such actions."

"You're one man. Lots of others out there will take his side." Mama sighed and rubbed her temples. She looked down at us. "Then where will we be?"

"Mama," I said, touching her apron. "Me and Jay will help keep the family safe."

She nodded, then looked up at the sheriff. "Is that all?"

"That's all, Mrs. Turner. Kids." He stepped back from the open door, put his hat on, nodded at each one of us. Then he clomped down the stairs, carrying his basket of food. A moment later, the car started, then pulled away.

Mama sighed and shut the door. She shuffled back over to the kitchen table and sank into a chair.

"What's he gonna do now?" Jay asked.

"Do we need to stop going to school?" I added.

"No!" That drew Mama's back straight upright. "You will keep on as usual. Go to school the same way you always do, but be sharp. Look around you, be aware of anyone creeping around. If you see anything strange, you get on back here, understand?"

"Yes, ma'am," we both said.

Jay went back to his breakfast, but I saw the worry on Mama's face. She looked out the window toward Doc's cabin and bit her lip. I knew what she was thinking. Deputy Collins would be coming back, and coming back mad, and there was nothing any of us could do about it.

I felt scared and helpless all at the same time. Seeing Mama worry when she almost always had an answer for everything was the worst part. My tummy felt wobbly, rough as the ocean during a storm. I pushed my bowl away toward Jay, and he dug into the rest of my breakfast.

Could we trust Sheriff Edwards to help us? Or would we have to fix this thing with Deputy Collins ourselves? Doc had left as soon as the sheriff arrived. Was he headed off to make a potion? Or was he leaving Mama to handle things, like Daddy did all those years ago?

Mama busied herself getting her last things ready for the market. She put Jay's lunch together, scooping Sea Island red peas on top of steaming rice. While I usually loved peas, I didn't want any today. I asked for my rice plain.

"You sure, Jez? Plenty of peas here," she said as she got a small bowl out of the cabinet.

"Yes, ma'am."

Mama shrugged, then scooped up the warm rice and covered it with a lid. "You kids head on off to school now, and remember what I said." She hugged both of us. "If you see Doc in his cabin, send him in here."

Jay scraped my dish clean and put it in the sink along with his. Then he grabbed his books and lunch and made for the cabin.

Mama was gathering up her blue metal cash box and getting her crates of jams and jellies and baskets ready to go. I touched her arm, and she stopped rustling around the kitchen long enough to look at me.

"It's gonna be okay, Mama," I said. "Do you want my bracelet?"

"No, thank you. That's yours, Jez." She smoothed her hands over my pigtails. "And you're right—it's gonna be fine. You go on to school."

I didn't want to leave her, but I grabbed my books and my lunch and raced off after Jay.

Classes were so much fun that morning that I almost forgot about Deputy Collins. Today was our first music appreciation lesson, and we listened to a classical opera song, followed by some big-band jazz tunes from Duke Ellington. I knew the answer when I got called up to the chalkboard in math. But my good day changed at lunchtime.

In the cafeteria, I sat with Susie again, at a sun-warmed table near the door to outside. The cool breeze coming inside rustled my paper bag. I took out my dish of rice and a spoon and sat it beside my thermos of tea. I lifted the tinfoil wrapper off, and a voice interrupted me.

"You're still coming to school, little witch baby?"

Lettie and her group of girls had already gone through the cafeteria line and were standing above me with their trays of food. Her nose was tilted up high in the air, like she was trying to make herself look taller than she really was.

Susie groaned. "Go away, and let us eat in peace."

I rolled my eyes and decided not to answer. I didn't owe her my attention. But ignoring Lettie didn't work.

"I thought you'd be in jail by now, with all the other witches."

Lettie was grinning when I lifted my head. But I wasn't looking at her. I was looking at the girls who surrounded her. Many of them I knew from last year, and most had parents who had come to Doc for something. I stared straight into the eyes of those girls pretending to look down on my family when I knew they benefited from our magic. A few of the girls turned their faces away.

I was tired of hearing her talk about how I was different because my family held on to our traditions and our history while we studied and learned and improved ourselves at the same time. I touched my Devil's Shoestrings bracelet and looked at each one of the girls as I said her name aloud. "Lettie. Wanda. Ruth. Brenda. Evelyn."

"What are you doing?" Lettie looked confused. Her girls all looked at each other, then at me, then back at their leader. It was like they were seeing her uncomfortable for the first time.

I smiled. I wasn't doing any kind of spell or anything, but making her feel worse made me feel better.

But Lettie quickly regained her composure. "Well, what can you expect from someone like *that*?"

One of her friends gave me a hateful smile. "Like what, Lettie?"

My head was light. Maybe it was that feeling Doc was talking about. The feeling something bad was going to happen. I held my breath.

"She's a bastard."

A gasp went up from the whole crowd that had gathered around the table when Lettie approached. It was followed by an "ooooh" that was just as loud. My face burned with heat and shame, although I didn't know what for. I knew she used a bad word, but it was one that I didn't exactly know the meaning of.

Lettie went on, "And one of those evil root people. Look at that ugly bracelet. It looks like it has bugs living in it."

"Root isn't evil!" I shouted back at her. "You're evil for all the nasty things you say."

Lettie cackled. "She admits it! She's one of those root witches that poison people's minds. My mom says you can't expect anything from them. They don't know any better."

Before I could open my mouth to respond, Susie shot up. She marched over to the whole group of girls to face Lettie. They were almost eye to eye, but Susie was taller.

"You will go away right now," she said. "Or else."

Susie fixed Lettie with a stare that made her take a step

back. I knew that look, but I'd never seen it on Lettie's face. She was scared.

She put her nose in the air and turned away. But I noticed her voice shook a bit when she spoke. "Come on, girls, we don't need to stick around here. The witch baby might turn us into frogs or something."

Susie sat back at the table with me. "Are you okay?"

"Yeah," I managed to say, even though my throat felt like it was closing up. "Thanks for sticking up for me."

"Of course," she said in a soft voice. "We're lunch buddies."

I nodded, but I didn't finish eating. The whole experience had made me lose my appetite.

9

I held tears in for the rest of lunch, and when I got back to class, I raised my hand. "Miss Watson, may I go see the nurse?"

I hoped she wouldn't ask me what was wrong, because nothing was. I just needed to get out of there. Miss Watson seemed to read my mind, and I breathed a sigh of relief when she nodded and handed me the hall pass without a word.

As soon as I got out of the classroom, the tears came. Then they ran down my cheeks, hotter than bathwater, down into the starched neck of my dress. I'd wanted so badly for this school year to be wonderful, and all I'd managed to do was make enemies and look silly in front of the whole class, every day. I wanted to disappear.

The dim hallway was empty. When I arrived at the door to the nurse's office and knocked, a voice called out, "Come in!"

"Miss Corrie?" I asked, peeking my head around the door.

The nurse sat in a chair with a padded back, different from every other chair in the school. She looked up from a thick hardcover book. When she saw me, she put an envelope in it to mark her place and closed the cover. The school nurse was a round-cheeked, dark-skinned woman with cat-eye glasses and a quick, crooked smile. It was said around school that she didn't have any time for children who pretended to get out of doing work. But if you were actually sick, there was no one better to help you.

"Good afternoon, Jezebel," she said. Her voice was gentle but serious.

"You remember me?"

Miss Corrie nodded. "Of course. You've been to see me before."

I hadn't been really sick before, but I had been to the nurse's office last year. It was when one of the kids poked me in the back of my neck with a pencil and the tip of the lead broke off in my skin. Miss Corrie cleaned it up and called the boy into her office for a talking-to.

She motioned for me to sit in a chair right across from her. "What seems to be the trouble?"

Suddenly my shoes were very interesting. The trouble was I didn't feel like I had a place in school, like I fit somewhere. But that wasn't something you could fix with medicine or bandages. When I looked up into Miss Corrie's cat-eye glasses, she pressed her thin lips together.

"Well?"

I took a deep breath. "I wanted this school year to be perfect. I wanted to make friends and not feel awful about myself. And I've already messed that up."

If she was annoyed that I didn't have a real medical emergency, she didn't show it. She just removed her glasses and wiped them with a cloth she took from a case on her desk. "Well, didn't you skip ahead a grade this year? That's a lot for a student to adjust to. And no school year is ever perfect. No person is ever perfect."

I thought of Lettie and her friends, with their beautiful new dresses and pressed hair and shoes without buckles. "Some people sure look like they are."

"That's how they look on the outside. Maybe what's inside them is very different." Miss Corrie looked like she wanted to say something, then thought better of it. She scribbled a note for Miss Watson and handed it to me. "Give this year a chance, Jezebel. It might surprise you."

It wasn't what I wanted to hear right then, but I appreciated her trying.

"What did I tell you about slamming that screen door?" Mama asked when me and Jay came in the house from school that afternoon. She was facing the stove, her back to us. "And James, you are supposed to let ladies in before you."

"Jezzie ain't no lady," Jay said.

I had done a pretty good job not crying anymore after getting back from Miss Corrie's office, and the whole walk home with Jay, while he ran and did cartwheels, having no idea how I was feeling. But at that moment, my tears burst into a wave like the big salt at high tide. I stood there in the middle of the kitchen and cried until I could hardly breathe. Jay looked uncomfortable and Mama put a dish in the oven before she turned back to look at me.

"What happened?" she asked him.

"I don't know," he said, scratching at a mosquito bite on his scrawny arm. "I didn't do nothing."

"Well, somebody did."

Mama poured a glass of lemon water from the icebox and came and sat in the chair in front of me. "Calm down, now. You're home. Drink this. Go on." She put the glass in my trembling hands and helped me tilt it back. I drank enough to ease the burning heat in my throat. Guzzled it until I choked on the water and Jay thumped me hard on the back. Mama put her cool hands on my forehead, my cheeks, and my neck, and I sighed. I took another long drink of water and set the glass down. Now I felt exhausted. Tired, ready to go to bed and sleep forever.

"Little better?" she asked. "Feel like you can tell me what that was all about?"

I took a deep breath of kitchen-warm air. "Yes, ma'am."

Jay sat in a chair on the other side of the table and chewed on a ragged wedge of sugar cane from the counter.

"I don't want to go to school anymore."

The gentleness in Mama's face disappeared. Her mouth twisted up like she had sucked on the lemon she'd put in my water. "Well, you're going to go to school anyway. And you're going to study and get the grades you need to make something out of yourself. That's it. End of story."

"But I—"

"No buts. You know how many Negroes are unemployed? Can't get jobs and have no money to live off? We don't have much, but I've always given you what I could. You and your brother have always had food and a roof over your heads. I don't want you to have to rely on anyone else for your livelihood, do you hear me?"

When I didn't answer or meet her eyes, she took me by the arms and gave me a little shake. "Do you?"

The look in her eyes was one I couldn't remember seeing before. I thought of the words to the sonnet-ballad poem Miss Watson read to us. There was a line about asking your mother where happiness was. I wanted to ask my mother about happiness, but right now, she didn't look like she knew. "Mama, you don't understand what it's like."

"I understand that you have to go through troubles in life and this is only one of them. You must, must, must go to school." She locked eyes with me. "So you have a chance at a future."

I pulled away from the grip Mama had on my arms, moved and stumbled, almost falling on my backside. I scrambled out of the screen door, letting it slam behind me as I flew down the packed-dirt path, then thought better of it and turned to the fields where the corn was growing taller than I was.

The neat rows reminded me of the braids Mama put in my hair at night to keep what she called my *wild hair* under control. I ran until my legs ached and muscles burned. Then I slowed down and sank to the ground. I lay on my back, looking up at the yolk-yellow sun in the sky, hoping to burn the tears out of my eyes.

I couldn't understand why Mama did that to me. She was always tough, but kind, especially when she was explaining why things had to be different for me than for my brother. Jay was a boy, and the world was different for men and boys, especially Negro men and boys, and he had to learn how to live in it. Doc had said that I felt things differently than Jay did because I was a girl. Gran always treated me and Jay the same, but even she admitted that the world wouldn't. She also told me I needed to be independent, learn how to do things for myself, even things men are supposed to do. If there was something I couldn't do for myself, I should find a trustworthy person to do it and pay a fair price for the work.

Maybe Mama was being so hard on me because Gran was gone. We didn't have someone who stayed at home all the time to make sure we were safe when Mama was at work anymore. This whole time, I was thinking of how much I missed Gran that I wasn't thinking of how Mama must feel.

How would I feel? On top of working every day, running a farm, and raising me and Jay all on her own, Mama had so much to do. She had to deal with the sadness of losing her own mother, and worrying about Deputy Collins, who could come to the house at any moment and take everyone she loved away. I was scared sometimes, and I didn't have to do everything Mama did. I bet she was scared too.

I waited there in the corn, expecting Mama or Jay to come looking for me and tell me to come back home. But neither one of them did. So after a while I got up slowly and walked through the tall stalks until I got to two posts pounded deep into the ground. The posts were about to my knee and as far apart as my arms when they were flung out wide. A long piece of wood lay on the ground next to the posts.

A smile twisted my mouth, a sweet and sad one, like remembering summertime during the winter. I pulled the board up, releasing boll weevils, pill bugs, and a small spider from their homes. It was damp and dark on one side, where it had been on the ground for who knows how long, and dry and beginning to crack on the upside that had been facing the sun. I placed one end of it on top of a post, then lifted the other end to the opposite post, connecting the two. I tested it with my hands, placing my weight on it little by little to see if it held.

When I felt like it was safe, I sat in the middle of the board, and it wobbled in a way that felt like bouncing. I jumped up a little in my seat and bounced on the board a bit more. It was lightweight and joggled easily, making me laugh out loud.

Jay and I had used this joggling board when we were little kids, spending hours on it in the blazing sun. We'd try and joggle the other higher, or joggle them off the board altogether. After a day in the sun, we'd go inside and compare our suntan marks, our upper arms and just above our knees. Mama would laugh and rub cocoa butter on our skin to keep it from drying out. Back then, there had been no corn; this field had been all covered by deep, thick, soft grass, and we had a few pigs that roamed this area, along with a clutch of chickens near the house. When one of us fell off the board, we would roll in the sweet-smelling grass, and one of the pigs would come over to investigate where the kukuing was coming from. They would snuffle and snort softly, rooting through the grass until they smelled us, and we would gather mud from the marsh bank and rub their skin with it to keep them from getting burned up under the sun.

I had forgotten this joggling board and I wondered now what had made me and Jay stop playing on it. It couldn't be that we thought we were too grown-up for it. Even now, I was having fun. We used to share our secrets here, and talk without anyone hearing us. It was more private, away from the sharp ears in the house. I struggled to remember the last time we'd used it. We'd come out here every day; it was always special because Daddy had made it for us—

Oh. Now I remembered.

When Jay and me were about six years old, Daddy had chopped the posts and used his big sledge to pound them into the ground nice and sturdy. He had also taken care to find just the right kind of board to go between them. When he took us out to it with Mama covering Jay's eyes and him covering mine, we had squealed like our little pigs and spent the rest of the day climbing on it and falling off into the fluffy grass over and over. It had been magic. And not the kind Doc made. This one was with hearts and light.

Then something had happened. One day, Daddy was there, and the next, he was gone. I put my head in my hands, trying to remember what had happened. I didn't remember any fights with him and Mama. No hard whispers in the night after they thought me and Jay were sleeping. We asked what happened to him. At first, Mama pressed her lips together and stalked off, not saying anything. But I saw her eyes were shiny with tears. We kept asking, and finally she said, "If I had anything to say about your father, I would say it, but I don't. End of story."

For what seemed like years, Jay and I would pray for him to come home. From wherever he was, we didn't care. If he would, we would all forgive him, even Mama. I prayed so hard, so often, my knees hurt from kneeling. Soon they turned dark, getting an extra covering of deep brown, like the color of the dark wood floor they rubbed against.

We were sitting outside the window one day, playing something—cards or jacks or marbles—and Jay said, "I wish Daddy was here."

He hadn't meant anything by it, nothing against Mama, but she didn't hear it that way. She leaned out of the window above us and said, "Wish in one hand, and spit in the other. See which one fills up first." Then she slammed the window shut.

The next day, things started moving fast. Mama sold our pigs, leaving the chickens as our only animals. When I asked if I could keep one piglet, just one, she pretended I hadn't said anything to her at all. With some of that money, she paid men to come and clear the land and dig rows for planting. When the rows were done, Mama sent the men on their way and planted the seeds herself. She didn't even want me and Jay helping her. I don't remember playing that day. I only watched Mama walk the rows that looked like my plaits and cover them with moist, black soil. It wasn't long after that Doc and Gran came to stay with us. And soon life got back to normal. Or close to.

Sometimes I wondered where Daddy was. But more often, I wondered what happened between him and Mama that made her want to erase him from her mind. In a few months, the corn grew long, hiding that whole field that used to be for our pigs. We would still go back there, wading through the young stalks, but as the corn grew higher and taller and stronger, it covered over all of those memories. Me and Jay made other hideaway spots, found other games to play, and soon we forgot about it.

As for Mama, she got upset easier now. Her laugh didn't happen as much. Her smile when she gave us our cake was the first one I'd seen in a long time. It made me sad. It made me want to try harder to make her happy. I made a promise to help her more, do more around the house. Maybe even bring her some of the wildflowers that grew along the road.

There must have been a reason, a really good reason, Daddy was gone, but Mama's mouth was shut up tighter than an oyster. We might never know, but whatever it was hurt Mama badly. Probably even worse than what I was feeling right then. Gran used to say hurt wasn't like a splinter that might work itself out after a while, it was a boil that had to be lanced—the hurt had to leak out before it could heal up. According to Doc, a swig of moonshine would help too, but I wasn't old enough for that yet.

The stalks of corn swung high and low, back and forth, like someone too big to squeeze down the rows was forcing them apart. There was the crunching of footsteps, the shuffling of drying husks. Someone was coming. I touched my bracelet to make sure I still had some protection with me.

But it was only Doc. His face appeared between some stalks, the top of the corn looking like it was growing out of his ear. I somehow couldn't smile, even though I wanted to. "Did Mama send you to talk to me?"

He shook his head. "But that tells me there's something to talk about."

I shrugged my shoulders and kicked my feet. I was too tall for the joggling board now, unless I held my feet up high.

He sat at my feet, stretching his bare ones out and lying back on the dirt. He moved his hat, a beat-up straw one with part of the brim missing, in front of his face. I waited for him to try and get me to talk. But he didn't. Doc lay up there with his rough, dark-skinned feet pointing at me while he folded and braided corn husks into the shape of a rose. When it slumped, he grunted and tossed it to the side. "Hmph. Easier with palmetto leaves. They're sturdier."

I'd seen both Doc and Mama weave strips of palmetto leaves and sea grasses into baskets and other shapes: flowers, crosses, and such. It was one of the things Mama did when our farm wasn't making as much money. While it was cold, baskets of all shapes and sizes, some with handles, some not, piled up in all the rooms in our house. When summertime hit and all the tourists came, Mama would head downtown and sell them in the market for good money.

Doc could lie there until nightfall if he had a mind to. I felt like I was hungry, but I knew it was the empty feeling in my chest and not my stomach.

"I told Mama I didn't want to go to school no more," I said, finally. "Anymore," I corrected myself.

"And?"

"She got angry and said I was going no matter what."

"Know why she said that?"

I shook my head no.

He took a pouch out of his pocket and laid it on the ground. "*Tote disya*," he said.

"*W'ymekso?*" I said without thinking. Why did he want me to carry his tobacco pouch? He never let me near it before.

"Do you know why you understood what I asked you to do?"

"No, why?"

"The same reason your ma is so adamant that you go to school." He sat up and removed the hat from his eyes, shoving it back off his face to look at me in mine. "Know how much teasing your ma and I got when we were your age? Even before that? When we started school, long time ago way back, neither one of us spoke what they called the King's English. We spoke Gullah, like your gran, and like you did just now. Everybody, including the teachers, laughed at us for sounding ignorant. They wanted to put us in a special class for slower children because they thought we couldn't learn."

"Did they?" I was shocked that back then teachers treated my mama and my uncle like they were stupid for speaking the language they learned first. "But you sound perfect when you talk either one."

"That's because your Ma and I made a decision together. We were going to learn how to speak what they called 'normal' English. Even if we had to do it with kids younger than us who didn't understand so well. We studied and we learned and no one ever saw us without a book or a pad and pencil. It was hard, but we did it. And once we started talking the way all those teachers said we were supposed to, know what happened?"

"Nobody teased you anymore?"

He laughed. "No! They teased us because we were poor. And I was skinny. And our skin was dark."

"The girls at school . . . they tease me about root," I said while I spun the bracelet on my wrist around and around. "Like there's something wrong with it."

"I'm not surprised. All skin folk ain't kinfolk. Ever heard that?"

I shook my head.

"It means just because someone is a Negro like you, it doesn't mean they agree with everything you say or do." Doc sat up straighter. "There are some of us who want to forget about our history and our past. Pretend we were not enslaved people who had to struggle to live. It makes them feel safer."

"But we aren't safe from Deputy Collins."

"You're right. But those people think if they act how Collins and other white people believe they should, they'll be safe from them."

"So Lettie—she's the girl at school—thinks I'm low-class because I believe in something that's from our history?"

"Pretty much," Doc said, lighting his pipe. "Thing is, Jezebel, people will find a way to make you feel bad about yourself if you let them. But it diminishes you. What does diminish mean?"

"To get smaller."

"Right. And that isn't what you want, is it?"

"No. But why are people like that?" I watched the smoke from Doc's pipe curl in the air. "Why can't we all try and understand each other?"

"You have a lot of strong people in this family, alive and not. Reach out to them. Learn your history and be proud of it. Become the best person you can be and don't spend any time thinking or worrying on the rest. It'll come."

"That wasn't what I was upset about."

He got up to his feet, slowly and without making any groaning noises like Gran used to. "Wasn't it?"

Then he left me there, wandering off sideways through the corn instead of down the rows, alternately whistling and humming a song I didn't know.

I pulled four ears off the stalks and shucked them before I headed back to the house. It was past dinnertime; the sun was dipping in the sky. When I got home, the yard was bustling with chickens getting ready to roost down for the evening and there was nobody sitting on the porch. I climbed up the three steps and into the house. Dinner was cleared off the table and all the counters had been wiped down.

As I searched for a place to sit my burden, I looked up and saw Mama leaning on the doorjamb to her room. We both stood there for a minute—her eyes wanting answers, mine all given up on ever getting them. I held on to my skirt, weighed down with ripe corn.

"A girl at school made fun of me for working root," I said. "But that wasn't all. She also called me . . . a bastard."

Mama let out a curse I'd never heard her say. I stayed still, ready for anything: a whipping for staying out, a tongue-lashing for missing dinner, getting my mouth washed out with soap for saying a bad word.

But none of it came. Mama lifted the ears of corn from my skirt and looked at them all over. "You did a good job on these," she said, wrapping the corn in a clean kitchen towel before putting it in the icebox.

Then she went to her room, and I heard her open and close a few drawers in her dresser. On the way back to the kitchen, she stopped at the door of our room and called Jay. He came out, frowning and scratching his belly.

"Sit, you two."

Jay stared at Mama for a minute, then glanced over at me. We both sat at the kitchen table and waited while Mama paced. Even the breeze stopped blowing, like it was also wondering what was going to happen next.

Mama sighed deep and long. She looked up to the ceiling, then back at us. "Jay, did you know this girl at school was calling your sister names?"

He looked at me, then back at Mama, and shook his head.

"Do you kids know what that word means?" She didn't wait for us to answer. That meant she was all fired up. "It means your father wasn't married to your mother when you were born. That's it. Understand? It doesn't mean you're better or worse than anyone else. The *only thing* that makes you a good or a bad person is how you treat others."

"But why would she say that to me?" I asked.

"To hurt you, Jez. But don't ask me why she wants to hurt you. I don't know." Mama sat at the table, between me and Jay. "Maybe she thinks you're different. Maybe she's jealous of you."

"I don't have anything to be jealous of," I said. "Lettie has fancy clothes and lots of friends. I don't have those things."

Mama smiled. "You have a lot more than you think. You just have to see it and value it. Believe you're important." Then she took an envelope out of her apron pocket and held it up. "In here is a piece of paper. If you need to look at it for proof you aren't . . . that word, then you can." The chair scraped as Mama stood up. "It's your choice. Bring it back when you're done." She left me and Jay sitting at the kitchen table.

"What should I do?" I asked.

Jay shook his head. "You have to choose. Wasn't me got called that name. You gotta think of how much knowing matters to you."

I thought of Doc's words as I turned the envelope over and over in my hands. *People will find a way to make you feel bad about yourself if you let them.* I was letting what the girls said make me feel bad. Even though they didn't know me at all. Even though they didn't even *try* to get to know me, either. No one except Susie, at least.

How I was born didn't matter. What mattered was what I did now.

I got up from the table and headed toward Mama's room to return the envelope. I wasn't going to open it. I didn't need to. As I stood, Jay grinned and gave me a thumbs-up.

"Mama?" I raised my hand to knock on her door, but it swung open before I could. Then she grabbed me up in a huge hug.

"I'm proud of you, Jezebel," she said.

I hugged her back. No matter what Lettie said or Deputy Collins did, I knew we would always be a family and help each other. It didn't matter where we lived or what we wore or what we ate, we were Turners and we were family.

My stomach rumbled, and Mama chuckled softly. "It's getting late, but would you like your dinner? I kept it warm in the oven."

"Yes, please!"

Mama put a big bowl of Frogmore stew in front of me. For the first time in ages, I attacked my dinner almost as hard as Jay usually did. Frogmore stew didn't have frogs in it, but it did have crab and shrimp cooked in a rich tomato broth with corn and potatoes. It was one of my favorite things that Mama cooked.

She sat with me while I ate dinner and I told her about the poems Miss Watson read to us.

"I'm so glad you're getting to learn about these artists, Jez." Mama took off her apron.

I finished the last of my stew. "We're learning about writers, not painters."

"Not only painters are artists. If a person is creating something with the work of their mind and hands, they are an artist, Jez."

"So is Doc an artist?" I asked.

Mama thought about that. "I guess he is. Now wash your bowl and get ready for bed."

Once I was tucked under the covers, I talked to Dinah about what I'd learned. Before long, though, Jay shushed me and said he wanted to get some sleep before tomorrow.

"Why?" I asked. "You never have trouble sleeping."

Jay groaned and pulled the sheet over his head. When I started talking to Dinah again, I kept my voice quiet. Soon I heard him snoring.

"Jay sounds like a lawn mower that ran over a penny." I laughed so hard at my own joke I almost woke my brother up. I could have sworn the edges of Dinah's mouth curled up.

I tucked her in next to me, her hair tickling my chin, and fell asleep still smiling, knowing that if I studied hard, one day I'd not only be a rootworker, I'd be an artist.

10

When me and Jay got up on Saturday, we shoveled hot Cream of Rice cereal into our mouths, then huffed and puffed to cool it down as the steaming grain burned our tongues. Doc sat at the table calm as can be, sipping on his coffee. Mama, though, was bustling about the kitchen, packing and repacking her items for the market. I had a feeling she had something on her mind about our training today. But the only thing she said when we got up from the table was "Listen to your uncle. And come home when you need to."

We both shouted that we would, as I grabbed my notebook and two new pencils, ready to write down everything.

"I see you all are eager to get started today. C'mon, both of you." Doc stood. "Down to the cabin."

As we walked across the dirt, tufted with dark green grass, Doc lifted his straw hat and wiped his brow with his fingertip towel. "Whew! It's a hot one, ain't it? But it's perfect weather for your first *real* rootwork lesson. Now that you know a bit of the truth about the family magic."

Me and Jay exchanged looks, excited and a little scared at the same time. We scurried after our uncle to the cabin so we wouldn't miss a word.

"You two grew up around me working root—laying tricks, mixing up potions and powders, picking out plants and such. But now you know there's more to it." Doc opened the cabin door and we followed him inside. "Some of it will be fun, some of it will make you nervous, some of it you won't like at all. But all of it you need to know." Doc clapped his hands. "And we're gonna start with some warnings about what you're gonna learn."

Jay's eyes glinted at the mention of warnings. I knew he was hoping to do something dangerous, like learn to throw a ball of fire at someone. I didn't think that was something Doc could actually do, but a few days ago I didn't believe spirits could come back from the beyond and talk to us, so what did I really know?

"When you start working with conjure—root is a type of conjure magic—you're opening yourself up to a part of the world most folks don't have access to. But: it also opens up that part of the world to *you*. Haints and spirits and all manner of things from the stories your gran told. And many of them—*most* of them—ain't friendly."

Doc reached up on a high shelf to grab something; as he did, he nudged aside the box I saw there on our first rootwork lesson, the one that had been full of Devil's Shoestrings. The vines that me and Jay now wore.

"And that can mean trouble," Doc continued. "Which is why you have to learn to protect yourself first before you can help anyone else."

Jay said, "You mean, like, fighting them? Are you going to teach us to use weapons?"

"No," Doc said. "You can find somebody else to show you how to fight. That's never been my thing. Besides, you can hit or stab at a haint all you want, but that won't kill it or stop it from coming after you."

Jay huffed at that.

Doc must have noticed, because he said, "I already told you both why we had to paint the house blue, and showed you how to lay graveyard dirt to deter spirits." I noticed he was trying not to grin when he said, "Suppose you forget to gather the dirt, and an evil ghost or a hag has chased you inside a cabin that hasn't been painted to keep them away. It's threatening to knock down the door and come inside after you. What do you do then?"

I shook my head while Jay shrugged.

Doc leaned back on his worktable. "Give up?"

We nodded.

"Want me to tell you?" he teased.

"Yes!" I had my pencil ready to write it all down.

"Lay a broom inside the door. Before a hag can come after you, they'll have to count each piece of straw in that broom. Or put down a line of salt, and it will have to count each and every grain. By then, the sun should be coming up, and the hag will have to leave or get burned up by the daylight."

Me and Jay followed Doc around the cabin like little ducks while he told us more ways to get rid of ghosts and monsters. I was writing so much in my notebook, I wondered if Mama would have to get me another one. Jay, though, wasn't so impressed. He didn't write anything down because he said he trusted his brain. He tiptoed and looked out of the window of Doc's cabin. "I didn't think learning root was going to be so boring."

Doc crossed his arms. "This might seem like a lot to know, but you'll be glad you did when a haint arrives. And *they will*. Your gran crossed some mighty high water to come see you. So you can see the spirit world is connected with ours. Other spirits besides your gran might be able to make the trip to this side too. You have to be careful now. You both do."

"We can't just ignore the bad ones?" I thought about how I was going to try to deal with Lettie and her friends from now on.

Doc placed his unlit pipe between his teeth. "Being a rootworker or witch doctor means you have to make some hard choices from time to time. Like a lot of things in life, you have to take the good with the bad. You can't only learn the fun, easy things. Tough things happen, and you need to know that they'll happen so you're prepared to make those hard choices."

"What kinda choices?" Jay looked worried.

Doc fixed me with a look, then Jay. "I knew we'd get to this point, but I didn't think it would be this early. Come on with me."

He got up and headed out of the cabin and down to a cluster of trees whose thick branches touched and tangled together to make a dense overhang. It was much cooler here, and so much darker under the trees that it didn't look like daytime anymore.

"I know you love animals, Jez, so you might not care for this bit of knowledge." As Doc crouched down by a little wooden cage, I tensed up, and he noticed. "Remember: Take the good with the bad. Sometimes the best way to get rid of a threat is to kill it off. Other times, we need to kill things for ingredients to use in our protective magic."

I threw a look at Jay, but he wasn't bothered like I was. For the first time today, he looked really interested. I turned away, back to Doc.

"Luck potions are my most popular," Doc said. He gently took a bat out of the little wooden cage. The creature flapped and struggled, but Doc held it fast and made a little cut on its back with a penknife.

"You're hurting it!" I cried.

He shushed me while he worked carefully. "Most root-workers will kill a bat outright. Cut out its heart to make a batch of luck potion." Doc collected some of the bat's blood in a little bottle. "I don't do that, because it's hard enough catching bats. No reason to reduce their numbers."

"Blood is enough?" Jay asked.

"Yes." Doc put a little salve on the bat's cut and let it go. It flew up into the blue sky, then faded from sight like a shadow. He took a different bottle out of his bag and showed it to us. "This is what the potion will look like when it's finished. Soon I'll show you all the ingredients and techniques you'll need to finish it."

Jay took it and pulled open the cork. He sniffed it. "I need some luck tomorrow. I'm playing baseball with Larry and them," he said. Then he tilted the potion up and took a drink.

"No, wait! That's not for drinking—"

Doc tried to grab his arm, but it was too late. Jay had already downed almost half of the bottle. His eyes got huge. Then he coughed. "Ugh, that tastes stink!"

"You weren't supposed to drink it, Jay! You sprinkle it on yourself. Like cologne." Doc was trying not to laugh. So was I.

Jay coughed and hacked and wheezed while he wiped his tongue on the hem of his shirt. "Why you laughing? I'm probably gonna die."

"No, you won't. Brush your teeth when we get home and you'll be fine." Doc took the bottle and shoved the cork back in it and put it back in his bag. "Love potions are made the same way, except you use a dove instead of a bat."

"That's awful," I said. "With all the roots and flowers and herbs around, why do you still have to use animals in some of these spells?"

Doc kneeled down next to me. "Animal sacrifice is a part of root, Jez. Always has been. We are thankful for their life because it helps preserve ours."

I stuck my lip out. "You're thankful, but you still take it."

Slowly, Doc nodded. "Yes."

"Aw, come on, Jez," Jay said. "It's just a bat. You don't like them anyway."

"That's not the point." I crossed my arms. "I wouldn't hurt a bat any sooner than I would a dove."

"Or a cat?" Doc asked.

"Is there a spell that uses cats?" I was going to be sick to my stomach.

Doc nodded. "The bones from a black cat are powerful."

"I won't do that one. Ever, ever! Even for magic." I felt

tears welling up inside me. "Why can't you use something from the cat, but not hurt it and let it go after? Like, the fur, instead of bones? Mama does substitutions for recipes all the time." I couldn't stop myself from talking. All I could think about was what happened at the marsh. How powerless I felt compared to such a strong force. I imagined that was how the animals felt.

"Is that why Mama doesn't do root?" I asked. "Because she doesn't like killing animals?"

Jay elbowed me. "Mama's killed chickens and all kinds of fish and stuff to cook before. And I bet she would kill any anything if it tried to hurt her or one of us."

He was right. I hadn't thought about food.

"You ever done it?" Jay asked Doc. "Killed an animal for a spell?"

"Yes, I have," Doc said, his voice serious. "I caught the animal, gave thanks for it, and I killed it as quickly as possible."

My mouth dropped open. "Gran too?" I asked.

"Yes, your gran too. She's the one who showed me how to do it."

"Is this why people think root is wrong?" I asked Doc. I was starting to wonder if this was really something I wanted to learn to do.

"Maybe. But lots of those people kill also. They stomp on bugs. They destroy trees because they're growing in an undesirable place. They kill animals because their numbers are too large. But they don't give thanks before they do." Doc shook his head sadly. "Some people take and never give back. Taking and not giving back isn't good, especially not for a rootworker. We are supposed to help care for the land around us."

Jay tapped his cheek like he was thinking. "Suppose someone gives things to you? Like when people brought bushels of crabs and dishes of cooked food to the house when Gran died?"

Doc nodded. "Exactly right. That's not taking. That's people caring for others—by giving freely."

It was a tradition people had on the island, to bring cooked food to people who had lost a family member as a way to ease their burden during a difficult time. I patted Dinah where she lay in my pocket. Learning rootwork was a way of honoring Gran. I would learn it too, and I would take the good with the bad.

But I still couldn't let go of the idea. "Isn't there another way to work those types of spells besides using things from animals?"

"If there is, I'm betting you'll be the one to find it, Jezebel." Doc looked up from his bag of roots and leaves. "Well, that's enough for today. It's almost time for your lunch."

"Aw, I thought we were gonna learn root all day."

"Yeah," I chimed in. "Mama isn't home waiting for us."

"You kids gotta do something else because I need to make some potions this afternoon. I gave you a lot to think about already today, I don't want to confuse you two with a lot more ingredients and instructions."

"Oh, we won't be confused! I wrote everything down in my notebook, even the stuff about the animals, so I can keep it all organized," I said. "Besides, I already have some of the potion names here." I read out the list I'd made, of all the labels on the bottles on Doc's shelves.

"Well, excuse me." Doc whistled. "I *am* impressed. Okay then. We'll go inside and have some lunch, then spend the afternoon learning about some more of my best-selling potions. Maybe you can even help me mix some. It'll help me get my stock back up faster, because I tend to sell out of them real quick."

11

The whole month of October flew by like a hawk chasing after a marsh rabbit.

So much was happening that I could hardly keep up with it. My very first root spell—the bag that I'd hidden, a wish for a friend—seemed to have finally kicked in, because Susie and I were hanging out every day at lunch and walking home from school together most days. Well, we left school together, but she and I separated at the top of the road that led to our house. She never actually came down the road with me. One time, I asked if she wanted to come over. She paused, like she wanted to say no but also didn't want to be rude. I didn't want to make her feel bad, and I definitely didn't want to embarrass myself, so I didn't ask her again. Maybe the spell would take a little longer than I thought.

At the same time, Miss Watson was giving me more homework than I'd ever had before, and it took me so long to get through it. Once Mama had seen how much I had, she insisted I do it immediately after school, and so Doc moved rootwork lessons to after dinner. Since then, me and Jay almost never walked home from school together; he didn't have nearly as much homework to do, and he had more friends than he knew what to do with.

To tell the truth, I started to miss him. We used to do everything together, talk about everything. Now it seemed he had friends and sports and games, all these things that didn't include me. When I told Dinah about it, after Jay had started snoring, her little red stitched mouth wobbled, but she didn't do anything except lay her tiny cloth hand on my arm.

Was this something I should have known would happen? How could we stay close when we were in different classes and he was so interested in things that had nothing to do with me? Jay loved the plane Mama and Doc gave him for his birthday and kept it in a special place in our room. He even talked about being a pilot one day. I wasn't sure I even knew my brother that well anymore. Not long after October started, he took his bracelet apart and stuffed a few of the Devil's Shoestrings into a small felt bag that he wore around his neck. I asked him what else was in the bag, but he wouldn't tell me. He said Doc told him that if he revealed what was in it, it would make the root bag worthless. I just nodded, feeling more alone than ever.

And I never went out to the marsh anymore. I didn't want to, not without Jay, even though I missed it. The rustle of cordgrass calmed me. I loved ebb tide, when the pluff mud bubbled, and flood tide, when the waters lapped gently against the shore. And now that I wore my bracelet for protection, I felt safer than I had before. I also carried a pouch of the graveyard dirt mixed with powdered brick dust from Doc. I didn't sprinkle it on anything, but I had it in case I needed to.

Before I knew it, November had rolled around, and that first Saturday, Doc set me and Jay to work making simple oils for him to sell in his shop. He said that Boss Fix, Steady Work, and Fast Luck oils were the most popular ones this time of year—he almost couldn't keep them stocked. When Mama got home from the market, she watched us measure, mix, and smell the oils, then make labels for each one of them. Jay was better at drawing the pictures and I was better at the handwriting, making the letters clear and even on the paper. Mama looked at the row of clear glass bottles lined up on the kitchen worktable.

"Hmph," she said. "People shouldn't place all their

hopes on these rubs and things. Maybe if they read about King Solomon in the Bible instead of using that oil with his name, they'd be better off."

I looked at her strangely while Jay went to grab some book. Probably to look up what King Solomon oil was for. I wanted to remind him that King Solomon was the one who was wise enough to get the stolen-baby fight worked out. Before I could ask Mama how she knew what that oil was for, she guessed my question.

"Just because I don't practice root doesn't mean I don't know a little something about what y'all are doing. Your gran was my mama too, you know." She pressed her fingers to her back and groaned like she was holding something heavy and somebody had just told her to keep it five more minutes. "Get on with it now."

She sashayed out of the kitchen, and a moment later, I heard her in her bedroom, humming "One Fine Day" by the Chiffons along with the radio and sweeping the floor. I moved on with my work, crushing up some cinnamon with a rolling pin, then tiptoeing to put all my weight on it so that it would turn into a powder. I scraped up most of it with my fingers into a little scoop Doc had given me and poured about a teaspoonful into each jar of oil in front of me. The leftover powder covered my fingers and part of the back of my hand. The cinnamon was the same color as me, so I pressed my fingers into it and spread some of the powder onto my face, like Mama did with her makeup when she went to church.

I looked into the side of one of her shiniest pans to see what I looked like, but I only saw a blur. Once the potions were finished, I would go to the mirror and look at myself properly.

Jay came in from washing more bottles and placed the box of empties on the table next to where I was working. "You making Follow Me Boy oil?"

I nodded.

"Smell like cinnamon in here," he said, sniffing. He sniffed the table, then the bottles, then he came close to me. "You smell like it too. What's that on your face?"

"Nothing," I said.

"Mama won't let you wear no makeup. You too young."

"It isn't— Ugh!" Before I could deny I was wearing makeup again, Jay had sniffed my face, then licked my cheek from my chin to my ear. It was like being licked by a happy dog, but one that smelled like peanuts. I pushed him off me. "What are you doing?"

He laughed. "You put cinnamon on your face!" He held on to his belly while he doubled over with laughter. "Like you a grown-up lady?"

"Shut up," I said, going back to my oil making. "You got the rest of the stuff? And leave me alone if you can't stop laughing."

Jay held out a bag of Devil's Shoestrings, his face still in a wide grin. When I took it from him, he giggled again before leaving me alone in the kitchen and heading outside. I had just finished crushing up and mixing in the last of the cinnamon and had screwed on the top to the final bottle of oil when I heard Jay call for me.

I went outside, about to tell him off for teasing me, when I saw all the funny was gone out of his face. He rubbed at a cluster of mosquito bites on his arm.

"Help me, Jezzie," he said.

"You should be helping me. I got to get labels on these—"

"Later," he said. "Go down to the marsh." His voice was trembling and his skinny body was shaking like he was standing in a strong wind. "I'll get Mama."

"For what? What's down there?" It had to be something terrible if he wanted to involve Mama. Usually we decided together what we could and couldn't get out of without asking the adults for help.

"Please, Jezebel, just go. Under the big live oak. Maybe you can do something before I can get Mama." His eyes begged me to stop asking questions. We both knew he would have to tell Mama the whole story before she would bring herself down to see anything.

"Okay," I said. I turned tail as he made for our house.

A pitchfork and shovel lay against the cabin; I took the pitchfork, just in case there was danger, and sped down the path. The sun was high in the clear sky, and I had to squint my eyes tight against the brightness. But I knew this part of our farm by memory; I could likely run from home to the marsh with my eyes closed.

Once the grass surrounding the marsh was in sight, I slowed down. I approached the old oak cautiously, my heart pumping in my chest.

I looked around, but I didn't see anything or anyone. I leaned the pitchfork against the tree. Was Jay playing a joke on me?

That's when I heard it. A muffled whimper. A whine, really. Something in pain.

I moved toward the sound slowly and carefully, still not sure what I would find out here. The noises were hushed and only came every so often. I had to stay still until I heard them again, then move in the direction of what I'd heard.

Grasses were tall near the marsh, even around tree trunks, and they grazed my knees. As I got closer, I heard a low *woof*.

Finally, I parted the grass near the foot of the tree. I saw the animal, lying on its side with its back against the tree. It wasn't moving.

It was a coyote. And it was hurt.

"It's okay," I said gently. I stepped closer, being careful where I put my feet. Daddy used to tell us to always have caution with animals. This was the same kind of animal we had to hide our chickens from, but it was still hurting.

It tried to sit up and move to see where I was, but it couldn't. It gave a pitiful cry, then lay back down. My heart broke. I wanted to run to Mama or out in the woods to find Doc, but I couldn't. My feet stayed where they were.

"Poor baby," I said. "I won't hurt you."

I knew what Mama and Doc would do. If there was an animal she thought would kill our chickens, Mama would kill that animal first. She wouldn't let a wild animal take food out of our mouths. And I knew Doc wouldn't hesitate to kill an injured animal from the marsh either.

But what would *I* do?

I spun my bracelet around and around on my wrist, thinking. Rootwork was about helping. No one had ever said anything about only helping *people*. Becoming the rootworker Gran said I could be meant making a choice, here and now.

I looked over the animal, and it was beautiful. Its fur was a mix of light and dark brown, thick and bristly, and it had a bushy tail. It gave another woof, but this one was more tired sounding than the first. I looked closer, and that's when I saw the trap. It was made of metal, with rusty teeth that sank into the coyote's back leg like monster jaws. Blood coated the metal and darkened the animal's fur.

I didn't know who'd set the trap, but I knew it was there to catch things like coyotes. Even though the coyotes tried to steal our chickens, I knew it was because they were hungry. It wasn't right for them to be trapped like this.

"It's gonna be okay," I whispered again. I wasn't sure it would be, though.

I looked back up the path to the house. No sign of Jay coming with Mama. I was on my own. I crouched down near the animal's head. Its ears tipped forward and its eyes followed me. I hummed to it in a low voice and held out my hand. At first, the coyote seemed unsure, but it sniffed me weakly. The scent of the oils and the roots stuck to my hands, so I smelled like the earth. I pulled my hand out of the bracelet Doc gave me for my birthday. Carefully I unbraided each of the Devil's Shoestrings he had woven together. Then I lay out them around the coyote in a big circle.

"This is to protect you, okay? I want to help. Will you let me?"

The coyote tried again to move, but yelped and gave up. It pressed itself into the ground like it wanted to die.

"Not yet, all right? At least let me try and get you out."

It snuffed and licked my hand. I took that to mean, *You can try.*

I grabbed the pitchfork and shuffled over to the rusted metal trap. Still humming softly, I placed the tines of the pitchfork into the narrow opening between the jaws of the animal trap. Careful not to touch the injured leg, I pushed the fork in until it touched the ground.

"Okay, little one." I breathed out a long stream of air. "Here we go."

My hands wrapped around the handle of the pitchfork, and I wiggled it back and forth. But the trap didn't move. It was shut tight. The poor thing whimpered.

"I'm sorry. That didn't work." I wiped my hands on my dress to get the sweat off. I had no idea how to open the trap. *Think, Jezebel, think!*

This time last year, we shucked oysters. Their shells were tightly closed, even after Mama steamed them. She let us try and get them open on our own. Then she showed us how to slide a knife in the side of the shell, then twist. If we got it right, the shell would pop open and we could pull out the soft, jiggly meat inside.

"Think I got it this time," I told the coyote, who was panting by now.

Again I gripped the handle of the pitchfork. With all my might, I twisted. The trap groaned, but didn't move. I wrapped both hands around the handle and ground my feet deep into the soft, black dirt. I gritted my teeth and twisted hard, harder than I ever turned anything in my life.

Heat built up under my hands as I turned the handle. In science lessons, Miss Watson called it friction. Force between two things trying to slide across each other. My palms were slipping, but I didn't stop. I groaned. My hands burned, and a splinter worked its way into my palm.

"Please," I begged. "Please open."

The trap groaned. The rusty metal jaws creaked, then started to separate. The coyote whined as the terrible teeth came out of its leg. Once the teeth were out, it drew its leg out of the trap altogether.

By this time, I could hear Mama coming down the path, telling Jay's head a mess about what she was gonna do if this was some kinda joke. When she got over the last rise, she started running, hurried over to where I was, and pulled me back from the trap, and the teeth snapped shut with a loud clang over the pitchfork.

"Jezebel, what in blazes are you doing? That's an animal trap!" Mama grabbed my hands and looked at them. My palms were red and sore. A few splinters peeked out of my skin. "Why were you messing with that horrible thing?"

"I was trying to get it open."

"Jay said something about a dog." Mama looked around. I did too, but there was no sign of the animal. It must have limped off when Mama and Jay came.

"It was a coyote, not a dog," I said. "It had its leg caught in the trap, but I got it out."

"Good Lord," Mama said. "You could have really been hurt. That animal could have bitten you!"

"It's my fault," Jay said. "I told Jez I needed help. I begged her to come down here."

"I couldn't let it die, Mama." The pain in my hands I'd ignored earlier was worse now. Burning. I looked at my hands, and some of the skin was torn, rubbed away.

Mama pressed her lips together. I knew she wanted to yell at me, but she didn't. "I don't see any coyote, you two."

I looked around. She was right; the coyote was gone. "It was here a second ago, I promise!"

I didn't want to get in trouble again, but I was glad I had at least saved a life. If I got more punishment or a whipping, I'd hold on to that fact.

"Stay back, both of you." Mama picked up a rock from under a nearby tree and pushed down on the side of the trap. The jaws sprang apart and we all jumped. Mama pulled the pitchfork out of the ground, then lightly tapped the open trap with the side of the fork. It snapped closed, empty this time.

"How did you know how to do that?" Jay asked.

"It's our trap," she said. "But how did it get out here? Doc usually keeps it in his cabin. We'd never set it out here where you kids could step on it."

The trap was mean looking, crusted with rust and edged with bloodied teeth. I shuddered. "Why do you even have something like that, Mama?"

"It belonged to my grandmama. Plantation owners used to set these same traps for our people—she had helped to take it off a man who was running away to escape slavery.

She tried to give it back to him, but he told her to keep it. He didn't want a reminder." Mama picked up the trap by its short chain. "Limped for the rest of his life, my grand-mama said."

We were quiet until a long yip and howl echoed through the marsh. *Wow-oo-wow, wow-oo-wow.*

"There it is!" I pointed. "Over there."

The coyote was at the edge of the forest surrounding the marshland. It was with another, smaller coyote that looked the same.

Mama's gaze followed my finger. "That isn't a coyote, Jezebel. That's a red wolf."

I gasped. *A red wolf?*

The wolf leaned its head way back and let out a howl. The smaller one followed. Their song filled the forest and drifted over the quiet marsh. Then they both edged away, deeper into the woods.

"I think that was a thank-you," Mama said.

I smiled, proud I had helped. That I had done what rootworkers were supposed to do—respect the earth and its creatures.

And I had done it on my own.

That night, I lay in bed with Dinah on my chest. I stroked her hair as I whispered to her.

"Why was the trap out there?" Dinah's mouth was

turned down, and her little cloth body shook. "Mama said the trap was usually in Doc's cabin, but I know he wouldn't have set it out there near the house."

She didn't have any answers. Me and Jay were really lucky we didn't get caught in that trap. If the wolf got caught, that meant it was set out in the open and dangerous position. Likely for the exact purpose of catching something. Or someone.

Then I remembered.

On the day of Gran's funeral, Deputy Collins had been at our house when we got home. There was no way to know how long he'd been there, but he had pried off the lock on Doc's cabin and gone inside. Could he have taken that animal trap and set it in the woods, for Mama or Doc or even me or Jay to step on?

There was no way I could know for sure. This time, I was the one shaking. The night was pleasantly warm, but I suddenly felt cold all over. I sat Dinah on the windowsill and turned her to face outside. Knowing she was keeping a lookout, I was finally able to get a little sleep.

12

Though I'd been falling asleep to pounding thunderstorms for three nights straight, when I woke up on the fourth day, the sky was clear. The land was flooded, leaving the scent of rainwater in the air. When I lifted the window, the whole world around me smelled clean and fresh as clothes from the washing line.

Still, it was terrible walking to school when it was wet. The mud got on my shoes and splashed up my legs, making my skin itchy and uncomfortable. Then I had to sit in class all day, unable to do anything about it.

There were a few whispers and smothered laughter when I walked down the hall. Some kids started cackling like witches, waggling their fingers to be scary. I pretended to grab at them and they ran off, screaming, which satisfied me. At lunch, I sat by myself and ate my rice, because Susie had been called into the principal's office. I didn't know why, but she said she'd tell me when she got back.

After I ate, I took out my root notebook to study what I had written. I was so deep in what I was reading that I didn't hear Lettie sneak up. I didn't even know she was there when she dumped an entire thermos full of water on my head.

I gasped at the sting of the icy-cold water. It soaked me from head to chest, then rolled down my arms to puddle on the floor. I sat there, dripping, wiping water out of my face, while she and the others laughed. Shame and anger burned at me, making my skin feel fever hot under the cold water.

"Why didn't you melt?" she asked. "Isn't that happens to witches?"

At that moment, it wasn't even Lettie's bullying that was bothering me, not on its own. After what had happened a few days ago, I couldn't stop thinking about Deputy Collins. He might be watching the house at night. Setting traps to hurt or kill us. Why was everyone out to get me and my family? We hadn't done anything to anyone. We were trying to survive and to live the best way we knew how. Fiery tears burned the back of my eyes, and I was glad water fell from my face so those girls couldn't see my hurt and anger.

"You're the witch, Lettie Anderson!" I yelled, jumping to my feet. Some of the water dribbling off my face got into my mouth and I coughed. "You're mean and cruel for no good reason at all!"

"Enough!" One of the teachers on cafeteria duty broke into the crowd of kids that suddenly surrounded us once the commotion started. She stood between us for a few seconds, sizing us both up. "Jezebel, go see if Miss Corrie has a towel. Lettie, you mop this spill up right now."

I sneezed, then grabbed my book and the rest of my things and ran out of the lunchroom.

Maybe I didn't melt on the outside, but inside I felt like I was melting. Did that make me a witch? Was I a witch because the only time I felt good about myself now, like a real, whole person, was when I was learning magic? I had a doll that ran around at night. An uncle who brewed potions. And I knew that black peppercorns could be used to protect you or to put a jinx on someone. Maybe those girls at school were right, and I was a witch. Maybe when I got older, I'd grow a huge nose with warts on it.

My footsteps echoed in the halls as I made my way to Miss Corrie's office for the second time this year. Even the small bag of graveyard dirt and powdered brick I carried in the pocket of my dress was soaked with water. Heavy and thick, it weighed me down as I squished along the hallway. From this moment on, I wasn't going to try and make friends anymore. I would go to school, do my lessons, and come home to learn root. I had bigger problems to think about than some stupid girls.

I knocked on the door.

"Come in."

I pushed open the door and Miss Corrie looked up. When she saw me, a little sound of surprise escaped her mouth. She got up and opened her ceiling-high cabinet. "Come to my desk," she said as she sat back down. When I did, she patted my face and neck with a white towel. It was scratchy and smelled like bleach, but it was clean. The gentle concern on her face and the careful movements of her hands almost made me cry again.

"Want to tell me what happened?" she asked, tenderly squeezing the towel around one of my pigtails, then the other.

Swallowing my sobs, I told her everything that had happened with Lettie. Once I was done, I sneezed twice.

"You feel cold. Here are some tissues." She opened a drawer in her desk, and I saw a bottle of Doc's Boss Fix potion sitting inside.

Before I could stop myself, I said, "I wrote that label!"

Miss Corrie looked down in her drawer, then back at me. Her face softened and she pushed back from her desk. The chair moved smoothly and without sound. "Is your uncle teaching you rootwork, dear heart?"

I hesitated, but only for a moment. I wouldn't share my family's secrets, but something told me I could trust Miss Corrie. I nodded.

"Would you like to share anything with me, Jezebel? Are you scared of something? Nervous?"

I shook my head. "I'm not scared," I said. "Not exactly."

"Tell me, then," she said. I could see my reflection in her glasses. "Exactly."

She already knew about the other kids teasing me. So I told her what I had kept inside. I told her about Gran dying and how much I missed her. I told her about how the police pulled rootworkers out of their homes, beat them, and put them in jail. Then I told her I was trying to learn enough rootwork so that when Deputy Collins came back, I could help Doc protect our family. I told her there were nights I was so tired, but I couldn't sleep. Tears burned my eyes, but I didn't cry. My throat got tight and I had to swallow hard to keep talking.

Finally, I said, "I'm not sure I can protect our family. Leastways not the way Gran did when she was alive."

When I was done speaking, Miss Corrie patted my hand.

"Do you know what stress is?"

My heart was pounding, and my stomach was fluttering like it was full of startled butterflies. I shook my head.

"It's when you have so much responsibility and so many things to do that you get . . ." Miss Corrie stopped while she thought about what to say. "You get frustrated and worried that you can't do all those things the way you want to."

I tugged at one of my damp pigtails and nodded. That was exactly how I felt.

"Stress can make you feel sick. Even make you lose sleep or get headaches. Do you know what this means for you?"

"That I'm grown up?" I asked.

"Not quite yet." She laughed, and I felt warmer inside. "But you're doing things grown-ups do, and it's a lot of weight on your small shoulders."

I tilted my chin up high. "But I want to do them. I want to learn."

Miss Corrie leaned closer to me. "Do you know why I bought that potion from your uncle?"

"No, ma'am." I shifted in my seat.

"Because I don't know how to make it. Many years ago, my family used to work the roots, like yours. But before I was born, they made a decision to leave those ways behind." She took off her glasses and cleaned them with a cloth before replacing them. I noticed there was a little brown speck marking the white part of her right eye. "So over the years, we forgot the recipes and the stories and songs. We lost them. You still have them, and that's a special thing to hold on to.

"Still," she continued, "everything you've told me, and being a magical girl on top of all that . . . Oh my, what a road you have in front of you."

"So what do I do?"

"Learn your magic. And your schoolwork too. Learn everything you can and become the person you want to be."

"What if people think—"

"Stop right there. One day, you'll have to make some pretty big decisions, and when that day comes, all that will matter is what *you* think, not anybody else. Best to start practicing now." Her voice held a firmness that made me stand up straighter. "Remember: what makes you different makes you special."

I thought of the looks the other kids gave me. "I don't feel special."

"Being different is hard, Jezebel. I know that. But you have to learn to accept what makes you different. Most of all, learn to love it." She looked at me, and her eyes seemed small and sharp through the glass of her lenses. "That's your power. Don't let anyone take it from you. Be strong and be yourself. Not the person you think everyone will like. Learn your power and learn to use it well." She looked at her watch, scribbled on a notepad, then ripped off the paper. "Give this to your teacher. And take care of yourself, Jezebel." Then she patted my shoulder and sent me on my way.

When I got back to Miss Watson's classroom, I found that the slip Miss Corrie had signed said I should be allowed to go home early. She didn't want me to catch a chill from sitting the rest of the day soaked to the skin, she'd said. After giving a wide-eyed Miss Watson the slip, I ran down the front steps of the school, only slowing when I reached the road. It was sunny and warm, and the shivering chill of the cold water was starting to evaporate.

But when I got home, something else sent a chill down my back. A police car was parked in front of our house.

I snuck in the back, being extra quiet. When I got inside and peeked around the doorframe of Mama's bedroom into the front room, I breathed a bit easier. It was Sheriff Edwards, not Deputy Collins. Sheriff Edwards and Mama were in the front room, talking.

Or, to be specific, arguing.

"How are we supposed to live?" Mama was saying, her voice rising. "Do you know what I found on Saturday out back in the marsh? An animal trap!"

"Miss Turner—" the sheriff began, but Mama cut right on in.

"Open and set where anyone could have stepped on it. One of my children, Sheriff! Only one person I know of would do a thing like that." She paced around the front room while Sheriff Edwards, big and tall as he was, stood in the corner, his hat in his hand.

"I am so sorry."

"Don't be sorry. Be about something. Fix this." Mama turned her face up to the ceiling and breathed deep, like she was gasping for air.

"I'm doing what I can," he said. His voice was gentle, careful.

"It's not enough. Can't you put Collins in jail or something?"

"I would, but he hasn't done anything I can jail him for. You know what the laws are." Sheriff twisted his hat in his big hands. "People like him have been doing this to folks for years, with no one saying a word. I have to operate within a certain chain of command to even get an investigation of Collins and his cronies started."

Mama had sunk down into a chair. She was nodding slowly. I didn't know what a chain of command was, but I could tell what it meant—Sheriff Edwards wanted to help us, but he would have to wait. And that meant we would have to wait.

"What are we supposed to do until then? Hope he doesn't catch wind of what you're doing and try to hurt one of us?" She plucked the strings of her apron, unraveling the thread. "I don't suppose you know my husband and Collins had a run-in a while back?"

The sheriff edged his way closer to Mama and sat across from her. He reached out, as if he was thinking to take her hand, then stopped. "No, I didn't."

"The kids were small. I'm sure they don't remember.

But Collins came here late one night and roughed him up. I thought . . . I thought he was going to—" Mama swallowed hard. "My husband left after that night. And I can't say I blame him."

I scurried back through the bedroom, through the kitchen, and out the back door. I hurried down the path, my heart beating fast, my head spinning with what I'd seen and heard. Daddy and Deputy Collins had it out one time? Then Daddy left us. He left us because he was afraid of what Deputy Collins might do. No wonder Mama was so hurt and angry. But why would she keep that from me and Jay?

I stood under our pecan tree, breathing hard. The rough bark of the tree scratched against my back through my school dress. I tried to figure out what to do, but I couldn't think straight. Should I go in and let Mama know what I heard? That didn't feel right. I let the cool wind blow over my skin. Secrets. Protection. Mama's story and Doc's lessons mixed together in my mind. Then I realized: while Mama didn't work roots, she thought keeping the story about Daddy a secret was protecting us. I didn't understand it, but I knew it, felt it with my intuition.

But Mama wasn't the only protector in the family. We all had to protect each other.

I started up the path, calling out, "Mama! Mama!" so she would be sure to hear me. I burst through the front door this time, giving her plenty of time to get herself together. When I got inside, she and Sheriff Edwards were sitting in the front room with glasses of iced tea, Mama fanning herself with the newspaper.

"Jez? Why are you home at this time?" She blinked, then stared at my coiled-up hair and wrinkled dress. "And what happened to you?"

I told her what happened and she looked me over. At the same time, Sheriff Edwards rose.

"I'd better be on my way now," he said. "If anything more happens, please let me know. It can all go in the investigation report." He took up his hat. "I'll let myself out."

"Okay, Sheriff," she said, her voice sounding far away. Our front door closed softly behind him, and as soon as it did, Mama spoke again. "Who is the horrible child that did this?"

"Lettie, of course." I told her the story as best I could without letting all the hurt and anger I felt earlier come right on back. My fists tightened as I told it.

"Oh Lord. How're you feeling, Jez?"

"I'm fine. Just mad at how stupid kids are."

"Go change your clothes and hang that dress up on the clothesline." She hugged me tightly and I snuggled close. "Bring your hair things when you come back and you can have a cup of hot tea while I redo your pigtails."

I changed into dry clothes and took the bag of grave-yard dust and powdered brick, still heavy with water, out of my dress pocket. I sat it on the windowsill to dry, along with my bracelet Doc had woven back together after I saved the wolf. I grabbed the small plastic bucket Mama kept my hair things in: pomades, combs, barrettes, and knockers. I set it on the chair next to me and sipped tea with honey and cinnamon while Mama loosed my hair, then oiled and combed and brushed it as gently as she could.

"Did you already sell out everything at your market stall?" I asked.

"Yes, I was home when Sheriff Edwards stopped by to give me some information."

"What sort of information?"

"That's . . . best kept between adults" was all she said.

She leaned over to look at me and saw me pouting. "Jez, you know why I sometimes tell you certain things are for grown-ups, don't you?"

I shrugged and focused on my empty cup. "Because you don't want me to know those things."

"Not only that. I have a duty—a responsibility—as your mother to keep you safe. Just like Doc tells you to protect yourself, I'm supposed to protect you and your brother." She stood up and refilled my cup with hot water.

"To me, that means I have to protect all parts of you: your body, your mind, and your heart. And there are some things I don't think you're ready to know. Not just yet, okay?" She smoothed her hands down each of my pigtails, the signal she was finished doing my hair.

I knew Mama was right. She already had so much to

worry about that I wanted to let her think I didn't know the story about Daddy. "Okay," I said.

"I'm glad we got that settled," she said, kissing my forehead.

That's when Jay came sprinting in the door. "Jez, you okay? After school, Susie told me what happened to you at lunch. So I ran home."

Mama looked grateful for the interruption. "If you are both home, why don't you two play outside for a bit? I need to do a few things before I get dinner started."

"Yes, ma'am," we said. Jay changed into his playclothes in a blink, and we ran out the door.

"Did Susie really tell you what happened?" I asked once we were a little ways from the house.

"Yeah, she said to tell you she was sorry she wasn't there when it happened." He grinned. "I think she woulda knocked that girl's lights out."

I couldn't help but smile at the idea someone wanted to fight for me. "Maybe she would have. Did she say if she might come by to check on me?" I asked hopefully.

"Nope. I asked if she wanted to, but she said she needed to get home or something."

We walked a bit longer, enjoying the warm afternoon, and I realized we were heading toward the marsh. "Do you think we need to worry about any more traps out here?" I asked.

Jay slowed down. "I don't know. I think we'll be okay

if we keep our eyes open."

"Yeah." I nodded. "Maybe you're right."

"I'm more scared of the things we *can't* see," he added.

I was thinking about that too. "But the marsh is our home," I said. "It has ingredients we use in rootwork. It's where we get some of our food. We can't stay away forever.. Come on—I'll race you!"

Jay grinned at that, and we took off, watching our footsteps as we did.

13

While we kept a lookout for any more traps, we soon relaxed, because it felt so good to be outside again. The summer had been dry, so the plants sucked up all the moisture they could from the early November rains, and extra water sat in a thin layer on top of the soaked dirt. The heavy rains had cooled the air some, and I took big gulps of it as I ran.

I wanted to run faster today than ever. Maybe I could outrun my thoughts. My heart thumped hard as my feet pounded into the muddy ground, and my arms pumped. At least tomorrow was Friday. Then I'd have the whole weekend to fix my feelings before I had to go back to school and all the kids there.

A chilly breeze blew up and I breathed it deep as it flowed over me, letting it power me on to follow Jay's lead through the marsh. After a storm, we always went down to the marsh, because the rains dredged up all kinds of weird stuff. Maybe I'd find something today that would take my mind off school. Some of our best prizes were a baseball cap, a beat-up weather vane shaped like a chicken, and a beautiful feather that looked like it might have come from a peacock.

"You find anything?" I yelled across to Jay.

"Not yet!" He high-stepped through the pluff mud, the hem of his pants rolled up to his knees, fishing for treasures. Jay could stay outside all day if he was able, searching the marsh's secrets. Only nighttime—and his empty belly—could pull him from a treasure hunt like this.

I skirted along the grassy bank, watching the water bubble between the stalks of grass, a sure sign that the fiddler crabs were scrabbling around just out of sight. The memory of the thing in the marsh holding me there to listen flooded my mind like a high tide. Being held in place was so terrifying, but I had Jay with me then. I looked up and out across the marsh, but I didn't see him anywhere.

Of course he'd wandered off. This was the first time in weeks when he was actually home after school and we were out together in the marsh like we used to be, and he was nowhere in sight. Mama and Doc had told us both to not leave the other alone. But I was alone. I was always alone, it seemed, these days.

Lonely girl. I am here.

The voice echoed around me, and I spun, searching for where it came from. No one was nearby.

Lonely girl.

I listened as the whispery light voice echoed. I couldn't tell if it was in my head or on the air.

I am alone too. I, too, have no one.

A flash of something caught my eye and I looked right, to an area within the thick rushes of the marsh where a tidal pool of water had gathered. There was something out there in the murky water: a glimpse of red that sank away as soon as I saw it. Moments later, it surfaced again before sinking out of sight.

"I see something!" I yelled, in case Jay was somewhere close enough to hear me. I didn't wait for him to answer, though; I just went on over to look. Around me, the blowing wind grew cooler, too cool for this time of year. And all I could see was the thing in front of me bobbing on the surface of the water: white, then red, then orange-brown, before it disappeared for the briefest moment.

I am so empty, lonely girl. Are you empty like me?

I should have been scared then, and I was, but that wasn't all I felt. I could feel the desperation all around me, hear it in the voice. It felt so true and so real. It felt like my loneliness, new and painfully fresh.

Something moved against me, and I found it was Dinah squirming in my pocket. I pulled her out; whether she was worried about me or encouraging me, I couldn't tell. I put her back in my pocket and gave her a pat.

As I got closer, the spot under the surface started to look like different things: a towel, maybe a scrap of a shirt, or a dress. Then I got close enough to see what it was.

Of all the things we'd found in this marsh, there was one thing we'd never seen: a body. I was afraid for a moment that we had finally found one. But then I realized exactly what I was looking at.

It was a doll.

The doll was nothing like Dinah; this one looked like someone tried to carve a real person out of wood. A shock went through my body, starting at my head like a lightning strike, then moving down, down into my legs, freezing them to the spot. I wanted to get a closer look at it, but it was in deeper water, a few feet out from where I stood. I searched around for a branch or something to use and came up empty.

"Jay," I called again, my voice ringing out over the stillness. "Got something here!"

Dinah was going crazy now. It felt like she was pushing against the pocket with her all of her tiny body. I didn't know what her problem was with some old doll, but I'd find out after I figured out a way to haul it in. Surely another step would be okay, especially if I kept the marsh's edge in sight. I stepped into the water and the mud smooshed under my feet. The water, cooler than the air, made me shiver, but it only came halfway up my calf. The doll looked so much smaller now that I was almost on top of it, as though I could pick it up in one hand.

My fingers waggled, barely scraping the muddy fabric of the strange doll's belly. Then my hand sank inside it.

My gasp was cut off quick as I was yanked forward into the tidal pool of standing marsh water. My knees hit the mud at the bottom of the marsh, splashing through the standing water left by the floods and the last hard rain. Then something strong—fiercely strong—gripped my right arm, still sunk inside the belly of the doll. It crawled up to my shoulder, adjusted its grip, then pulled harder.

I screamed out.

"Jay! Doc! Help me!" My voice was swallowed up by a roar of air from the doll. Dinah thrashed around, the tug of her flailing keeping me off-balance. I couldn't get free of the thing that had me and I couldn't get to her. She was in my right pocket, and I was using my left arm to brace myself as I was pulled closer and closer to the surface of the water. I pulled back with all my strength, but whatever had my arm was stronger. I reached for the protection powder I'd made with Doc's graveyard dirt and powdered brick—maybe if I sprinkled it on the water, I could get free—but then I remembered I'd taken the bag out of my pocket and left it on the windowsill to dry. Along with my bracelet of Devil's Shoestrings.

Doc had told me never to go out without protection and I had done just that. I tugged harder, screaming until my voice cracked and my throat was raw and sore. The puddle of water churned now, and I saw glimpses through its cloudy surface. The smell of the marsh surrounded me. Usually I loved the scent of it, rich with bubbling life, but there was something in it now that smelled burnt and bitter. I could taste it on my tongue.

Whatever it was drew my head closer to the pool. I writhed and punched the water, but nothing I did made any difference.

"No! No, no, no!" I cried out. My heart was in my throat. I felt like I was choking on my fear. Cold water covered my lips and nose. Dinah was scratching against the inside of my pocket, but all the sounds around me were drowned out by the voice pounding into my head. The one coming from the doll.

Got you!

And then, laughter. Hard, cruel laughter just like the kids at school.

My body tightened up and I flailed around, trying to get loose. *I can't die like this! I can't leave Mama and Jay and Doc.* I had to get away from that voice that sounded like creaking floors and smelled like used oil. Where was Jay now?

I don't care about the boy. But a girl? I can use a girl. A lonely, scared little girl.

I screamed again and my mouth filled with muddy water. I jerked away enough to lift my lips clear of the water and spit out the thick liquid, and that movement pressed my tummy forward into the puddle. I was soaked in an instant. The water was so cold, and the shock of it raced through me.

Yes, you're my poppet now. My little doll. I'm going to fill you up.

Dinah wiggled frantic against me, pounding her gunny-sack body into my side. I kicked my legs, tried to get up, but my feet kept slipping in the mud and I couldn't get enough of a grip or a foothold to move away.

Full of pretty pins.

Something sharp poked, then pierced my side. It felt like a branch sank into my skin, then through the muscle, layer by layer. I gasped at the pain. But when I looked around, then down at my body, there was nothing. No branch, no pin, only the dirty, heaving water.

I tried to settle myself, breathe deep, and think as Doc told us. What could I do?

Another stick, this one needle sharp, entered my hip. When I hollered, the thing clutching my arm yanked hard.

My left elbow gave way, and I crashed face-first into the icy-cold water.

Eyes open, I saw a face in the water, smeared and wobbly. What I could see clearly were the teeth: white and large and sharp, exposed in a sneer. The grip felt like bony skeleton fingers. I couldn't breathe. I needed air. And another sharp needle worked its way into my shoulder, bumping off the bone, then moving off to find softer muscle.

Bucking and struggling, I knew, would make me run out of air even faster. My lessons flashed in my head like fireworks. Doc had told me that I had to bring my calmest self to the magic. It was okay to be eager and excited, but the negative emotions like fear and anger were not good when working root. "Bad draws bad, Jez," he'd said. "Try to let those bad thoughts go."

Anything that would steal power surely was evil. I didn't want to make evil stronger, but how could I keep that from happening?

I ceased moving. I focused and let my body go still. I felt the pain, but it seemed far away now, like I'd closed a window between it and me. My mind raced around, trying to work out this puzzle. *Think, Jezebel!*

Mama and Doc had both said rootwork takes intent. Even Mama knew that, and she didn't work root. *That's your power. Don't let anyone take it from you.* Miss Corrie's advice came to me now. The words echoed in my mind, weaving in and out around the doll's triumphant laughter.

I knew I didn't have the strength to get my body loose from this grip. But maybe that wasn't the only way to get free.

At that moment, my body felt light, lighter than the water surrounding it, like a balloon lifting into the sky. I let that floaty feeling move into every part of me: my arm and legs, my belly, blotting out the pain as another pin slid inside my skin. It filled me up, and I felt a part of me break away. Up, away from my body in the marsh pool. Separating itself from the grip keeping me in the pool of water.

No! Get back here!

The grip yanked at my arm, the voice shrieking in anger, but I was free of my body. Floating above it, I looked down and saw me, a brown girl in a blue dress surrounded by green-gray water. I wanted to stay like this, apart from everything. Safe. There was no pain here, as there was down in that pool.

You can't have me, I gasped. My breath was coming in pants, like a dog's that had run too fast and too long. My heartbeat was fluttering, making me think of trapped butterflies, but did I even have a heartbeat right now? It was down there in my body. I knew in that moment my power wasn't only in my body. It was deeper, embedded into my spirit. Separate, I could feel the source of the wind. In the air, I could feel the big salt where it kissed the beach.

And even deeper inside, I could feel a part of Gran

with me. And not just her. I felt surrounded by warm, loving people. My people who had been on this land even before Gran was born. I could hear their voices in English and in Gullah. They were inside my head and my heart.

Wi binya, gyal.

We're with you now.

A gentle breeze surrounded me, and I felt its pressure only, not its temperature. I felt—no, I knew—I was connected to everything around me. As if I could push a button and make something happen. When that thought flowed out of me, a flock of ducks rose up from the water, taking to the air with furious honks and squawks. Their wings created a small windstorm that rippled the surface of the water.

"Over there!" a voice cried.

Then I saw the marsh grass part, and two other brown bodies trampled through the grasses and mud. Jay was in front, running up to the tidal pool, with Doc close behind holding a big jar close to his chest. Doc pointed and mouthed something I couldn't hear; then he gave the jar to Jay. I recognized it as the one from his cabin that was filled with that dirty, muddy liquid. Jay poured the contents of the jug into the water while Doc yanked me free by my ankles.

I didn't know if Doc or Jay could hear it, but a screech, somewhere between a person's scream and a bird's cry, filled the air around me. The water blackened and rose up in hurricane waves.

Then, just as suddenly, it froze in place before dropping back down and lying still. Doc shook my body as he held me upside down, while Jay thumped me on the back.

I dropped like a stone back into my body as a river poured out of my mouth. I coughed and Doc laid me on the ground. I blinked the grit out of my eyes.

They waited until I could talk. When finally I could, I told them of the body that was a doll, and the teeth in the water.

Jay touched my shoulder and I flinched away. "Look," he said, holding up his hand. I stared at it, then looked at my own, stained reddish-brown. I saw my dress poked through with holes, all rimmed with rusty-looking blood. His face, when I looked back, was drenched in fear.

But, for some reason, I didn't feel scared about what had just happened. I felt . . .

Strong. Like I had conquered something.

A smile started to form on my face, but it stopped when I saw Jay's look of worry mirrored on my uncle's face.

"Are you gonna tell Mama about this?" I asked.

"No," Doc said. "You are."

14

"Janey," Doc said. "Your daughter has something to tell you."

Mama looked at Doc, then back at me before she put down the sweetgrass basket she was weaving. She settled herself back in her rocking chair and pressed her lips together like she knew it was gonna be something bad.

I didn't know how to tell her. How could I tell her I almost died?

Doc seemed to read my mind. "Just say it straight out. Easiest way."

Beside me, Jay's face was solemn. I shoved my hands in my pockets and wrapped Dinah's hair around the fingers of my right hand. My shaking eased up, but only a little bit.

"Jez?" Mama prompted.

Then I told her what happened in the marsh. It came out fast, like pouring water out of a bucket. I told her everything—about the pins and the marks on my skin, about the face in the water, about how it wasn't the face that scared me so much, but the teeth. I kept the part about floating up out of my body to myself.

A few times, Mama opened her mouth, but she stopped herself from saying anything. One time she tried to sit forward in her rocking chair, or maybe get up, but Doc put a hand on her shoulder and she stayed seated.

At the end of the tale, I puffed out a breath, tired from talking. My shoulders slumped, and I felt an ache like a bruise where the ghost hand grabbed me. The whole room was quiet, waiting for Mama to say something.

She closed her eyes tight, like I did when I didn't want to see something scary. But hers was like she was also trying to hold something in. When she opened her eyes, I saw what it was: tears.

"Jezebel, listen to me very carefully, hear?"

"Yes, ma'am."

"That was no doll in the water," Mama said.

"How do you know that?" I asked. "You don't even do root magic."

Mama pressed her lips together again. I wondered if

she was about to tell me it was grown-folk business, like she did when I asked about Daddy. But she surprised me by answering.

"I don't work root by my own choice." Her fingers wove the sweetgrass in her lap, twisting and tugging the strands into perfect place. She did it without looking at her hands, because her gaze was on me. "But your gran taught me lessons just like your uncle is teaching you and Jay. I simply decided I didn't want to learn anymore. For reasons I will tell you when you're older."

Never did I think of Mama as getting root lessons from Gran. I never thought of her even being my age at all. "Oh," I said. "Well, if it wasn't a doll in the water, what was it?"

"That was a poppet."

Poppet. That's what the thing in the water called *me*. I rubbed the ache in my arm where one of the ghost pins had gone through me. Beside Mama, Doc was nodding, and I realized she really did know a whole lot more than she told us.

Jay piped up. "What's a poppet?"

"A poppet looks like a doll but is filled with magic." Doc answered this time. "They can be used like traps, left by someone to do harm to people."

"Is Dinah a poppet?" I asked. I put my hand in my pocket to make sure she was there. If she could talk, she would probably say, "Nah, I is me!" I could hear her voice in my head, and I smiled and rubbed my hand over her hair. But when I looked back at Mama, she wasn't smiling at all.

Her hands clutched the half-made basket so tight, I could hear the sweetgrass crunch. "I want you to stay away from that marsh from now on, understand? I shouldn't have let you go out there today at all, what with the trap you found last time. Besides, you're growing up and there's no reason for you to be running and ripping around that place."

"But I—"

"No buts. No backtalk. You know what this poppet means? It means there is something out there, and that something is trying to capture you. Trying to take your magic. So you stay out of that marsh—am I clear?"

"Yes, ma'am," I whispered, glancing beside me. Jay's face crumpled like he wanted to give me a hug, but he didn't dare risk it. Not when he wasn't sure what Mama would do. And I was nervous too when Mama rose from her chair. But when she got over to me, she just kneeled down.

"I appreciate you for telling me this story," she said. "I know it wasn't easy. So thank you."

I looked into Mama's face and she was smiling. It was a wobbly smile, but it was there. "You're welcome."

She hugged me, and I breathed in the sweet orange

scent of her hair dressing. My arms wrapped around her too. Finally, I felt Jay's skinny arms around me, and Mama embraced us both.

"The scariest thing I can think of is something bad happening to one of you. That's why I have to give punishments." She let me go and looked me in the eyes. "This isn't your fault, Jez. But you have to be careful. Promise?"

"I promise."

Magic hummed inside me, warm and full. Before, I wasn't sure I could be a rootworker, but now I was. I thought about the marsh—not the poppet grabbing me, but what had happened when I tried to get away. When I lifted out of my body. I was getting stronger.

Someone wanted that power. *My* power.

My magic was what made me special. What made me a Turner. I wouldn't let anyone take that away.

———

The "punishment" Mama had mentioned wasn't too severe—I had to help her out on the farm early in the mornings for the next week. Nothing too much, because I was sore from my run-in with the poppet yesterday. The balm Mama smeared on my cuts and bruises made them feel a little better, though. When I got out onto the porch early that morning, I heard Mama at the chicken coop talking with one of her customers. About me.

"Have you ever had a child that wanted to eat nothing

but rice?" Mama asked the woman as she packed her eggs up. "Just plain, no gravy or butter or nothing?"

The woman was older than Mama, closer to the age Gran was when she died. Her thick, gray hair was a wig; I could tell that even from where I was, across the yard from the coop.

"Just rice? That all?" The older woman lifted her bony shoulders in a shrug. "Chirren got all kinda foibles nowadays. Running around wild, doing all they wanna do." The old woman stopped to count the number of eggs, her lips lightly moving. "Least rice is cheap. Be glad the chile ain't only eating meat. Then you'd have a time." She pulled a few coins out of her snap purse and put them in Mama's hand.

She turned away to go back down the road, then stopped. "Is it the gal?" she asked. "Only wanting the rice?"

"Yes'm," Mama said.

"Then keep eyes on her. Might be time for her woman trouble."

The look on Mama's face was open and understanding. What trouble did women get that men didn't get? Babies? Were they trouble? I guess me and Jay could be difficult sometimes, but I didn't think we were trouble as babies.

As the old woman passed the porch, she gave me a close look. I greeted her and she returned it, peering at me until she eased along up the road, leaning on her dark wood cane.

Before Mama could leave the coop, I went to find Jay. He was shoving his feet into his socks and yawning.

"That old lady who buys eggs from Mama thinks I'm getting *woman trouble*," I told him.

His face knotted up. "What's woman trouble? You ain't no woman."

"I'm getting to be."

"Mmph," he said, thoughtful, as he wedged his feet into his shoes. "Maybe. You scared?"

"No," I lied. Then, "A little."

I didn't want things to change. If I had woman trouble, that meant I was a woman and I couldn't carry Dinah anymore, because dolls were for kids. I thought of the things Mama and my teachers didn't do. Climb trees. Run in the marsh. It didn't seem fair, and I made up my mind to ask Mama what the trouble was with being a woman.

As for the rice, Mama was right—it was all I seemed to be hungry for lately. I usually loved all of Mama's cooking, and most of Doc's when Mama let him use the kitchen. But lately, things changed. I tried eating other things, but they felt wrong in my mouth. I only wanted the rice and I ate it at every meal. We had rice most days for dinner, but I didn't want it with peas or butter beans, or even collard greens. I wanted it all by itself. I didn't see anything wrong with that. The old lady said it was cheap, so why was Mama worried? I couldn't understand it and I told Jay so.

"I don't care as long as I get to eat the rest of your

food. But why do you want that much plain rice? Ain't you tired of it?"

I just shrugged as we went out the back door to do chores. Today, I fed the chickens, gathered eggs, and plucked the ripest tomatoes before the birds got to them. I was sweeping the kitchen floor when Jay came in lugging two peach baskets full of ripe vegetables and plunked them on the table.

Sure enough, at breakfast, Mama made oatmeal with spoonfuls of her scuppernong jelly, but I pushed at the bowl until Jay grabbed it and shoveled it into his mouth. Mama then made me a bowl of Cream of Rice, and I happily ate it. If I had to go back to school today, at least I could eat what I wanted.

No one bothered me that day, but the school day still took forever, and when it was finally over, I got a long cold drink from the water fountain in case Jay might want to walk home together. We hadn't done it in a while, but after yesterday, I thought maybe he might leave his friends and walk with me instead. When he didn't show, I looked in the cafeteria and out on the ball field.

No Jay.

I dragged myself toward the front gates, tired from the early-morning work mixed with the long school day. That's when I saw Susie. She stood there against a tree, to the right of one of the gates. Her body didn't move; only her eyes did. I slowed down my steps. Her dark eyes stayed on me as I got closer and closer to the front gates of the school. A breeze blew up, and it smelled like the marsh.

"Are you waiting for me?" I asked.

"Yep!" Susie said.

Since I'd gone home early after lunch yesterday, I hadn't had a chance to talk to her about what happened, or hear why she had to go to the principal's office. And I spent lunch today talking with Miss Corrie.

"I heard about what happened yesterday, and I was worried about you," she continued. She rubbed her lips together like Mama did when she put on lipstick. "Do you want to walk home together today?"

I smiled. "Sure! I was going to see if Jay was around to walk too, though. Have you seen him?"

That was when I saw some branches rustle on the chinaberry tree across the road from the school. Then I heard a shout. When I moved closer and peered through the gates, I saw what looked like Jay's bag on the ground.

If he was hurt, I didn't know if any teachers would leave the school to help. I held my own bag close, ran out of the school gates, and jogged across the road toward the tree. I felt someone next to me and saw Susie at my side.

It was quiet for a moment, and we stopped to listen. When I glanced over at Susie, she nodded like she understood the thoughts going through my head. Slowly, I moved closer.

"You sure?"

It was Jay's voice. I breathed in relief and walked over to the tree to tell him off. But what I saw stopped me in my tracks.

Jay was sitting under the chinaberry tree with a boy I didn't know. I guessed he was from Jay's class. The other boy had his back to the tree and Jay was in front of him, holding out his hand. The boy whispered something I couldn't hear, then he pulled out a small knife.

I gasped out loud, then covered my mouth with my hand to stop the noise. But it was too late. They heard me and jerked apart like they were caught having cookies before dinner.

"Jez! What are you doing here?" Jay asked, a guilty look on his face.

"Looking for you." I frowned at both of them. "I thought maybe you'd want to walk home together today."

Jay looked embarrassed, but the other boy spoke up. "I was just gonna make a small cut on his hand, like mine." He held up his hand to show me. "Then we shake hands and mix blood, so we can be blood brothers."

"Blood brothers?" I shook my real brother's shoulder. "You're already somebody's brother—mine!"

"It's not for true," the boy said, reaching out with the knife again. "Are you stupid or something?"

That's when Susie made a sound in her throat like a growl. "No, she's not."

The boy gulped, then bent down and grabbed his books before running off, back to the school gates.

"What did you do that for?" Jay said, his eyes angry. "I wanted to have a brother."

"Why? I'm—"

"My sister. But you ain't no boy, so you ain't the same." He grabbed up his books and ran off toward home, leaving me standing there with Susie.

My mouth dropped open in surprise, my heart sinking into my stomach. I knew things had gotten strange between us, but I didn't know Jay wanted a brother. Was I not . . . enough?

"Jez?" Susie nudged me with her shoulder.

I didn't answer. I couldn't. After all the times Mama and Doc had told me and Jay to look out for each other, after the poppet in the marsh had almost got me . . . I stood there, frozen. The poppet's words echoed in my head. *Lonely girl.*

Then Susie touched my arm, turned me to face her. Her eyes looked like little flashes of lightning. "Are you okay?"

"I don't know," I told her.

"Come on, let's walk home."

My bag slid down my shoulder and I hitched it up. We walked the path side by side. Birdsong accompanied us, along with the scuttle of fat-cheeked squirrels searching for nuts among the trees. I took a deep breath of sweet-hot air and blew it out. The worry about Jay was slowly flowing away, like the tide ebbing back out to sea.

Susie cocked her head in my direction but didn't change her steps. I noticed her hair wasn't in the usual crown of braids. It looked almost exactly like mine: parted in the middle with a Goody elastic on each plump, twisted pony-tail. "Are you mad at your brother?"

I thought about it for a minute, letting the fresh wind blow over me. I could smell the last of the heavy, ripe watermelons on the vine in the fields as we passed. "More surprised? I didn't know he wanted a brother."

"Doesn't mean he doesn't care about you," Susie said.

"I know, but we—" I stopped, not sure I wanted to tell her everything in my head.

Susie looked at me with her eyebrows raised but didn't say anything. She waited for me to speak, but I didn't know what to say. I thought I'd found a power inside myself when I escaped that poppet in the marsh. I'd felt *connected*—to my ancestors, my past, and my future. This business with Jay made me think that it was my present that was the real problem.

While I walked with Susie, all I could hear was the sound of home. The wind through the live oak trees. Our shoes scuffling on the hard-packed dirt. Shirts on nearby clotheslines snapping in the wind. The splash of birds fishing in the water. Susie stayed next to me, let me walk without saying anything until I was ready. It felt comfortable. It felt good. It felt like what having a friend should feel like.

"Me and Jay used to tell each other everything," I said finally. "Do everything together, look out for each other. We're twins." I looked down at my shoes as I said the words, barely missing stepping on a dead grasshopper. Ants marched all over it, on top and around, taking pieces of it home for the winter. I rubbed the goose bumps that prickled on my arms away. "I don't know if he wants me around anymore."

She nodded. "You feel like a part of you is gone."

I nodded.

"I understand." Susie sounded as sad as I was. "What about rootwork? Is there, I don't know . . . some spell that can help you fix it?"

I hadn't considered that. A root bag might work, but it also felt strange to think of using magic to make Jay care about me again. "I don't know," I said. "I'm still new to it. There's a lot to learn. Do you have a sister or brother?" I asked, changing the subject.

Susie shook her head. "That's one of the reasons I'm glad I found you to sit with at lunch this year."

I smiled. "Me too."

"Can I ask you something?"

"I guess," I answered, shrugging. "About what?"

"Rootwork." Before I could say anything, she spoke

again, quickly. "I'm not going to be nasty, I promise! It's just, I can't help but hear kids talking about your magic, what your family does. Some of them are mean about it, but it's not like their families do magic, so how would they know?" She met my eyes. "So I wanted to ask you person- ally."

This was more than anyone else at school had ever done. *Asking* me about root, instead of joking about some- thing they didn't understand.

"Sure, you can ask."

"What is root? Is it real magic?" Susie asked.

I didn't answer at first. What should I tell her? She wasn't family, but wasn't it a good idea to try and edu- cate people who didn't know about root but wanted to? Wouldn't that help to fix the problems I'd been having, the ones Mama and Doc had spoken about all rootworkers hav- ing? That no one—not even other Negroes—understood what it was we did?

I thought about it for a long time without talking; soon we'd be at the road that led to my house. Susie kicked at a mound of fine dirt, and a flood of reddish ants poured out, but she walked through them without a blink. "My family doesn't do root magic," she said, like she was confessing something. "They don't even talk about it. Except to tell me to stay away from anyone who does it because they can hurt me. But I don't think you'd ever hurt anyone."

"Is that why you can't have me over to your house?"

Susie sighed. "Yes, I'm sorry."

"Thank you for being honest with me," I told her. "But you don't have anything to worry about. Root is . . . a part of my family, part of our history. A connection to the earth and our ancestors." I didn't know if I should tell Susie much more than that, about haints and boo-hags, and all the other strange things I was learning about, the strange things I was learning to do. Maybe someday.

"But is it *real* magic?" she asked, looking at me with her black patent-leather eyes.

I thought about what Doc said to me and Jay when he first told us he was going to teach us root. "It is to me," I said and smiled.

We walked faster the closer we got to home, where the live oak trees spread their branches wide, giving cooling relief from the sun's embrace. At least I think we did, because the time seemed to fly away faster than usual. When we got to the edge of the marsh near our farm, where Susie usually stopped, she kept walking with me.

"Do you want to come over?" I asked. I could see Doc's cabin and our haint-blue house from where I was.

When Susie looked up, her steps halted. "No, not today, Jez. I only wanted to walk with you a little longer."

"Sure you don't want to come in? My mama probably won't be home, but we could have a snack."

"Sorry, I can't. I have to leave now," she said. Tilting her head toward me, she waved. "See you later, okay?"

Susie seemed to glide when she moved away. After a few steps, she turned back and gave me a strong hug. Then she ran off, disappearing into the thick stalks of corn bordering one of the farms that led around the opposite side of the marsh.

15

I watched the place where Susie had been, then turned around. I walked slowly the rest of the way home, knowing Jay would be there. Now that Susie was gone, my anger had popped back up, like weeds after a hard rain. I didn't want to see him right now.

I jumped over a black-feathered chicken in our yard and stomped up the front steps and inside. I was right that Mama wasn't home. As I put my books down on the table, Jay cut his eyes at me and went back outside, letting the screen door slam behind him.

If he wanted to be like that, fine. I grabbed the metal canister of rice Mama kept on the counter, the shaking grains sounding like a rattlesnake's warning. Mama was probably still at her stall; she'd be home soon to start dinner, but I didn't care. I was hungry, more than I could ever remember being, and I wanted a bowl of rice now. I pried the tight lid open, working it back and forth. A powdery smell hit my nose, along with a light puff of rice dust.

Before I could start cooking, I heard a voice and froze.

"I'm telling." Jay stood in the doorway, a slight sweat stain ringing the neck and underarms of his shirt. A smudge of dirt ran from his front pocket to his waist. "You know we ain't supposed to eat anything this close to dinner."

I jerked back, mad at myself for not thinking Jay might come back before anyone else. I put the lid on the canister. "Don't you dare tell on me, James Turner."

He laughed, his mouth wide open like a barn door. "Oh yeah? Why not?"

"If you do, then I'm gonna tell about you and that boy with the knife."

His laughter stopped and he almost turned white under his brown skin. "You wouldn't."

"I would so!"

"That's wrong. You a mean, hateful sister."

"No I'm not!" I yelled so loud my throat hurt.

"Or you jealous, that's what it is," he said, sticking his nose up in the air. "Jealous because I got lots of friends and you ain't got none."

"You never walk home with me after school. You're

never there for me *at school*." I shoved him and he rocked back against the kitchen counter, but he didn't fall. "Maybe that's what Mama was talking about, with woman trouble. I get bullied every day for working root, but you're my brother, and no one gives you a hard time."

He didn't push me back. He just rolled his eyes. "That's because I got *friends*."

"Well, I have one now too. Susie."

"Ooooh! One friend. So what?"

I was hurt and angry all at once. And I was a little scared. Was Jay going to turn his back on me too? "Of all people, you know what the other kids are like. How could you forget about me?"

Jay sighed in that heavy way he had before he knew what to say. But I didn't have any patience for it. I punched him in the arm with all my strength. His face was furious, but he didn't hit me back like he usually would.

"You're not gonna hit me back?"

He shook his head slowly. "I shouldn't hit you because you only a girl."

I saw red, I was so mad. I jumped on him, sending him to the floor. He pushed me hard. I kicked out and my foot scraped his cheek. Jay made a sound like a growling dog as he scrambled up and ran at me. I swung at him, and he ducked out of the way, but he smacked his head against the counter. I laughed until he threw the canister of rice at me. Then it was my turn to duck.

The canister flew across the room and hit a cabinet, spraying rice grains all over Mama's clean floor.

"Uh-oh," we said at the same time.

That took the fight out of us. We both stood there, breathing hard, staring at the wash of rice grains that had tumbled out of the canister and spread to almost every corner of the kitchen. I pressed my back against the counter and slid down to sit on the floor. "We never used to have secrets from each other, Jay. We used to have them from other people."

"Okay, okay." He sat down on the floor across from me and ran his hands over his face like Doc did when he was thinking really hard on a problem. "It's just I been—I don't know how to talk to you about this stuff."

"You can tell me anything. We're brother and sister. Even more, we're twins. That's supposed to be special."

"I know. I'm sorry, Jezzie," he said.

"Me too. I'm really sorry." I felt sick to my stomach. My belly churned from worrying. This fight with Jay, on top of everything else, left me feeling so cold inside. I shivered thinking about Lettie, Deputy Collins, and that voice in the marsh. Was I a witch? Was I evil? "I just want us to be like we were before. Telling each other things. Being friends."

He rubbed his arm where I'd hit him. "I want that too."

"Okay," I said. "Does that mean I can ask about your . . . your blood brother?"

He shrugged, then leaned back against the other side of the counter. Our legs both stuck out in front of us, making an L shape. I didn't press him about it, because he could be stubborn and not want to talk at all. But I was so curious—nosy, Jay would call it.

"Only if I can ask you about Susie."

"I guess so. She's new this year, in my class. She's been friendly to me since the first day, and we sit together most lunchtimes. She's . . ." I hesitated, realizing I didn't know a lot about her. Not what school she went to before, or who her family was, even though it seemed to me they probably had money. All I knew was that she was a little strange, like me, and she didn't seem to care about what any other kids said. After a moment, I could only come up with a not-good-enough word. ". . . nice," I finished.

"Yeah. Tony is nice too."

"Mmm," I said, to keep him talking.

"I dunno," he said, lying back on the floor. "Tony asked me and I been knowing him, so . . . I figured why not?"

He still looked like my brother, but there was something in his face now that made him look a little older. I was fascinated and terrified and I wondered if he could see the same changes in me.

"I don't want us to grow apart," I blurted out. "I still want us to be close, even after we grow up. Like Mama and Doc."

"But Doc didn't come here until after Daddy was gone, when Mama needed help. We only had stories about him before that."

"Do you think he didn't like Daddy?" I asked.

"How could anybody not like him? Nobody in their right mind, anyway."

"Suppose," I said, my body feeling light and heavy at the same time, "suppose our dad left for a special reason. Like he was a warrior who got called for a mission and he had to go save the world."

"Like, a secret mission?"

"Yeah." I pulled my legs under me and sat up. "We would have to cover up any signs of Daddy, so the bad guys wouldn't threaten us because we're his family."

"Oooh! Maybe he's a spy."

"Or maybe someone like Dr. King."

He laughed hard now. "You think Martin Luther King is our daddy? That he secretly run around calling himself Danny Turner, out here in South Carolina? You crazy."

"No, not that he's *actually* Dr. King. That he's someone who—" I lay back on the floor and looked up at the ceiling, frustrated. "You don't understand."

"No, no, I get it. I'm just messing with you. I think the same thing sometimes. Like Daddy had to leave without telling us anything to protect us." His voice sounded far away. "But other times . . . I don't think that's what really happened."

I stayed on my back, then put my bare feet up against the wall. My toes were straight, but dirty. The cuts from scratching mosquito bites I got over the summer were now fading thanks to the cocoa butter Mama made me rub on my legs at night. She said no one would want a girl with scarred-up legs. I used the butter to make her happy, but I really didn't care about anyone wanting me. Maybe when I grew up, but now I had more important things to think of.

"Then what do you think he is?" I asked Jay.

"Maybe he was like Doc. A magic man. A witch doctor."

"Was?" I asked, sitting up fast. I wished I hadn't, because the whole room started spinning and I felt my stomach twist. Good thing we hadn't had any dinner yet.

"He might be dead, Jezzie," he said. "We don't know."

Jay shook his head, and watching it move didn't help my dizziness. I'd never thought of him as dead before. My stomach had felt like it was a used trash bag, and someone was crunching it up in their fist. Now it felt like they were stretching and shaking it out. I shuddered.

My brother must have known what I was feeling. He smiled. "It's nice to think of him alive, though. Fighting bad guys like a hero."

"Yeah," I agreed. "You have blood on your face."

"And your dress got a rip."

Jay was right. I'd have to sew it up really fast. "We better get this rice and us cleaned up before Mama gets home."

"Too late for that now." Mama's voice boomed across the room, filling my chest up with sound.

16

"What in the world were you two thinking? Fighting like street cats!"

I looked at Jay, but he was staring at his hands. I was surprised he hadn't already said it was my idea. And I wasn't going to admit that to Mama.

"Huh?" she prompted. "Neither one of you got a thing to say? Fighting in here while I'm busting my hump at that market. And you two are eleven years old!"

"We already worked it out. It's over. We're friends again, right?"

Jay nodded. "Right."

"Were you going to eat rice instead of your dinner?

I'm sure that was you, Jezebel. You know better." She put her hands on her hips, and one of her feet tapped an impatient rhythm. "Never in my life have I seen the like. What I ought to do is whip both of your tails."

I prayed she wouldn't do that; I already felt bad enough. Plus I was hungry. So hungry I couldn't think straight. I sat there waiting to see what else was going to happen.

"Well, get to cleaning this rice up, you two." She gave me the broom and Jay the dustpan, then wiped her hands on her apron. "Lord Jesus, give me strength."

We went to work sweeping up the rice. Since Mama said her floor was clean enough to eat off, she made us put the grains in a bag to save them, while she boiled fresh rice and reheated okra and tomato soup. We were almost finished when Doc came in.

"Did I miss the dinner call?" he asked, scanning the empty tin of rice on the table.

"No, I just gave the kids something to do to keep them from killing each other."

Doc's eyes got real wide. "A fight in the house?" He stroked his salt-and-pepper beard. "Now that is bad. Would have been better if you had a tussle in the front yard. Get it outta your system."

"Will you stop? They don't need any encouragement." Mama dished up bowls of okra soup over the rice and placed them on the table.

"Can I have my rice plain, Mama?" I asked.

She sighed and handed me another bowl. "I swear, with these kids."

"Just remember, Janey. That's all they are—kids. They're growing up mighty fast, but inside—heart and mind—they're only young."

Mama sat down to her dinner and didn't reply. A few minutes later she nodded, almost like she was talking to herself. "Both of you finished? No rootwork lessons tonight; you're going to bed early."

"Aw, Mama," we both said.

"No, not after that fight. You both have to learn to get along, so you're going to your room to spend some more time together." She crossed her arms, so I knew we didn't stand a chance of changing her mind. "Go on."

We didn't argue; we just washed our dishes, then headed off. Jay went to wash up first, but I climbed straight onto my bed. The night was hot for November, so I lay down on top of the covers. When I picked Dinah up, I could feel her disappointment like a heavy weight inside me.

"I know, I know," I said, feeling ashamed. "Mama told me."

Even though Dinah didn't have eyes like real people, I knew she was looking at me. I couldn't look back at her. I twirled her crepe wool hair around in my fingers instead. "I'm sorry I argued with Jay. I was upset and hurt." My voice became a whisper.

Dinah made a sound to herself, a low rumbling sound like faraway thunder.

"I shouldn't have yelled," I whispered.

I felt a tug on my fingers where they were wrapped in her hair. When I looked down, Dinah was nodding.

I knew I had to start making good choices if I wanted to make it to being a grown-up. Even Miss Corrie told me that. I hugged Dinah close, not sure I was ready for what being grown meant. Mama and Doc both worried about being able to take care of the family. Now that me and Jay were getting older, we needed to start helping more.

"Dinah, am I a witch?"

"Sho," she said, her creaky, squeaky voice in my head. "Da famblee is two-head."

Two-head. A name Gran used for a witch doctor. It was an old name, meaning you had one head in the real world and one in the magic world. I wondered if I would be able to live up to the name.

For a while I watched the lights from the sky play around the trees and listened to the crickets singing. Then I closed my eyes and let everything fall away from me. I was tired from the day. Drained like I had been working on a chain gang, breaking rocks in the hot sun.

As I lay there, I felt my body want to move. I started to get up, but my belly full of food kept me in place. One of my feet hung over the side of the bed but didn't touch the floor.

Both of my arms were flung out on the mattress, touching nothing. I breathed deep, taking in the smell of the marsh, the night, the wind outside. I relaxed every bit of me.

And that's when I felt myself rising like a balloon above a fair.

I was rising out of myself, like I had at the marsh. I lifted, feeling the warm, moist air hold me up. I was drifting above my body, floating there like a bee above a flower. I didn't weigh anything, and I felt—

"Ow!" Jay yelled suddenly.

At the sound, I lost the floaty feeling and dropped back down into my body with a thud. I struggled to sit up, confused. I grabbed Dinah for comfort.

"What? What happened?" I didn't know if I meant with Jay or with myself. Probably both. I hadn't heard him come back in the room. Dinah squeaked as I tugged her hair too hard, her mouth in a thin, hard line. "Sorry," I muttered, untwisting my fingers from her coils of hair. I hated when Gran had been rough with doing my hair, and I was glad I wasn't the only one in the family who was tender headed.

"I stubbed my baby toe! I think it's broke!"

I watched Jay sit on the bed and hold out his foot for me to see.

"It isn't. Just rub it really good to get the pain out."

He frowned, but he did it, wincing the whole time. "Don't know how I missed the edge of the bed."

I grunted at him, upset now that I'd gotten interrupted.

He gave me a look, then laughed softly. "You okay? You look strange in the face."

What could I say? That just before he went and stubbed his toe, I was actually floating? I still hadn't told him about what I'd been able to do at the marsh pool, separate myself from my body, so it would be a long story that I didn't feel up to telling tonight. And how would I explain it anyway? *I came out of my body and—* What was it that came out of my body? My soul? My spirit? This made me even more worried about the separation . . . but at the same time more eager to try it again.

"I'm fine. Just dozed off and woke up to you yelling about your stupid toe."

"You fell asleep? You never sleep that quick."

"It was a long day."

"That's the truth." He slid back toward the head of the bed and got under the flat sheet. He took out a magazine I'd seen him reading the last few nights, with a plane on the cover. "We're still okay, right?"

"Of course," I said, ready to get back to floating. "Always."

Once Jay's light snores started, I kept ignoring sleep, instead trying and trying to lift out of my body again, but I couldn't.

The next morning was Saturday, and I woke up with drum-beats in my head. The sun coming into the room felt like knives going through my eyes, and I rolled over, hoping to get away from the pain. Even moving my head made it hurt. Maybe staying up most of the night trying to fly again wasn't the best idea.

"Ughh!" I groaned, hunching over and curling up like a grub to avoid the light.

Soft laughter greeted me, and I realized it was Dinah. Faint giggles seemed to be coming through her red stitched mouth. The mouth stayed in a smile, but I heard her chuckles clearly in my head.

"What's so funny?" I asked. "I'm dying."

In a fading echo, I heard the words *Lib eb'uhlastin*.

Life everlasting? What was that? It sounded like a potion Doc would sell.

I stumbled up out of bed, past Jay, who was still sleeping with a pillow over his face, and into the kitchen. Mama was humming a song, and the tune was cracking my skull open like a nut.

"Good morning," she said, her smile unusually bright as she handed me a peach basket.

"Morning," I grumbled, taking the basket and shuffling outside to fill it with the ripest vegetables and fruit I could find. Then I came back in and handed her the over-flowing container, sat down at the table, and put my head in my hands. Already I could tell the day was going to be hot, and I wanted to go to the bathroom and press my face against the edge of the tub, where it was cool. "You're happy today," I said.

She didn't seem to notice that I wasn't. "I am, Miss Jezebel. How are you?"

"I feel like dirt." Dug up, turned over, raked through.

Mama put a cup of tea in front of me and I held it between my hands; it felt like it would burn me. I groaned as she placed a bowl of hot grits in front of me. She'd cracked an egg into it and stirred it up, so the steaming-hot cornmeal softly scrambled the egg. It was one of my favorite breakfasts, and I sprinkled the top with a pinch of salt and pepper, but I couldn't eat it. "Can I just have some rice, please?"

"We don't have any left over from dinner, I'd have to make more."

"Please!" I begged.

"I'll make you some Cream of Rice," Mama said. "That'll be faster." She put a pot of water on the stove. When it boiled, she sprinkled in the fine grains and stirred.

I yawned. "I don't feel so good."

"Hm," she said, putting her hand on my forehead to check my temperature. "Think you caught a little cold from those kids at school?"

I shook my head. I didn't get close enough to any of

them to catch a cold. But I wasn't going to tell Mama that maybe I made myself sick on rootwork and flying. "Do you know what 'Life Everlasting' is?"

"It's a medicine." Mama watched me closely. "You got a fever or something?"

"No, just tired. I didn't sleep," I answered.

She felt my forehead again with the back of her hand. "Hmph. I don't feel a fever. But you might need to skip lessons with Doc today."

"We can't, Mama!" Jay cried from the doorway. "If you don't let Jez go, Doc won't do a lesson today at all. We need to learn this stuff." Jay was even more eager to learn after this week; he'd brought to school one of the dried snakeskins we found out in the woods when we were gathering them for Doc's storeroom, and it impressed all his friends. As for me, I had a long way to go before I was able to create my own spells beyond the root bags we'd made and a few of the basic potions Doc had taught us. Because of that, I didn't want to miss a single lesson.

"Jay's right," I agreed. "We can't miss a lesson. Doc is counting on us."

"I don't know . . . ," Mama said.

"I want to go. We'll be fine." When she hesitated, I added, "It's one of the only things that make me feel closer to Gran."

She nodded, then got up to spoon steaming Cream of Rice into a bowl for me. "Want butter on it?"

"No, ma'am." I dug into the bowl like it was the fanciest dinner I'd ever had.

"James, go wash up while your sister finishes breakfast. Then you two can go. I need some time to myself today."

He rushed off to the bathroom while I finished the soft, tender rice, then nodded at the pot on the stove as I stood up.

"Thanks, Mama," I said. "I'll finish the rest of it later."

"Okay," she said softly as me and Jay ran outside to Doc's cabin. It was on the way that I realized she had never told me what the Life Everlasting was for, but I didn't need it now. The rice had fixed what was wrong with me.

I was especially focused on lessons, scribbling down everything Doc said. He was glad to see it. Much of rootwork from the old people way back wasn't written down—it was passed on only by word of mouth, which made each telling a little bit different. But it also meant the stories could be lost. Preserving our people's stories, Doc said, was the most important thing.

I still wasn't sure I was ready to tell Doc about my flying, but I hoped something in his lessons, at some point, could tell me what it was, and if I could ever manage to do it again. I'd felt afraid at first, then realized what a freedom it was. I wanted to know if I could go places when I was like that. Go outside, maybe follow Dinah if she ever went on another one of her outings.

"Jezebel!" Doc's voice cut through my daydream.

"Yes?"

"Were you listening to me?" Doc and Jay were both turned toward me, but only Jay was grinning. He got in trouble more than I did, and it must have been a real treat for him to see me get a talking to.

"I'm sorry, I was . . . umm . . . thinking, I guess. I didn't get a lot of sleep last night."

Doc moved his pipe around in his mouth. "This feels like you're back in the classroom, doesn't it? No wonder you're drifting. Come on, let's go do some real work."

We followed him out of the stuffy cabin into the humid air. It was still warm for November. Not burning hot like the middle of summer, but warm enough for me to not need a coat. Jay followed Doc first, and I tagged behind him, crossing the fields. The garlic stalks, which Mama hated and Doc loved, had recently blossomed into fat flowers, adding their sharp, stinging scent to the air.

To the edge of the woods we headed, finally coming to the base of a fig tree. Doc motioned for us to sit while he showed us how to measure the strength of the herbs and roots that would go into the potions and incense he made.

"The strength you need depends on the strength of the problem," he said. "Less for a gentle potion, more for a particularly rough or evil spell."

"How do you know when you need a little or a lot?" Jay asked.

"If it was a situation like a removal of a jinx—that's a trick that is hurting someone—you need something strong. A person's health, even their life, is on the line. What you'll be left with after you remove the jinx is tainted, and until you learn how to keep the tainted water safely, be sure you dispose of it somewhere so you don't get anything sticking to you or the customer. Bury it." Doc's eyes slid over to me. "That's what I used against your attacker in the marsh. Some tainted floor wash I had from cleaning a bad spell out of a client's house. The old magic in the cleaning water interrupted what the attacker was doing to you. It's one of the uses of tainted water." He stroked his beard thoughtfully.

"Will doing that always work?" I asked.

"Most times, it's enough to interrupt someone's magic. I was hoping it would break the hex and give me time to pull you out." His eyes got a faraway look and he squinted them a little. "Glad I was right."

"What about doing jinxes ourselves?" I asked. Hoping for a spell to use on the kids at school, I held my pencil ready over a fresh page.

Doc tapped his finger on his chin. "What sort of tricks you talking about?"

"Oh, I don't know." I fidgeted and scribbled a drawing in my notebook, a circle of vines and roots that looked like my bracelet from Doc. "I mean tricks like . . . giving somebody bad luck or something like that. Or make some-one scared of you."

Doc replied with seriousness in his voice. "Listen to me really close. When you lay a trick like that—one that has evil intentions, or is made to injure somebody—you better be very, very careful. They are dangerous, you hear? And not just to the person you're jinxing. I don't do them unless I have a good—no, a *perfect* reason."

"But why?" I knew I sounded frustrated, but I couldn't stop myself. "Isn't that part of why you do root? To get back at people who hurt you?"

"Yeah," said Jay. "Then they'll be scared of us. It's protecting ourselves, right?"

Doc shook his head. "No, and I don't know where you got that idea. The point of root is to try and make this world a better place to live in. Sometimes it means ridding the place of a person, but most times, it's giving people strength, a reason to be better. Do you understand?"

"But you said *sometimes* it means getting rid of some-body. Why can't we learn that?" I tapped my notebook with the eraser end of my pencil.

"You will learn it, just not now. Once I feel like you have a good understanding of the ways of this magic and how to use it right, then I'll teach you everything I know. But those magics—the bad ones, the destructive ones—are dangerous even for me to use." He drummed his fingers on his worktable. "Among other things, it is powerfully easy for a haint or a decent rootworker to reverse a spell back onto you. And that's something I don't want to have to deal with."

I nodded, a little bit embarrassed. I got so angry at the kids in school for not understanding what I could do, and here I was trying to force the information out of Doc. It wasn't right. I needed to be more patient. Study hard, and let Doc guide us. I listened to the rest of the lesson and made my notes without any more questions.

We finally finished the day in the late afternoon, before the sun started to set, and the air cooled enough to carry a slight chill. Jay went off to play with Tony for a bit before dinner; I hesitated only for a moment before heading down to the marsh. I had a shiver inside when I thought of the poppet, but the marsh was part of my life, and I wanted to watch our neighbors' boats come in with nets full of shrimp and crabs. I'd be careful, but I couldn't be afraid.

I sat alone on the marsh bank for a while, my back against the thick trunk of the old live oak we called the boar hog tree. Warmth radiated from the ground, and the breeze was just the right kind of cool. It made such a pleasant combination that I closed my eyes. I must have drifted off into sleep, because the next thing I knew, something was nudging me and I jolted.

"Susie!" I hadn't heard her at all. I thought the tall grasses would give me a signal someone was coming, but they didn't. First there was nothing, then she was right in front of me. "Hi," I said.

"Is it okay if I sit with you?"

I went to move my notebook so she could sit down but couldn't find it. I spun around, afraid I'd misplaced it.

"Is this what you're looking for?" Susie said. She had my notebook in her hand.

"Yes!" I said. "Thanks."

"It slid down the bank." She sat next to me, our backs against the rough bark.

"What did you do today?" I asked.

After a pause, Susie said, "Chores." She shifted on the hard ground. "You?"

"Some of that. And some rootworking lessons."

"What did you learn today?" She tucked her dress under her legs and bowed her head like she was praying.

"Um, it's kinda private." Back and forth, I rocked my heels in the soft dirt near the water's edge. I didn't want to tell her about jinxing people; I didn't need to give her any reason to think rootwork was scary.

If she was put off, she didn't show it. "Okay. Want to skip rocks?"

"Well, I want to, but . . ."

"But what?"

I looked away, out over the calm water. "I can never get my rocks to skip. Jay always teases me about it."

"Is that all?" Susie sprang up from her seat. "I'll show

you the trick to it. You have to find the right kinda rock first. Small, flat ones."

We searched the ground near the edge of the marsh and gathered up as many flat stones as we could find. Most were no bigger than my thumb. Susie showed me how to crook my arm just the right way to get the best distance. Me and Susie took turns seeing who could skip them across the water the farthest. I even beat her a few times.

A loud, angry cackle sounded from the edge of the reeds after my last throw, and a goose marched out. It stomped through the marsh grasses, wings spread wide, honking loudly. We must have disturbed its nest. It rushed toward us, flapping its huge wings.

We ran and didn't stop until we got back to the edge of our farm.

Finally when we caught our breath back, me and Susie laughed so hard we had to grab our sides. Then we headed to the pecan tree near our house for a rest. I dropped my notebook and flopped down on the cool grass, and Susie did the same.

"That was fun!" I felt light and free and excited from the run.

Susie turned to me. "That was the most fun I've had in a long time. Maybe ever."

We talked for a while, lying in the shade of that tree. We talked about our favorite things to do. Susie told me that she spent whole summers running through the marsh barefoot, and I told her Jay and I did the same. I couldn't believe we'd never seen each other; the marsh was big and wide, but it seemed so unfair that we'd never met before.

Soon the sun was dipping low in the sky, and the cicadas were singing. It was almost time for dinner.

"I have to go soon," I told her.

Susie looked disappointed, but she nodded. "I'm glad you're my friend, Jezebel." The words rushed out of her like she had been holding them in for a long time.

"Me too." An idea popped into my head of something I could share with my friend. "Oh! Stay right there. I'll be back."

I hopped up, ran up the path to the house, and burst in the front door. Mama looked at me the way she would when I did or said something she didn't expect. But I didn't have time to explain what I was doing. I put a palmful of salt in my pocket, kissed her cheek, then took off out of the back door. Over my shoulder, I yelled, "Thanks, Mama!"

I sped back down the path to the fields. It felt good to be among all the plants and herbs. I walked along the edge of our farm, past the beans and peas to the corn and the watermelons across from them, until I got to the tomatoes. Even though we were getting closer to the end of their growing season, ours were still full and round and deeply red. Their scent was strong and rich, especially when you rubbed their leaves.

"I thought you weren't coming back out."

I jumped at the sound of Susie's voice. "You scared me! I didn't hear you coming."

"Sorry," she said.

"I . . . um, wanted to say I had a good time too. I, um—" Nervous, I pulled on one of my pigtails. "I don't have lots of friends. Any, really."

Susie pulled on one of her braids too. "That's okay," she said. "Me either." Her dark eyes reflected the fading light like a mirror.

I cleared my throat. "So I wanted to give you something."

"You don't have to—"

But I was already tiptoeing down the rows of coiling tomato vines. "Come on."

She followed, careful and silent, until we got to the biggest tomato plant. I pulled the green, fat-bodied hornworms off the stalks and tossed them into a patch of weeds. Then I twisted off a ripe tomato and presented it to Susie.

She looked at it like she was afraid it was poisoned.

"It's okay," I promised. "This is the best way to eat them. Fresh off the vine and still warm from the sun." Even though I wasn't craving any food except rice, I took a tomato so Susie wouldn't feel like she was alone. I wouldn't want someone offering me food they weren't going to eat. I bit into it. The firm skin popped, releasing its sweet liquid. "And here's the best part." I sprinkled some of the salt from my pocket where my teeth marks were and bit again.

Susie took a tiny bite from her tomato. When she looked up at me, her grin was wide. She didn't want any salt, but she ate the whole thing up.

"That was great!"

I giggled. "I know. It's one of my favorite things."

Susie placed her hand on my arm. "Say we'll be friends no matter what. Promise?"

"Jezebel!" Mama's voice cut through the early evening.

"I have to go."

"Promise," she urged.

"I promise!" I trotted back toward the house, but when I looked over my shoulder, Susie still stood in the middle of the twisted vines, almost like she was trapped and didn't know how to get out.

17

At bedtime, Jay fell asleep right away, snoring as usual. It was the sound I was waiting for. I wanted to see if I could float again. I put Dinah on the windowsill and lay down on the bed, again not touching anything. Deep breaths in and out helped me to relax enough to try and forget all my worries.

After a few minutes, I just felt . . . not tired, exactly, but more like my mind was wandering and going nowhere in particular. *Practice, practice,* I reminded myself, so I wouldn't get frustrated. I closed my eyes and counted backward, letting go of everything my mind and body was tied to.

Up.

I lifted, slow and steady, until, once more, I was up in the air above my body.

For a moment, I was scared to open my eyes, wondering how it would work. Would my real eyes open? Would it be like the time in the marsh? I couldn't remember exactly how it happened because that day was a fight to survive. It was a reaction—I wasn't concentrating and trying to float then like I was now. Worry crept in again and I felt myself sinking.

Deep breath in and out. Relax. Loose, feel loose, stay loose.

I bobbed up again, and this time, my ghost eyes were open. I didn't remember doing it, but it was like I wanted them to open and they were. The room was almost dark, but there was no need for light. A little streamed in from outside: the moon was full and I could see me lying there on my single bed, Dinah looking up at me.

My body's eyes were closed and my arms and legs were slack like I was deep in sleep. Jay sprawled out on his bed, mouth open and snoring. I floated up and over his bed. He didn't wake up. I sorta wanted to know if he or anyone else could see me, but I also had more I wanted to do.

Turn.

The spirit of me turned toward the window.

Open.

Nothing happened. I guessed I would have to open it, so I reached out to grasp the handle. But my hand went through the closed window, quickly followed by the rest of me.

Now I was outside the house, hovering like a dragonfly. I couldn't feel the temperature of the air outside, but I knew it must be pleasant and sweet with late-year crops. Moving in this spirit body took time for me to get right, even though I was eager for this new freedom. I looked down and saw the damp dirt road leaving the farm, hard-packed in the middle of all of that moist dark soil. If I could just . . .

Suddenly, I was moving. It was slow and I was, for a moment, nervous of what would happen. Could anyone see me? The chickens, shut up in the coop for the night, cooed to each other as I went by but didn't make too much fuss.

Intent. That was the word Doc always used. He had said root worked with intent, and you had to have what you wanted to accomplish in mind.

I looked at the pecan tree Susie and I had sat beneath earlier. *I want to go there.* I thought it, and then I lifted and moved to the tree without a care in the world. From there, I raised and lowered myself, up over the top of the highest branches, and down under low-hanging ones.

I lost track of time, until the thudding crack of something dropping inside Doc's cabin scared me. I gasped and felt my body pull back on the free part of me, drawing me in like a crab on a fishing line.

My spirit plunged back into my body like jumping into a cold lake. I shivered hard and I woke up with a shout.

No one woke up, not even Jay, which made me wonder if I'd cried out in real life. I sat straight up in bed, looking around the quiet room filled with moonlight. I blinked, and the world looked different through my eyes for a moment, thin and see-through; then I blinked a few more times and it was back to normal.

Dinah was at the foot of the bed. I picked her up gently and rubbed my face against hers. Everything else around me was still, and I didn't feel any different. But what I did feel was hungry.

That was how Mama found me: barefoot and in my nightclothes eating out of the pot of rice from dinner, Dinah propped up against the sugar bowl facing me, in the dark kitchen.

And that was when she called the doctor.

A short, sturdy brown man in a bow tie and a starched white jacket over his white shirt came to the house. He looked me over: eyes, ears, mouth, and nose. He had me go to the bathroom in a little jar and he put it in his black leather bag.

"Nothing wrong with the child that I can see, Mrs. Turner. But once I hear anything back about this"—he patted his bag—"I'll let you know."

"But she won't eat," Mama said, biting her lip. "Nothing but rice."

The doctor nodded. "Be okay for her for a while. We'll see about it."

Mama didn't look any less worried, but she left me alone about it.

A week later, my test came out clean, and there was nothing the doctor could say about what they called my strange habits.

I wondered what he would say if he knew of my *traveling*.

Every night now, as soon as Jay was asleep, I'd fly. I'd gone to other farms at night, down to the marsh, even along the main road to the houses of a few neighbors. And I saw some crazy things there. Games of dice and dominoes, people dancing and partying till all hours. But not all my visits were happy. There was screaming and fistfights, little kids left alone at night, and animals being hurt.

I thought about quitting flying and staying home. But something always drew me outside. One night, I was tired of all the trouble I saw on the island, and so I just floated on my back in the middle of the air above the dying cornstalks, looking up at the sky. And somehow, I knew that was where I wanted to go. But wasn't that where heaven was? You could only go there if you died. I didn't want that at all. I felt the pull, but I was afraid I'd die up there and never find myself or my family again.

I felt a tug from a different direction—from the string that bound me to my body. The tug increased, yanking me back. And I fell, faster and faster, dragged back through the air into my body.

I woke up again with a start, like I'd hit the ground and knocked the wind out of myself. I panted, barely able to sit up. My blood was swirling in my head and I could hardly hear anything outside of the rush of liquid. But a small sound came through to me, a little girl's voice.

He'p.

I felt a pressure in my chest ease up, and I was able to breathe regular and deep. What was that voice asking for help?

For comfort, I reached for Dinah, but she was already looking at me. Her head was turned in my direction in the moonlight, staring at me, almost like she didn't know me. I froze.

"Zar," Dinah said.

I gasped and my hand flew to my mouth. "D-did you actually talk? I mean, really talk just now?" Maybe I was confused from the flying, but I definitely heard a voice. Even if her mouth didn't move.

She kept staring at me, her head tilted a little to the side like she was trying to figure something out.

"Zar." I heard the voice again, and I realized it wasn't Dinah talking. The voice was inside me. Inside my head, talking to me.

What was zar? And this voice . . . where did it come from? It wasn't like when I heard the voices of my ancestors at the marsh. This was like someone speaking from within me.

He'p, the voice said again.

Dinah stood up from where she sat on the windowsill and pointed at me. I grabbed her up and lay back on the bed. I held her over my face and she looked at me, deep in the eyes. And I could tell she didn't like what she saw.

I imagined a stream of Gullah words coming from Dinah. They were almost impossible for me to follow, they came so fast: *Gwine ta da Buzza'd.*

I needed to tell Doc what was happening. But what was happening?

He'p.

The voice came again, louder this time. More urgent. I set Dinah on the bed, and she waddled along it, sliding off the end and down to the floor. I shoved my feet into my shoes and followed her through the ink-dark night to Doc's cabin.

When we got there, he was at his table, scraping bark into a bowl, humming to himself. A candle was lit, smelling of a protection oil, and I wondered if it was one of the ones me and Jay had made.

"What are you doing up so late? Or early, I should say." Then he looked down and saw Dinah. His mouth opened and he dropped the branch he was scraping. For a moment, his mouth moved, but no sound came out. Finally, he said, "Seeing is believing, I guess. Well, your gran was stronger than even I knew."

Dinah tapped my leg with her cloth hand, and I knew she wanted me to tell Doc my story. I did, going all the way back to the marsh, all the way up to how I'd been feeling and the voice I'd heard tonight. The words flowed out clear and easy, even though I trembled hard, I was so scared. Doc and Dinah glanced at each other like they were having their own conversation without words.

My uncle listened without interrupting me, and even though he tried not to show it, I could see the worry in his eyes. "Sounds like you picked up a little haint on your travels."

My eyes went wide, but Doc's voice remained calm when he asked, "Jezebel, honey, how are you feeling?"

"Fine," I said, but I was scared. Doc had been teaching us to be cautious of spirits and beings we didn't understand. They could be tricky and dangerous. I picked Dinah up and held her close.

"Are you hungry, thirsty?" This time when he looked at me, he chose another candle from the shelf behind him and anointed it with oil. Then he mouthed a few words while he lit it. Smoke began to trail up to the ceiling and the scent of cloves filled the room. "What do you want?"

I breathed in the scented smoke. I was about to tell Doc that I wanted him to maybe pick a different scent when I heard the voice inside me again, speaking as if we were sitting together talking over tea and cakes.

"She's not hungry anymore. She wants to go home now."

My words shocked me as much as they did my uncle.

I remembered the haint in the marsh that had tricked me with the poppet doll. That haint was outside me, trying to steal my power. What could this one do if it was already inside me? My heart beat like I had run miles. Had I really picked up this ghost as I was traveling outside my body? I had never felt anything bad inside me. No evil, no pain. Just the hunger.

"Oh my God," I said, now letting the fear sink deeper. I could feel what this ghost wanted. It was living inside me! I started to breathe really fast.

"No, no, no. Don't get scared. Don't get tight, honey." Doc took me by the arms, gently. "I'm sorry I didn't see this before. I should have. But I'm going to fix it, okay? With your gran's help."

I nodded, afraid to speak in case it came out as someone else's words. I focused that same way I did when I escaped the haint in the marsh. I reached out, felt the presence of my family, my ancestors surrounding me. My breath calmed down. I had support. I had help. I had love.

"Now tell me a bit more about what you've been doing when you leave your body."

I told him about my trips, my adventures around the

island at night. About how I lifted out of my body and flew.

"You're sharing your body right now, Jezebel," Doc said. "Can you feel it?"

"No . . . ," I started, unsure. I didn't feel any different, except for that new pull I felt tonight. The one to go up, up, farther up into the sky than I ever had. The one that scared me. "Yes. I felt like going up to heaven."

"Lord Jesus," Doc whispered. "Did you feel like dying?"

"No, just going up into the sky. Like I was being pulled up there. But I got scared and I fell back."

"Back into your body?"

I nodded.

He rubbed his beard, then got up to search his shelves. Glass bottles clinked and metal bowls clanged, so loud that I was sure it would wake up Mama and Jay way over in the house.

"Is there really a ghost inside me?"

"Possibly," he said. "But something was attracted to your ability. To your power. It wanted to have some fun. Did you have fun with them?"

"Um, I think so?" I said, unsure how to answer.

"Okay, good. But like when you play outside, with a friend, there is a time for everyone to go home. Do you understand what I mean?"

I wasn't sure if he was talking to me anymore, or to . . .

the haint. So I didn't say anything. But for some reason my mouth opened anyway and a voice that was not mine spoke.

"Please for Zar."

I clasped my hands over my mouth to keep any more words in.

Doc jerked back and Dinah's little stitched mouth fell open. Doc recovered first. He stood up and came across the table to stand in front of me, motioning for me to lie down on the little cot he used when he was working all night.

The mattress was thin and clean, and it smelled of sage and cinnamon mixed with Doc's peach tobacco. I lay down on it, my eyes closed, listening to the sounds around me: matches lighting, glass jars tinkling together, liquid falling into glasses. He placed Dinah on the cot, next to me but not touching, and asked, "How do you do this flying, Jezebel?"

"I just relax and . . . let go, I guess. Then I lift up like a balloon."

"Go on, do that now. We'll be here with you, okay?"

"Okay," I said. My bed wasn't much bigger than the cot, but I didn't have the sheets here to cover me up and make me feel secure. I ignored that and concentrated on flying.

I closed my eyes and breathed deep, trying not to fidget. My worries about Deputy Collins and Lettie and everything else faded away. I let my arms and legs relax, and after a few more breaths, I felt like I weighed nothing at all. There was a freedom in this feeling, rising like warm air. Nothing could harm me, not with Doc and Dinah keeping watch. I lifted up, over the cot, the tiny thin string holding me to my body stretching like chewing gum.

Up I went, above the room where Doc and Dinah guarded my body, up above the cabin. The night was clear, and I could see what must have been millions of stars. One of them looked especially beautiful, and so far away.

"Zar," I whispered.

I floated up, not afraid this time. Through trees and higher. I rose past clouds, fat with rain. I didn't feel cold or scared; I felt wonder stirred with anticipation and a sense of homecoming.

I must have lost myself for a while to the haint, because soon I was farther than I'd ever been. So close to that star, on the other side of far. And I finally felt what she felt. Happiness. Joy. Relief. And then I—*we*—were there.

A place full of beauty and celebration. A place filled with children. I felt a warm tightness around my shoulders and I realized someone was hugging me. Then I saw a burst like a flare of sunlight pull away from me. It was the spirit—her spirit—separating from mine.

"*Tenki,*" the haint said. *Thank you.*

"You're welcome," I replied. A trickle of sadness came over me. I wondered how long that haint had been with me. I thought of Susie's words, asking if I felt like a part of me was missing, and I felt that now. But the haint's flare of sunlight embraced me again, my arm this time, pulling me forward.

"*Hunnah. Kumya.*" You. Come here.

I followed the haint to a gathering of lights just like hers. They were all different sizes and shapes and they welcomed me to join them. I did, laughing and happy and full of the warmth of friendship. Colors swirled around me, and while I didn't remember eating, I felt full—my belly, my heart, all of it. I listened to stories and shared them, playing and running and—

A tug pulled me out of my fun.

The scent of sage and cinnamon.

I looked up and another spirit formed in front of me. This one was larger and fuller and it spoke to me in English.

They are calling you back, child.

"I want to stay," I said, not caring about the whine in my voice. I would miss it so much, being with the other children's spirits, even for the little time I'd been here. I knew they all liked me.

Yes, but you want to go back as well, don't you?

I thought of Doc and Dinah waiting with my body on the little cot. Mama and Jay sleeping in bed, or maybe now up making breakfast. Or with my uncle and my doll, worried about me.

It wasn't fair. I wanted to stay. I wanted to not be the weird little girl in school. The one with the faded clothes, the dresses made out of Gran's old things. The one who tried to ignore the jokes. The one who was studying to be a witch doctor.

Then I thought of making fruitcakes with Mama before Christmas. It took us two days: chopping candied fruit, mixing the cake by hand, and lining cake tins with cut-up brown paper bags. Those were my favorite days of the year, even better than playing in the marsh or listening to Miss Watson. I already missed her. I also missed Doc, and even Jay. And Susie, my friend. My sight burned and I realized it was the start of tears.

"Is this heaven?" I asked.

The older spirit shimmered like heat on the road in summer.

The old people used to call this Zar. A place . . . beyond the farthest place you can think of. I don't know how you found us, but you did. Although I can guess, she said as the small spirit that had shared my body came over next to me.

Sage and cinnamon was strong in my nose now. Tugging, tugging.

You are already going back. Please tell Benjamin she is happy and well. But before you do, I give you this in thanks for bringing her back to us. Her shimmery, blurry arms swirled around with mine, and she placed a kiss in the center of my palm and closed my hand around it.

I felt myself losing my grip on this place. On Zar.

You are strong, child. This will make that voice inside you louder. Use it with care it will—

But I was gone, returning to my body. I was falling again, farther and faster than ever. Faster, through air yellow, then pink, then clear. I opened my hand and looked inside to see a coin that looked brand-new. It was beautiful and I'd never seen anything like it. I couldn't wait to show it to Doc.

I closed my hand again and let myself continue to fall, unafraid. Through thin, then thick clouds, through treetops, and landing with a thud. I didn't jerk awake this time; I settled into my body, happy to have it back and all to myself. I relaxed into it, wiggling my toes and fingers, then snuggling into the mattress.

"Oh, thank God!"

I heard Mama's voice and I opened my eyes. I wasn't in the cabin anymore but in my own bed. It had been moved to the middle of the room, so everyone could sit around me.

And they were: Mama, Doc, and Jay were staring at me so close, I pressed my back into the pillow. Dinah was snuggled against my side, her crepe wool hair standing on end and her dress wrinkled and in need of a wash. Jay pulled and tugged her hair back into place while giving me sidelong looks.

"What?" I asked, yawning. I felt happy-tired, like I had done a lot in one day and had nothing else to do but rest.

Doc said, "You were gone a long time. We were worried."

It didn't feel like a long time. I'd been having the best time of my life, but looking around at the faces, I could see they were all worried. "How long was I . . . gone?"

"All day." Mama put her hand on my head to feel my temperature. "How do you feel?"

I felt relaxed and pleased knowing somehow I'd helped someone—or something. Under the covers I made a tight fist, feeling the thick edge of the coin in my hand. I'd been so excited to show it to everyone, but I decided maybe later would be best. For now it would be my secret.

With a start, I recalled the message I was supposed to give. "Doc, will you please tell Mr. Benjamin that his daughter is happy?"

Doc blinked really fast, like he couldn't believe what he was hearing. "How do you know that, Jez?"

I covered my mouth with one hand and let out a huge yawn. "I played with her today, and I could feel it."

"Okay, Jez. I'll go see him tomorrow and let him know." Doc rubbed his beard. "You know, not everyone—very few rootworkers or witch doctors—can leave their bodies like you do. I can't."

"Really?" I asked, sitting up.

"Really," he confirmed. "You're learning fast, and you've learned something I could never teach you."

"And you helped somebody today," Jay added. "You always been wanting to do that."

Mama folded a handkerchief that was sitting on her lap and tucked it into the pocket of her apron. "I was so worried. But I'm proud of you. We all are."

"Thanks." A warm feeling flooded my face. Mama, Doc, and Jay were looking at me so closely, I had to look down at my hands. "I'm hungry," I said, knowing this time it was only my belly. My heart and spirit felt full.

"It's almost dinnertime. Want some rice?" Mama asked.

For the first time in a while, I didn't.

While Jay helped Mama cook dinner, I took out my root-work book. I wanted to make sure I didn't forget anything during the whole day I was in Zar. And I could write down what Doc said about my flying being something that even he couldn't do.

As soon as I opened my notebook, though, I knew something was off. It felt wrong in my hands. Thinner and lighter. I went back all the way to the beginning and turned each page.

Certain spells I knew I wrote in my book were missing. My notes on how to keep a boo-hag out of your house—the haint-blue paint, the broomstick across the door—were all gone! When I looked close, I could see the raggedy edges where the pages had once been. All the time and effort I took to write down the information Doc gave me, and so much of it was gone.

"Jay!" I shouted.

"What?" he said, turning from the counter where Mama had him cutting out biscuits with a cookie cutter and putting them on an oven tray. "You ain't gotta yell, I'm right here."

"I *do* have to yell. What happened to my root book?"

"How I'm supposed to know?"

Mama dumped a colander full of cleaned shrimp in a pot. She wiped her hands on a kitchen towel. "What happened to the book, Jez?"

"Half of it's gone," I cried. "Well, not half, but a good bit of it."

"Gone?" Both she and Jay came over to look, and I turned the pages that were left.

"See? Some of them are missing."

"Don't look at me. I ain't rip up your book." He held his hands, covered in flour, up in the air. "No reason to."

Jay was right. There was no reason for him to tear pages out of my book. If he needed a spell or to know an ingredient, he could have asked me to see the book. Or just ask Doc himself. Besides, he teased me at times, but he wasn't cruel.

"Sorry, Jay," I muttered. "I was wrong."

He came over and hugged me with his elbows, so he didn't get flour all over me. And I knew he had forgiven my too-quick words. "Question is," Jay said, "who would wanna tear your stuff up?"

Mama tilted her head to the side like she was considering. "I can only think of two reasons someone would tear pages out of a book. One: they want to destroy the book. Two: they want the information for themselves." She flipped through my notebook. "These pages look like they were torn out carefully, not ripped apart. So I think whoever did this was after what was on those pages."

"But who wants my rootwork spells and stuff?" I thought of Lettie, but she always acted like rootwork was some kind of evil, so I didn't think she would take the pages.

"Maybe the question you should ask yourself," Mama said, going back to her pots, "is when was the last time you let the book out of your sight?"

I didn't have it when I went to Doc's cabin about the haint inside me. . . . But then, it had been in my room, where Jay had been asleep. When I thought back further, a sinking feeling took over me.

The last time I had left the book somewhere was when I fell asleep against the tree near the marsh. Susie was there when I woke up.

But—no. It couldn't have been Susie. We sat together every day at lunch. Well, she hadn't been to school since that day at the marsh. I didn't know if she was sick, if it was just a coincidence that she happened to be out of school right after I discovered that my notebook was missing. She listened to me when I was upset about Jay. She walked home with me after school. She stuck up for me in front of Lettie and all the popular girls. She wouldn't do this to me. She was my friend.

But at the same time, I couldn't think of anyone else who could have done it.

If it was Susie . . . she must have had a reason. And I was going to find out, either way.

"How long before dinner?" I asked.

"A half hour," Mama said. "Why?"

"I'll be back on time!"

I grabbed my torn-up book and raced outside before Mama could stop me. I needed to find Susie. My feet pounded on the ground as I ran toward the marsh. When I got to the edge where the seagrass met the water, I stopped. I didn't know where she lived exactly. She'd never told me. She was the closest I'd ever come to having a real friend, and I didn't even know where her house was. I didn't know anything about her, really.

But when I thought about it, hard, I did know something. I knew that the last thing I wanted was for her to be the person who did this to me. It wasn't only a notebook—it contained connections to my past. To Gran. And even if she wanted to know what was on those pages, I couldn't believe that she wanted to take those connections away from me.

I shouted as loud as I could, "Susie, where are you?" I shook the book in the air. It was ridiculous, because I knew she couldn't hear me, but I yelled again anyway. "I need to talk to you!"

Only the sounds of the marsh answered, croaking frogs and singing cicadas. A splash of water that meant a fish leaped up and dived down again. Leaves on the trees rustled, and our clothes waved and snapped on the clothesline. Of course, Susie didn't appear.

My shoulders slumped as I turned to walk back home. The orange root bag I'd placed under the house hadn't worked. Or maybe I did it wrong. Or maybe root just didn't work like that.

It was as I was drifting off to sleep that night that I heard the crunching of car tires on dirt and rocks outside our house. I blinked and tried to focus on the sound. It was getting closer. Who was coming to our house at this time of night?

That was when the car picked up speed, racing toward our house, tires screeching. I shrieked, then slapped my hand over my mouth to stay quiet. I sat up right as the headlights came on full bright, shining straight into the window. The sudden light stole my vision for a few moments and I put my hand up to shield my eyes.

"What the—" Jay scrambled up out of bed, his head bent down against the light. "Jezzie?"

"I'm here! On my bed."

The car moved around to another side of the house, and I saw that it had blue and red lights on top of it.

Jay climbed up next to me as a horn blared, cutting through the gentle night sounds of the marsh. Shrieks of laughter came out between the horn blasts as the car circled our house three times. Then something hard slammed against our front window, and the car pulled away.

Mama burst into our room as the horn and laughter faded into the night. I could feel Jay shaking next to me, and I was trembling too.

"You two okay?" She hugged us tight.

We nodded, our faces buried in Mama's nightgown. She smelled like Ivory soap and her sweet orange hair pomade, and I breathed deep to try and relax.

She rocked us back and forth, whispering, "He's gone for now, okay? He's gone."

18

I got so little sleep that night that Mama had to shake me to get me out of bed the next morning. I dragged myself to the bathroom, then got dressed for school. I ate whatever Mama put in front of me—grits or eggs, I don't even remember. The table was strangely quiet, Mama and Doc sipping coffee and Jay eating up his breakfast without the usual clattering of his spoon against the bowl. I guess we were all just thinking about that car zooming up to our house with the lights on. We all knew it was Deputy Collins, even if we couldn't prove it.

Then Jay asked me something that woke me right up.

"Suppose Susie is back to school today. What you gonna say about your book?"

I hadn't even thought about that. "I guess I'll ask if she took it."

Doc made a sound of agreement. "That's the best way, Jez."

But it turned out I wouldn't get to, because Susie still wasn't at school. And I didn't know where she lived to go and try to find her. I was so caught up in my thoughts that when Lettie said something to me, I didn't even look at her and just shouted, "Your mama!" over my shoulder.

After school, Jay and his friend Tony waited for me outside to walk home. It was nice, and unexpected, even if they did spend the whole time laughing and running, acting silly, mostly ignoring me. I couldn't help it—I missed Susie. In spite of her doing what she did behind my back.

"Can you stay out and play?" Tony asked Jay, tossing a ball to him as we reached the path that led to our house.

"No," he said. He tossed the ball back. "I gotta get on now. See you after dinner, okay?"

Tony smiled and rushed off to his own house, probably to stuff down food and get back outside. Me and Jay walked until we were out of sight and then ran the rest of the way home.

When I walked in the door, Mama smiled and handed me a brand-new notebook. I hugged her and then got to work rewriting everything I remembered from my old book. Doc sat with me to go back over a few things I missed. I finally had a change to add some notes about my time in Zar.

When it was bedtime, I climbed in with my notebook to keep writing. And even after Jay fell asleep, I still worked. Mama came in and made me turn off the light, saying I could get back on it tomorrow. But I couldn't sleep. Thoughts swirled around in my head and I tossed in bed.

Dinah wiggled next to me, and I patted her head. Finally, I sat up. There was no way I could sleep now. Maybe there was enough moonlight for me to read some of my root notebook. Or I could light the hurricane lamp me and Jay used when we lost power because of a storm.

The room felt hot and sticky, so I kneeled on my bed to crack the window open. That's when I saw it—a flash of something outside. I leaned closer, till my nose almost touched the window. It happened again: a swatch of pale light, like a shadow made of moonlight, darting through the dark toward the woods.

I eased out of bed and into my shoes, then woke up Jay. He started to protest loudly and I clamped my hand over his mouth. When he realized it was me, he pushed my hand off. I told him what I saw, and then he got up as well, grabbing his shoes and pulling on his overalls.

Me and Jay tiptoed out into the dark night, following the moonlight shadow that was slipping and dipping between the trees and bushes. All I saw was a flash of color in the darkness, then it was gone. Again it came, dashing in and out through the woods quicker than a rabbit. Jay and I froze.

"What is that?" I whispered, soft as I could.

"Shhh," Jay said, creeping closer and bending forward to get a better look. "Just watch." He stared for a while, then straightened up. We fell silent as we got closer, quiet as the bubbles breaking in the mud of the marsh.

But what I saw almost made my jaw hit the ground.

"It's Susie!" I hissed.

Jay looked like he was going to yell out to her, and I clamped my hand on his mouth again. This time, he licked it. I took my hand away and pinched him.

"I'm gonna go ask her who she think she is," he whispered. "Playing with your emotions like that."

I grabbed his shirt and pulled him back. "No, no. Wait, I want to see what she's up to. Why's she in the marsh behind our house in the middle of the night?" We eased closer and took up a spot with our shoes in soft black soil and our backs against the bark of a tree.

Susie was standing in the moonlight in a space of trees, looking up at the sky. We watched in shock as she took off her dress and shoes, leaving only her underwear on. Then, she reached up to her head, and there was a ripping sound.

It was like when you pull apart two pork ribs that weren't quite finished cooking yet. The sound made my stomach do a flip-flop. My legs felt wobbly-weak, and Jay squeezed my hand tight as we watched Susie split her scalp straight down the middle and continue right down her back.

Then, she just shuffled out of her skin, like it was a winter coat that got too hot to wear. She folded up that skin and left it tucked up near the base of one of the largest trees.

Beside me, I heard Jay gasp and felt his body slump, but he stayed on his feet. As we watched, the thing that used to be Susie stood there, all meat and blood, and shook itself like a wet dog, then stretched its arms up to the sky. She—it?—took a running jump and leaped up into the air. For a while it hung there looking at the skin it was leaving behind. Then it flew away, off into the night.

I couldn't look more. I couldn't breathe.

Susie was . . . a boo-hag.

"Oh my Lord!" I said, the words feeling like they were not enough for the images I just saw. I stared up at the sky where Susie had disappeared, my head spinning. Boo-hags were real. And Susie was one of them.

Jay was speechless. His mouth opened and closed, but he didn't say anything. Then he grabbed his head, pushing at his ears, and cursed. "She's a monster! What we gonna do?"

I tried to get my thoughts straight. Doc told us that boo-hags would remove their skin when they went out to terrorize people. They loved to prey on rootworkers and suck up all their strength. And it was best to get rid of them as fast as you could.

I knew what we had to do. "Let's get the skin," I said.

"You fool up? I ain't touching it," Jay said. "That thing is nasty."

I screwed my mouth up. "It's just skin. It wasn't nasty when Susie was in it a couple minutes ago. Help me get it."

As we tiptoed over to the tree, Dinah wriggled up a storm in my pocket, a warning to be careful. We brushed off the few leaves that had fallen on the pile of clothes and skin, then got on either side of it to drag it away. At first, we tried grabbing the hands, but the skin's fingers flopped like they were holding our hands and I squeaked like a scared mouse. Instead, we grabbed it under the arms. The skin itself was heavier than I thought it would be. We couldn't lift it all the way up, so we dragged it along from the marsh to Doc's cabin.

We knocked on the door, but we didn't hear anyone moving inside; it didn't seem like Doc was there. So we laid the skin down and I lifted the latch. I held the door open with my back while Jay and me dragged the heavy load inside.

I didn't even need my notebook—I had just rewritten the information about how to deal with hags. To keep them from coming inside, you painted the house haint blue, or you laid a broom across the entrance to the house. I also remembered what he said about hag skins—there was no way I could forget something so yucky. "Salt," I told Jay. "We're supposed to cover the skin in salt."

We ran around the cabin looking for salt. We knew it had to be here somewhere because Doc used it all the time in his spells. We grabbed all manner of jars, boxes, and bags until finally, Jay found the paper can with the little white girl's picture on it. We poured a stream of the white crystals into our palms, just like Mama taught us in cooking. And then, together, we sprinkled salt all over the skin.

We almost screamed when the skin reacted to the salt, jerking and jumping like it was caught in a trap. But after a moment, it went still. Jay and I finally relaxed, sucking in deep breaths to get our heartbeats to slow down to normal.

"Now, let's take it back outside." Sweat beaded up on my forehead and I swiped at it with the back of my arm.

"We just dragged it in here. Why we wanna to take it out? One time touching that thing is enough." Jay was wiping his hands on his overalls.

"Well, I don't want to touch it either. But we need to take it outside. I have a feeling Doc won't be happy if he comes back to find a hag skin in his cabin."

Jay sneered. "Jez Turner, always the teacher's pet."

I jerked back like he'd hit me. "What'd you say?"

"You heard me."

I could feel the blood rise to my face. "Just because

I'm a good child doesn't mean I'm a teacher's pet. You'd know that if you actually listened to Mama or Doc or your teacher for once."

"So, you're perfect." He frowned. "Perfect Jezebel, with a name of a street walker."

No one had ever said that to me. Especially not my brother. Not even when we were fighting really hard. I pulled my hand back to box him in his dirty mouth.

"Stop! Stop it right now!"

Both me and Jay froze. We hadn't heard Doc come up from the cellar of the cabin; we were too wrapped up in our fight. But there he was, half in and half out of the trapdoor. He had heard everything we'd said. "Don't you see that this is because of the skin? You two aren't like this. Think. It's affecting your mind."

He came fully out of the cellar and slid heavy gloves on his hands. Then he grabbed the skin around the belly area and took it outside himself, throwing it several feet from the cabin but where we could see it from the window. Coming back in, he took the gloves off before he poured water from a pitcher into a basin, then added a pouch of dried plants to it. He dropped the gloves into it and then plunged his hands in.

Doc motioned for us to do the same, and we washed our hands in the smoke-scented water. An oily residue rose to the top of the water. I shuddered.

"Now what I want to know is how did you two manage

to get hold of a boo-hag skin?" He poured the dirty liquid into a jar and closed it up. Then he poured salt in the bowl and scrubbed it. "They are very protective of their skins and usually only keep them in a place they feel is safe."

Jay and I looked at each other, but didn't say anything for a few heartbeats. "It was in the marsh," I said, not sure where to begin.

"And what were the two of you doing out there this time of night?"

"We were . . . following someone—" I began, but then Jay jumped in.

"It's Susie's skin," Jay said. "That girl in Jez's class."

Doc's eyes grew huge. "What? You've been going to school with a hag in disguise?"

I nodded. "I couldn't sleep, and I saw something from the bedroom window. When me and Jay got to the woods, Susie was there. We watched her take off her skin and leave it. You said boo-hag skins should be salted."

"That's right." Doc looked concerned, and he bit at his bottom lip. "Well, I suppose we just figured out why she stole those pages from your notebook."

I'd completely forgotten about that. The way she'd befriended me, all the questions she had about root-work . . . she'd only been trying to get at me, at my magic. Tears stung the back of my eyes, and I was glad it was too dark for Doc or my brother to see.

Doc took a peek at the sky out the window. "The sun

is only a little while away. About an hour or so, I'd say." He peered at the sky again. "Maybe a coupla hours."

Just as he said that, the trees rustled. A wind came up that was from a different direction than the rest of the sticky air. A chill ran through me, but Doc and Jay didn't react.

The thing that was Susie had returned. A screech filled the air—part owl, part hawk, part something I couldn't name—and it made me tremble, because I had heard that exact same sound before on many nights when I couldn't sleep. When I was little, Mama used to tell me it was night birds fighting each other. Did she just tell me that because it would make me feel safe?

We all tensed, watching the thing from the window. It looked like a skinned person creeping on all fours, bent, a horrifying open gap where a mouth should be. It looked around frantically, then saw the cabin light in the distance.

It came toward us, walking its hop-limp, until it saw the skin lying in a heap outside the cabin. It touched the skin like sinners touch the Bible, screeching again. Then it bent over the discarded flesh and fussed over it, doing things with its hands that I couldn't see.

"What's it doing?" I asked, scared to breathe.

"It has to pick out every grain of salt before it can wear the skin again," Doc said, his voice a tobacco-scented whisper.

Jay laughed, but I cut my eyes at him and asked, "And

when it's finished, it'll just put the skin on and be Susie again?"

Doc sighed. "It won't finish, Jezzie."

"Why not?" The thing seemed focused on the task. It looked so small now, tiny and fragile.

"The sun will be up soon. And if that hag ain't finished picking out every grain of that salt so it can get its skin back on, the sun will burn it up. Ashes'll be all that's left."

I stared out the window to Doc's cabin, letting that sink in.

"Do we . . ." I swallowed. "Do we have to watch her?" I couldn't watch a creature frantically trying to live, knowing it only had a short while—an hour or two, maybe. I wasn't that . . . strong.

Both Jay and Doc were silent. Maybe they didn't know what to say. I tugged on one of the braids Mama put my hair in to sleep.

The thing outside was a boo-hag, a monster I'd been hearing about my whole life. One that could feed on the power of rootworkers. But . . . it was also Susie. Who had spent hours running and playing with me. Who had sat with me at lunch every day. Who had stood up to Lettie and her friends when no one else would. I could still see the edge of her striped dress poking out from under the pile of her skin.

Even if she'd done those nice things to get at me and

my magic . . . she still did them.

Jay looked on, his eyes dark and closed off, as what used to be Susie continued to clean the salt out of her skin. The creature's fingers worked faster than humming-bird wings, pinching and tossing each particle over its left shoulder.

"We can't watch her burn up," I said, barely louder than a whisper.

"*It*, Jezebel," Jay said. His voice was cold. "Remember, its skin tried to turn us against each other a few minutes ago."

"Yeah, but . . ." Doc was quiet and I shook his arm. "What do we do?"

Faster and faster, the little hag's fingers flew, but the dark was already lifting from the night. What used to be Susie was shaking, crying. And it began to speak through the tears in a sweet, singsong voice.

"I'm sorry," it said. To itself or to us, I couldn't tell. "I didn't want to. I'm so sorry."

I stood up.

"Jezebel, where are you going?" Doc asked, reaching for me.

I sidestepped him, opened the cabin door, and walked out to Susie. I didn't care in that moment what she'd done to me, what she'd tried to do. I couldn't sit by and let her burn up to nothing while I watched.

"Susie?"

The monster didn't look up from its movements. *Pick, toss, pick, throw.* It looked like the drawing of the skeleton with muscles on it from my science book, only covered in red paint. If I thought about it like a science lesson, I wasn't scared at all.

"Susie?" I said again.

"What?" she choked out. "You did this, didn't you?" Her voice was hard on the edges, still soaked in tears, but somehow accepting. "I should have known."

I couldn't lie to her. "Me and Jay did it, yes."

She stopped then and looked toward the cabin, her body without skin slick under the still-dim light. Then she went back to her picking.

"Did you take the pages from my notebook?"

She nodded, still picking salt. "I didn't want you to know how to do this, in case you found out."

"I remembered it anyway." I rocked back on my heels. "What did you mean before?" I asked.

"When?" *Pick, toss.*

"When you said you *didn't want to.* What did you mean?"

Susie-thing sighed, her arms moving slower now, but still faster than mine ever could. "You wouldn't understand."

"I understand from my uncle that boo-hags are a threat to rootworkers. You try to take our power."

"I know how most of us treat most of you. Sometimes

we have a choice about that; sometimes we don't. But I never wanted to hurt *you*."

I poked out my bottom lip. "But you did."

"I am sorry, Jezebel. But I was desperate."

I waited until she spoke again. The dark was lifting, and we both knew there wasn't much time. "I'm trapped," she said. "For years now, I haven't been able to leave this island, even after my kin departed. I think . . ." She swallowed hard. "I think a rootworker—one of your kin—stole a piece of my skin. I don't know how they got it. Maybe they wanted it for a spell. I thought if I could understand your magic, I could find out what they were doing with it and how to get it back, so I can be whole again."

"A piece of your skin? But no one—" I began. I was about to say that no one in my family would do something like that, but I knew that wasn't true. Doc had said that animal sacrifices were a part of rootworking. And several spells, ones I didn't know yet, used animals. I didn't like the thought of it, but that's how it was. It was a practice older than I was, older than anyone I'd ever known. And if they used animals, I imagined they wouldn't hesitate to use parts of a monster, especially one that they thought was a threat.

"Who has it?" I asked instead.

"I don't know who. I just know it's here, hidden somewhere on this land. For a long time, I didn't know where it was, I couldn't see it." Her fingers moved as she talked.

"But a few months ago, I started having visions about where it is."

A few months ago? That was when Gran passed away. Could Gran have been the one who took a piece of the hag skin? "What's it for? I mean, what could a rootworker do with it?"

"I don't know how root magic works, that's why I took your notebook. I wanted to see if there was anything in there that could tell me what my skin would be good for." She chuckled, but it wasn't a happy sound. "All I know is not having a whole skin keeps me from going where I want to. Keeps me from seeing my family." *Pinch. Throw.*

I understood that. Despite all that had happened, my heart ached for her. I couldn't imagine never seeing my family ever again. I still missed Daddy and Gran, and I guessed I always would. But the thought of never being able to see Mama and Doc and even Jay again too was terrible. "Keeps you from being free," I whispered.

Being held down by the poppet. Being forced to watch as Deputy Collins searched through our house. The trapped feeling I had from those experiences still made my breath catch in my throat and my heart thump in fear. I wanted to be free of those situations, and they had only lasted a short time. I couldn't imagine how Susie felt being trapped in one place, alone.

"Yeah." She stopped trying to clean out her skin for a moment and sat back on her heels. The muscles moved easily under the slick layer of what I thought must be blood. "I guess I'm going to die here, huh?"

"Not if you tell me how to help you." I couldn't let her stay trapped in a place she didn't want to be. And I couldn't let her die here.

"If I knew that, I would do it myself." She sounded older than twelve now, older than Mama or Doc. "Then I could get my skin back and go home."

I bit my lip, thinking. The sky was getting lighter and I saw Doc come out of his cabin, the door creaking softly.

Susie-thing, a monster with a beautiful singsong voice, looked up at me. "Can I tell you something? You have such wonderful, strong magic. I can feel it."

"I do?"

"Yes. You and Jay both do, though he doesn't trust it yet. He likes the newness of it, he likes being able to show off, but . . . well, I guess we'll see how it develops in him." She looked up at the sky and I saw her eyes were a solid, tarry black. "Or maybe *you'll* see." She went back to picking.

"If I can get that piece of skin for you, will it help?"

She let out a sob then, so full of tears that it broke my heart. She swallowed, and the muscles in her neck tightened. "Would you really do that for me? Even though I—hurt you?"

I didn't answer in words but in actions. I turned away and went toward the water pump in the yard, filling the bucket we used to give water to the chickens.

Doc approached me while I was trying to lift the full bucket. "What are you doing?" He pulled my hands away. "Her kind feed on rootworker magic. Some have even killed us."

"I think we can trust her." I pressed my lips together. My intuition was telling me that I should take the chance on Susie. Another creature trapped in a situation she didn't want to be in. Alone, without any of her people around. Desperate to feel whole again. I understood those feelings. "Yes. We can."

Doc stared at me hard for a moment, and something seemed to shift in him. He picked up the bucket I was struggling with, and I thought he was going to toss it off into the trees, but he didn't. He carried it over to the skin and poured the water out in a huge wave, washing the rest of the salt away. Susie let out a glad cry and picked up the skin, shaking it like a coat that had been in a storage box all winter. She stepped into it and it closed around her, sealing shut just as tiny smears of yellow touched the sky.

"Thank you." She looked like the girl I'd gone to school with, mostly. "I have to go now, but I'll be back. Thank you for saving me."

We watched as Susie ran off, her feet barely touching the ground as she did.

"Y'all stupid." Jay's angry voice came from behind us.

His arms were folded over his chest and a frown creased his face as he looked at me. "Why you let it go? To kill somebody?"

I hated that he called Susie *it*. "She's never killed anybody. She had plenty of chances to kill one of us, didn't she?"

Doc just looked at the road where Susie had disappeared. "I hope we did the right thing."

"Nope," Jay said. "She'll be back all right. With an army of them things."

I took a deep breath. No matter what they said, I *knew* we did the right thing. Watching someone, or some*thing*, suffer wasn't in me.

I didn't think Susie would be coming with an army. But something told me she would be back.

19

When we got to school on Thursday, Miss Watson asked us if anyone had heard from Susie. I didn't answer, knowing that there was no reason for her to ever return to school.

For the first time, I didn't care that the other girls whispered about me, or that they put their books on the seats next to them when I walked by their tables at lunch. I ignored them all and took my bag to an empty table, where I thought about places I could look for Susie's missing piece of skin. If Gran or Doc had taken it, it could only be in Doc's cabin or in the house. I supposed it could have been buried in our fields, but if that was the case, there was no way I'd ever be able to find it. Those girls' whispers faded away as I ate, the sound like wind ruffling marsh grass. Soon, lunchtime was over and I went back to class.

"I wasn't even paying attention to those mean girls at all today," I told Jay as we walked home. "Even without Susie there, I was okay."

"That's good," Jay said. "Them girls ain't nothing noway. Who cares what they think?" He picked up a rock from the path we were on and threw it sideways. It sliced through the air and hit a young tree hard enough to make the branches shake. "Plus Doc says if you wanna be a rootworker, you gotta get used to doing things all by yourself."

"Yeah," I agreed. "I guess so."

I wondered if Doc was lonely before he came to live with us, but I guess it didn't matter now. He was here and we were all family. As we came up the path, I could see the flash of white fabric on the porch of our house—Mama was outside. And she wasn't alone.

"Jay, is Mama supposed to have company today?"

He looked up from the June bug he had caught and tied to a string. "I don't think so. Who is it?"

"I can't tell from here."

"Probably someone from the church or somebody to trade their catch for some fruit or something."

But when we got closer, we found we were wrong.

Susie was there, on the porch, talking to Mama.

She was sitting there pretty as you please in a white blouse and striped skirt, sipping on lemonade and eating Mama's benne seed cookies. Me and Jay looked at her, then at each other, then back to Susie. I bit my lip and clenched my fists, glanced into the trees all around. There was no hag army; Susie was alone. Why was she here?

Jay was about to tell her head a mess until he noticed Mama was all smiles. "Look who stopped by, Jez," she said. "Would you like some cookies while you visit with your friend?"

"Mama," Jay said, "she ain't welcome around here."

"James!" Mama scolded. "How dare you say that about your sister's company. You be nice to Susie."

"But she ain't even—"

I put my hand on his arm. "It's okay. Me and Jay were just wondering if we'd see her again so soon." I said it with a strong voice so Susie would know what I meant: that me and Jay were ready to fight if we had to.

"That's better," Mama said with a smile. I could tell she was happy we had a visitor. We hardly ever had anyone come to visit us. The boys who wanted to play ball and such with Jay played in the open field away from the house and the crops so they didn't damage anything. Mama went back inside to fix a plate and Susie turned to us.

"I really am sorry, Jezebel," she said. "I just wanted to tell you that in the light of day, when I can't take off my skin. So you'd know I meant it."

I crossed my arms. "Why did you lie to me? You pretended to be a person and pretended to be my friend."

Susie twisted her hands in her lap. "I didn't think you would help me if you knew I was a boo-hag. You would've run away, or told your uncle or your mama. And I was afraid they would kill me. I had to do something." She glanced in the screen door to see where Mama was, then turned back to me. "And I did pretend to be human, but I didn't pretend to be your friend. That was real."

I sucked my teeth the way Jay did when he didn't believe something. "But a friend wouldn't steal from a friend."

"No, you're right. I shouldn't have done that. When I saw the instructions, on how to kill boo-hags, I just . . . got scared and ripped them out."

I nodded. I could understand that. "I've . . . I've been thinking about where your skin could be."

"Really?" she said. "You'll really help me get it back?"

Jay shot me a nervous glance, but I ignored him. I'd explain my thinking to him later. For now, my intuition was telling me to trust Susie. "I'll try. Is there anything you can tell me about where it might be?"

"I don't know exactly. There are always protections around this place, so I can't tell. Your house is painted blue, so I can't go inside. But maybe, this close, I can use my power to see where it is."

She closed her eyes and sat still as a statue for a while. I reached out to poke her in the arm, but a second before my fingertips reached her, her eyes opened. "It's . . . in some kind of fancy wooden box, carved or something, but I can't see more than that." She shifted on the rocking chair.

"Okay," I said. "That helps."

"When do you think you can get it back?"

Jay had been staring at Susie for the last minute without speaking, quiet anger on his face. I was afraid I'd have to do this all myself. "As soon as I can."

"Please hurry. I've been stuck here such a long time." She sipped the lemonade. Sweat clung to the glass and the coldness slid down in drops.

"I will," I said. "But we have to be careful."

Susie's eyes flashed from black to golden, then back again. "You mean because of that policeman?"

I had been thinking more about Doc. "How do you know about Deputy Collins?"

"I see him around the rootworker farms and houses. Sometimes sneaking. Sometimes not."

I shuddered, but I couldn't let myself get distracted now. "How long has it been since that piece of your skin was stolen?" I asked.

"Twelve years."

"Twelve *years*?" I exclaimed. That was longer than me and Jay had been alive—but she looked the same age as we did. I knew Susie wasn't a human, but I realized then how little I knew about boo-hags. Maybe even Doc and Gran didn't know everything about them.

Instead of accepting what the girls at school had said about rootworkers, Susie had asked me directly. Maybe it would be okay if I did the same.

"So . . . what exactly is a boo-hag?" I tugged on one of my pigtails.

She shrugged. "I don't know. I'm just . . . me. I'm a spirit with a body. Does that make sense?"

"Sorta. Are you alive?"

"As alive as you. My skin has magical properties. I can change how it looks, but losing a piece of it means losing a piece of my power. Because that piece of skin is gone, I've been stuck looking like this. And I've been searching for it ever since."

Then I asked a question I wasn't really sure I wanted the answer to. "Where is the piece of skin from?"

Susie knew what I meant. "Here." She pulled up the right side of her blouse and there was a patch of skin missing, about the size of a large walnut, from her side. In its place was a deep, empty dark space. It didn't bleed. I reached a finger toward it, then stopped myself and drew back. Susie pulled her top back down quick and tucked it into the waistband of her skirt.

"Does it hurt?" I asked.

"No," she said. "But I can't be myself. I can't change or leave here or find the rest of my family. That part hurts."

I couldn't find my daddy, and that hurt a lot. Maybe

if I knew where he was, that would help the whole family deal with his being gone. There was no way I could refuse to help Susie find the rest of her family.

"There's one more thing." Susie pulled a square of folded paper from her dress. After a moment, she held it out to me. "These are the pages I took from your journal. I'm giving them back. Along with something else."

I took the paper. Sure enough, it was the missing pages from my notebook. I flipped through them until I got to the last page, where I found words in handwriting I didn't recognize. At the bottom was a blob of dark liquid. "What's this?"

Susie took a deep breath. "That is my promise to you, sealed with my blood: if you ever call me to help you, I will come."

I ran my finger over the drop. I thought of my idea to use black cat fur instead of the bones. Here Susie was, giving away her promise and her blood freely to me, a rootworker. She was taking a risk—that I wouldn't use it against her, like other rootworkers might. She trusted me, even though we were from different worlds.

She finished her lemonade and called to Mama through the screen door. "Mrs. Turner? I have to go now. Thank you for the cookies and all."

"Wait a minute, sweetie." I heard Mama scrabble around in the kitchen for a bit, and then she came out with a mound of folded tinfoil that she handed over to Susie.

"Here, I want you to take these with you, since you loved them so much. Come visit Jezebel anytime, hear?"

"Yes'm." Susie turned to me, and her smile was shaky but real.

From deep inside my heart an ache started, a hurt for Susie and for her loneliness. Even though she stole from me, I understood why. To protect herself. It was the same reason I was learning rootwork.

I think I gave her a smile back, but I'm not sure. My mind was already focused on finding that piece of skin.

Mama told us dinner was just about ready and went back inside. Susie stepped down off the porch, heading for the path. As she passed me, she whispered, "Thank you."

I was quiet all through dinner. So much that Mama asked why. She understood when I said I was thinking about all I had to do; she probably thought I meant homework and chores. But I meant helping Susie.

"We have to do this tonight," I said to Jay when we were in our room later. We were supposed to have our lights off, but I couldn't sleep and Jay was awake too, picking something from his teeth with a fingernail, then looking at it.

"No, we don't have to do nothing for that . . . *thing*. How we gonna find a box when we don't know what it looks like anyway? Could be anywhere."

"It's somewhere on this property. Susie said she could see it. And it's not like we have a lot of carved wooden boxes it could be in." I pulled at one of my braids. "I wonder if she could just be thinking of our house? Technically, that's a wood box."

"So, our house fancy?" Jay raised his eyebrows at me.

"No," I admitted. I flopped back on my bed with my arms over my face.

I wondered who in our family would have a carved wooden box. Mama wasn't one for pretty things that didn't have a good use. And Doc's idea of fancy really wasn't at all—he had what he liked to call *simple tastes*. I rolled over onto my belly to think. Most of the special items we had belonged to Gran, and we'd placed several of them on her grave after her funeral.

A memory rose up in me, and I bolted upright.

The box. The one I thought was beautiful the first time I laid eyes on it—on the first day Doc let us inside his cabin to start our lessons. He took it down from a top shelf, where it was pushed all the way back. When he'd opened it, it was full of Devil's Shoestrings.

"What if it's that box in Doc's cabin?" I said.

Jay's eyes got big and round. "Oh no, we ain't getting in there."

"Doc's going to go out tonight to gather plants in the marsh, so we'll have some time to look."

"'We'?" Jay shook his head. "What's-its-name done

got *you* doing its work. You on your own."

This time I wasn't going to argue with him. Not about how he was wrong, or how he had promised to not let me go anywhere alone. I just said, "Fine." I held up Dinah, whose mouth was turned way down at the moment. The new dress I got for her was already starting to look dingy. Had Dinah been going out when I couldn't see her?

Then I stood up and patted Jay on the shoulder. "I didn't expect it anyway."

"How you mean?" His look was suspicious.

"I mean I understand. You think Susie is a monster. But I can't stand to see people, or animals, or even monsters, in pain."

I shoved my feet in my shoes. Then I put Dinah's old dress, which Mama had washed and ironed, back on her. The new one I left on my bed to put in the hamper later. I tucked her in my pocket as I looked at the clock, then raised the bedroom window. I'd oiled it earlier, and it slid open without a sound.

"What you fixing to do?" He watched me but didn't make a move to get dressed.

"I'll figure it out," I said, climbing out of the window and dropping softly to the ground. "Hand me the flashlight."

He placed it in my hand. "I hope you know what it is you doing," he said.

"I do." I marched off, the flashlight swaying. The movement created shadows that crept toward me, then away, and I shivered. I thought for a moment I might hear Jay following me by the time I got down to the chicken coop, but he didn't. And that was okay. I didn't want him to get in trouble for a decision that I made anyway.

I crouched next to the coop and waited until I saw Doc leave with a basket on his arm, headed for the deeper part of the marsh. I ran on my tiptoes to the cabin and eased the door open. The scent of bark and herbs surrounded me. I breathed in deep, holding it inside me for a moment before breathing out.

The cabin was dark and warm, the boards holding on to the heat from the day. The place felt empty without Doc in it, like it was missing an important ingredient. I walked all around the space, being careful not to knock anything over. A bowl of pomegranates with ruby-red skin and some waxed-paper-wrapped peanut candies sat in one of Mama's sweetgrass baskets on Doc's worktable next to a deck of playing cards.

I looked to where I last remembered seeing the box, and found it almost immediately. It was still up on the highest shelf. There was no ladder, so I pulled over Doc's straight-backed chair and climbed onto it. Still, I couldn't reach the box. I stretched more, and the chair started to wobble. If I fell, all the glass bottles and jars on his shelves would come crashing down around me and make a huge racket. Surely Mama would hear it and come running, and then I'd be in for it.

I needed something to—there! The sharpened cane I used when I thought an evil spirit was chasing me and Jay. I hopped down and grabbed it up, then returned to the chair. When I used the hooked end, I found I could snag hold of the box and drag it to the edge of the shelf. One more yank, and the box was falling. I caught it in my outstretched arms.

"Oof!" It was heavy. The solid wooden box had a thick metal plate on each corner. I climbed down off the chair and sat on the floor.

It didn't seem to have any way to open it. There was no lock or keyhole or hinges. "What in the world . . . ?" I tilted the box, looking all over. Something was rattling around inside. As I fiddled with the box more, a thin piece of wood slid away. I gasped, thinking I broke it, but when I looked, the sliver of wood revealed a keyhole.

Resting the box on my legs, I pushed and pulled at all the panels of wood. My back ached from hunching over my task for so long. Then another sliver moved and I felt something fall into my lap. A key.

Fast as I could, I shoved the key into the lock and turned it. The lid creaked open when I lifted it. Once it was open, I held it close to the flashlight so I could see.

Empty! The box was completely empty. Only the scent

of cedarwood lay inside, and I realized the rattling that I thought came from within the box was the key in its hidden compartment. If the skin had once been in here, it wasn't anymore.

I slumped down on the floor, defeated. It was getting late. Doc would probably be back soon. I reached for the box and noticed writing in its lid:

PROPERTY OF ANNIE FREEDMAN

That was Gran's name. When she passed away, Mama and Doc went through her things, deciding what to keep, what to place on her grave, and what to give away. Mama took all of Gran's clothes and things. But Doc had taken all of her rootwork possessions: her potions, her perfumes, and all of her jars and baskets. And this box.

I leaned back against the wall of Doc's cabin. Right after Gran's funeral was when Deputy Collins came to our house, searching for who-knows-what. For as long as I could remember, Gran had said her magic would keep us safe. How could I think that, knowing other families of rootworkers had been dragged out of their homes, beaten, and jailed? Even though we mourned when other people on the island lost family and friends and property, the deepest part of me trusted that Gran would protect us. I realized why: It was because I had never seen those horrible things happen myself. Until a few months ago, I had never been face-to-face with someone who truly had the desire to hurt me. Gran had done everything in her power while she was alive to protect our family and keep me and Jay from knowing how much danger we were in every day. If she knew a spell to protect the entire house and farm by using a piece of hag skin, she would do it without a second thought.

Raise the family, she'd said to me. That was what she had done for me and Jay our whole lives. Raise up our family in the traditions of rootwork and use it to keep us protected.

But now that Gran was gone, was her spell gone too? Was our whole family without protection? I shook my head. Gran wouldn't have left us without anything to help us. But if that was so, where was the skin? Gran had been pretty sick toward the end of her life, and she didn't have much strength to do things. The last thing she did was make Dinah and breathe into her.

Dinah.

I pulled her out of my pocket. She was made of crocus, but she never felt as rough all over as a real gunnysack. I looked at her and saw her red stitched mouth was in the tiniest smile. I had changed her clothes before, but I'd never touched her headwrap. . . . My hands shook as I removed it.

There it was. Right at the back of her head, where the bright wrap covered it. The hag skin was a smooth blue color against the brown fabric and felt cool when I touched it. I'd had the skin all along. As I went to remove it, I stopped. Suppose this hag skin wasn't just for protection but was also what made Dinah move? The thing Gran used to connect herself to me? I didn't want to lose that. If I took off the hag skin, would Dinah be just like any other doll?

A wind blew up off the marsh, bringing its dark, muddy scent. It also brought the memory of the haint in the marsh that tried to steal my power. When I floated up and out of my body that first time, I understood what Doc had been telling me this entire time: Rootwork is a connection to my ancestors, my traditions, and my heritage. It is a practice I share with people from hundreds of years ago. I felt them around me, watching and supporting, waiting for me to call on them for guidance. Now I knew I could call on my ancestors for guidance at any time, even Gran. I didn't need Dinah. It would be okay.

I got up and found Doc's sewing kit and took out a pair of tiny scissors. With care, I snipped away the stitching that held on the hag skin. It came away easily, and I put it in my pocket. Then I gently replaced Dinah's headwrap. Her smile was exactly the same as before I removed Susie's skin. I gave her a squeeze.

Through the woods I walked, shining the light on the ground so I could avoid any traps that might be hidden. It made my progress slow, but finally, I got to the tree where

Susie had left her skin that night. I ran my light back and forth, then down and up, only managing to irritate an owl. It blinked at me, then gave an unhappy hoot.

"Sorry," I said, returning the light to the ground.

"Hi, Jezebel."

I managed not to shout in surprise, but my heart beat like ten drums. "Susie!"

"Did I scare you? I didn't mean to." Her eyes looked black as Mama's patent-leather pocketbook.

I eased the square of skin out of my pocket and held it out to her. It shimmered in the moonlight, turning all shades of blue, from indigo to haint blue and back again. "Here," I said.

"You found it!" She took it gently and lifted the hem of her blouse. When she touched the skin to that empty space, it wobbled, then sealed itself right onto her side. I couldn't even tell where the space had been only seconds before.

Tears flowed from her eyes and I felt mine start to burn too. "Thank you. I'm whole again, because of you."

I nodded. "You're welcome."

The owl hooted again, making us both jump. We giggled, exactly as we did when we ran along the marsh, ate tomatoes out of the garden, and skipped rocks. Exactly as we did when we were friends.

"You are an amazing girl, Jezebel."

I looked down at my feet, embarrassed at all her praise.

When I raised my head an inch, something had changed. Her feet were no longer in shoes. And they were floating a tiny bit above the ground.

My head snapped up. "Susie?"

She stood in front of me, looking somehow the same but different. Her face and eyes looked older, less scared.

"I'm free now." Susie looked at the night around her. "I can leave this place."

Part of me was sad to hear it, but pride also swelled up in me. "Where will you go?"

"Wherever I want. I'm not bound anymore. Nothing was made to live like I did. I felt— It doesn't matter. Maybe I . . . I might fly until I'm tired and see where I am. Then I'll try to find my family."

My smile was wide and real. I knew what it was like to fly. "Good luck, Susie."

"Thank you again."

"It was the right thing to do."

Her face changed into something I couldn't read. When she spoke, her voice sounded far away. "I wonder if you'd say that if you knew some of the things I've done."

My blood turned cold. I didn't want to ask, but the question slipped out anyway. "What did you do? Susie?"

She looked away and I remembered Jay saying, *She's a monster.* She didn't answer, but she said, "I consider you a friend, Jezebel Turner. I won't forget what you did for me."

The monster walked away, her feet no longer in buckled

Mary Jane shoes, floating just above the dirt. In a few breaths, I couldn't see her anymore. She faded into the distance and into the air of the marsh.

"Goodbye," I said, sure she could hear me.

The monster.

My friend.

20

When I got to school, Miss Watson told us that Susie wouldn't be returning because she and her family were moving out of the area. Then she went on with the lesson. I was so busy wondering if I was ever going to see Susie again, I didn't hear Miss Watson call on me to answer a math question. She had to call my name twice more before I answered.

"Sorry, Miss," I said, my face going hot at the laughter from the other kids in the class. I swung my feet, letting them hit the legs of my desk.

"Where were you, Jezebel?" she asked. She sounded annoyed.

"I'm here. Now."

Giggles came from the class, and Miss Watson frowned. "That I can see. Where were you a moment ago?"

"Worrying—or, wondering," I corrected myself. "I'm sorry."

"Don't be sorry," she said, sharp as lemon juice. "Tell me the answer to the question."

I said the first thing that popped into my head. "Eighteen?"

Miss Watson's eyes rounded into two soup spoons. "That is correct." She smiled, then turned back to the class and went on with the lesson.

I breathed out, knowing I was lucky for the answer coming to me so quickly. For a moment, I wondered if I had more things on my side than I knew about.

After school, a few boys asked Jay to walk with them. I told him he should go on ahead. Truth was I wanted to be by myself for a while. I didn't know what to think about Susie. I didn't know if Susie was evil or not. She'd said there were things she'd done that she couldn't tell me. What could those things be? The memory of that sharp-toothed smile in the water, hearing that terrible voice echoing from the pond, made my stomach twist. Quick as lightning, I remembered the taste of that murky water as it went in my nose and mouth. There was no way Susie did anything like that. She'd admitted she never wanted to hurt me.

The whole time I was worrying about these things, I walked home slowly to the sounds of Jay and his friends tossing a ball and laughing fifty yards ahead of me. A chilly crosswind came up and I shivered, pulling my little jacket closer over my dress. From the corner of my eye, I saw a shadowy movement, a swift blur of beige, blue, and brown. When I looked, it was gone. After that, I clutched my books close, keeping my eyes on the road in front of me.

Both me and Jay were surprised when Mama came out of the house with her black leather Sunday pocketbook. She locked the door and scurried down the steps.

"Where are you going?" It was strange for Mama to be home at three thirty in the afternoon, right when we were getting home from school, and even stranger to see her leaving the house again. I couldn't be sure, but I thought I saw tears in her eyes. When she spoke, her voice sounded like she'd been crying. "Come on, kids. We're all going to the church."

Jay made a face. "Church? Ugh, do we have to? It ain't even Sunday!"

I almost stumbled trying to catch up with Mama as she headed off at a high-stepping pace. "But we're supposed to have root lessons. I—"

"Listen to your mother," Doc said in his no-nonsense voice. He seemed to come out of nowhere, but I knew he had his own hiding places. "Today is not a day to talk back. There will be no root lessons today, but you'll learn something all the same."

"Are you coming too?" Jay's face was slack, his eyes wide. He turned to me with a look that said, *What is going on?*

I shrugged and mouthed to him, *I don't know.*

"We're all going together as a family. Just like we did for your gran." Doc cleared his throat, then placed a hat on his head and strode off after Mama. His legs ate up the distance, and he was soon next to her.

Oh no, I thought to myself. If we were going to the church and it wasn't a Sunday, it was because someone else in our community had passed away. Jay came up close to me, his shoulder touching mine. It felt good to feel him next to me then.

"Who died?" I shouted after Mama and Doc, but they didn't answer.

The church hall was so crowded we could barely get inside, and once we did, it was overheated with the crush of bodies. So many of the island's people were there, crying and mourning. Even some of the girls from school who teased me were there. I tensed up, but they were with their own families, heads down, arms wrapped around themselves. Others looked lost and afraid as they watched their parents cry. Most didn't see me. Those who did searched my face for answers to what was happening. I didn't have any.

Lots of folding chairs were arranged in front of a TV screen, and I found an empty one for Mama at the end of a row, near a cracked-open window. I directed her there, then sat on the floor at her feet. Jay plopped down next to me. Doc stood next to her and yanked his hat off.

Me and Jay looked at each other, his face showing the same confusion that must have been on mine. We didn't have a TV in our house; even so, we had never gone over to the church just to watch a TV program. What was going on?

Pastor Robertson turned the set on and adjusted the antennas to bring the picture in clearer. He turned a knob to make the sound louder. We all watched the newsman's serious face as he took off his eyeglasses and looked directly at the screen. His voice boomed across the hall.

President John Fitzgerald Kennedy is dead. A nation mourns as it has been confirmed that he was shot and killed as his motorcade passed through Dallas, Texas, today.

A wail went up from the people gathered. Cries erupted throughout the church hall. Weeping filled the close room. People leaned on each other for support.

At Gran's funeral, Pastor Robertson had said President Kennedy had helped pass laws to make life better for many people, including Negroes. We had hope that the country would start to become a better place for us because of him. He was a powerful man who wanted to help. Now he was gone.

Mama cried silently, rocking back and forth in the creaky folding chair. "Not one more thing, Lord," she whispered. "I can't take one more thing right now, please."

I hugged her leg and pressed my face to her knee. "It's gonna be okay, Mama," I said.

Jay lay his head in her lap without saying a word. We didn't know everything this meant to the island or for Negroes or for the whole country, but Mama breaking down in front of people was something we'd never seen before. I felt helpless, like there was nothing I could do to fix anything.

One of the women of the church came over and hugged Mama. I thought she might try to pull away and straighten herself up, but she leaned into the older woman and cried.

"Mama?" I asked.

Doc kneeled down then and took me and Jay by the hand. "Come on, you two. We're going on a little trip."

"Where?" Jay asked.

"I need to stay with Mama," I told him.

"She has support right now," he said as he led us away, nodding to the older woman rocking Mama back and forth like a baby. "Come with me. I need a few things from the graveyard."

When we stood there staring at him as he headed off, he called back over his shoulder to us. "Come on. I'm not telling your mother I left you here."

We walked down to the church cemetery.

"Why is everybody so sad? None of those people knew that white man," Jay said.

Doc let out a heavy sigh as he walked. Cooler air blew off the sea, surrounding us as we marched behind him. "It isn't because we knew him like a friend or a family member, Jay. It's the loss of a man who had tried to help our people. It's the loss of an idea that one day we will finally be equal in this country."

"And safe."

"Yes, Jez, and safe," he said. "Now I'm going to show you another way to help keep yourself safe. And since we don't have anyone else to help us here, we have to help ourselves."

The graveyard faced east, all the stones and markers laid out in a fan shape bordered with saw palmetto and evergreen trees. When we got there, Doc unwound the chain from the ironwork gates and pushed them open. They didn't squeak at all. Jay elbowed me and I jumped, but managed not to yell out. I cut my eye at him something serious and he stopped. I realized he was scared. I grabbed his hand and we followed Doc.

There was no one else paying respects to the dead in

the cemetery; all of that was going on inside the church. Even so, Doc said that people mostly didn't come here unless it was a new grave, or a holiday, like Christmas, when the graves would get fresh red poinsettias, or Easter, when they would get white lilies.

Doc leaned over close to one of the headstones and whispered to it. Then he took out a small bottle and sprinkled the liquid over the grave.

"I haven't showed you how to pay for graveyard dirt yet," he said.

"You don't just dig it up and take it?" Jay said, making a face.

"I told you before, that's stealing." Doc ignored our frowning faces. "When getting dirt from someone's grave, you must be respectful and do it right. First, you have to ask permission to take some of the dirt. This is a person's final resting place. You wouldn't walk into someone's house and take anything, would you?"

Me and Jay shook our heads.

"Well then. Once you do that, you give the person a gift. Best if you're familiar with the person—then you'll know what they like." Doc pointed at the grave he sprinkled the liquid on. "That's one of my friends I used to play cards with. He loved root beer."

"Is that it?" Jay was unimpressed.

"There's other ways to pay for graveyard dirt, but until you show you got a little bit more between your ears"—he poked a finger at each of our foreheads—"I'll keep them to myself."

I smiled and Jay pouted.

"Go fill those pouches and we'll head on back."

We filled pouches with the graveyard dirt and tied them up tight, putting them in Doc's big bag. Doc said a prayer and instructed us to walk backward out of the graveyard because we didn't want to bring any haints home with us. As we did, we thought we heard Mama talking.

Doc heard it too and put a finger to his lips to keep us quiet. We crept slowly closer, finally coming around a tall tree, and there we saw Mama sitting in front of a head-stone. Gran's headstone. She was talking, but we couldn't see who she was talking to. When we tried to get closer to see better, Doc told us not to bother.

"She's not talking with anyone on this side; she's talking to your gran."

I had never heard of Mama doing that with anyone else, especially not in a graveyard. Sometimes, we put flowers or dolls or other little gifts on the graves of people we knew, but we never stayed to talk. But here Mama was, sitting and talking to her mother. Since Gran's spirit had come to wish us a happy birthday, I guess there was no reason Mama couldn't visit her and spend time.

We heard Mama give a soft cry, then blow her nose. I started off toward her, but Doc put a hand on my arm and shook his head. "Let her be. We'll go home now. If she wants to talk to us, she will."

In a line, the three of us wound our way through the cemetery and back to the house. Since we didn't know when Mama would come home, we all started the jobs she usually did. Jay went to feed the chickens and get a few eggs, and Doc went to dig the vegetables out of the ground: sweet potatoes, mustard greens, onions. He even pulled up a few of our peanut plants, so we could boil them for a snack later. I knew how to make a cornbread and I got to doing that so Mama wouldn't have to. The batter was all mixed up and in the iron skillet when Mama came in, her eyes looking red and tired.

Without a word, she washed her hands in the sink, then took the skillet from me and put it in the oven and set the little white kitchen timer next to the stove. Then she collapsed onto a chair and sat there looking at me and at Jay across the table. Doc sat next to her, and he made a point to keep his eyes elsewhere while she slid her gaze away from us kids and over to the window.

"What is it?" I asked, not able to help myself any longer.

She looked back at us and smiled. The biggest smile I'd seen on her in a long while. "Sometimes," Mama said, "a little talk makes things all right."

21

By the next Thursday, Mama was still in a good mood, and she had both me and Jay working for her in the kitchen from the time we got up. There was so much to do on Thanksgiving Day that she needed as many hands as she could get. Especially since she didn't like doing any of the work the day before.

The meal we made wasn't only for us. We would deliver some of it to other people on the island who were too sick or elderly to cook for themselves. We would also return the dishes to the families who brought us food after Gran died. But we would never return them empty, because it was bad luck.

After a breakfast of grits with flakes of fried shark steak, Jay washed dishes while I snapped a whole colander full of pole beans. Mama kept an eye on both of us as we moved on to peeling sweet potatoes, then layering them in the pan. The stove was burning so hot, it felt like the middle of summer in the house. All the windows were open, but the cool breeze that managed to make it through got warmed up by the time it hit us.

Doc brought in a large chicken for Mama to season and put in the oven. Jay and I gathered up pecans from our tree as Mama made the crust for a pecan pie. We spread a sheet of newspaper between us on the kitchen table and started shelling them. It was one of the few jobs we never needed reminding to do. Since our tree made papershell pecans, Jay and me would take two of the oblong nuts in one hand and press them together until the shells cracked. Once there was enough of an opening in the nuts, we would pull the sweet-tasting meat from the shells, doing our best to keep each half in one piece. We would race to see who could open the most nuts the fastest, but it didn't matter who won, because we all would have some of Mama's pecan pie after dinner.

Once the pies went in the oven, we helped each other wash a bushel of collard greens straight from the field—we did it three times to get all the bugs and dirt out. Mama fried a piece of salt pork—what my gran called "streak o' lean"—in her great big pan, then took out the strip of hot, crispy meat and sat it on a folded paper towel to catch the grease.

My mouth was watering, but we couldn't have it until all the work was done for dinner. We dumped huge handfuls of chopped collard greens into the thin layer of pork fat until they overflowed, then we pushed them down in the pot and topped it off with water, seasoning, and the lid.

"I think that's it, y'all," Mama said, wiping her hands on her apron. "I'll do the rice and gravy when we're almost ready to eat." She took her sharp knife and cut the slice of salt pork in half, the crisp sound of the meat making my belly rumble.

Me and Jay each took our half and went out on the porch, chewing and licking our fingers. The air outside the house was cool and fresh, and we dragged it into our lungs to clear the heat and smoke from the kitchen.

There was no need to bother with our jackets or shoes—the work would keep us warm for a while still. Since I knew Mama was going to tell us to bow our heads before dinner and say what we were thankful for, I asked Jay what he was going to say when it got to be his turn.

"I dunno." He looked down at the porch step and picked at a bit of loose wood. "What you gonna say?"

So much had happened to us in the last year, both good and bad. It didn't seem right to pick just one or two things to be grateful for. It didn't even feel right to only choose the good things, because you could learn from mistakes.

I leaned back on my elbows on our front porch and looked out over the farm. I closed my eyes and breathed in, letting the beads of sweat on my skin dry up in the cool air. Behind me, I could hear Mama's slippers shuffling around on the hardwood floor, and she was humming. I didn't know the song, but it didn't matter.

"Home," I said.

Jay nodded. "Me too."

When we finally went to bed, it was dark. In spite of everything that had happened, we'd had a good day visiting people on the island and bringing food to those that needed it. Some of the people were worried about how life would be now without a president who wanted to make us Negroes equal in the eyes of the law, but Mama and Doc told them we would do what we always did: help each other and try to survive. It seemed to cheer people up, hearing those words, and I realized that Mama and Doc were doing a little something to fill the gap that Gran left behind too.

The last person we visited was Mr. Benjamin. We brought him a batch of Mama's peanut candy and half of a pound cake. He accepted the gifts with thanks and invited us in for a drink of sweet tea. He also held out his hand for me to shake, then gave me a special thanks for telling him that his daughter was doing well and was happy.

On the way home for our own dinner, Jay was unusually quiet. I nudged him in the side to get him to race me home, but he didn't move any faster.

Finally, when we got to our road, I stopped him. Mama and Doc kept walking, knowing we were within earshot if me or Jay needed them.

"Well, what is it?" I asked my brother, who wouldn't look me in the face.

He didn't answer for a few moments. "Jez, do you think you growing up faster than me?" He asked the question so quietly, I knew he felt ashamed to be asking it.

"What do you mean?"

"You know, you're a grade above me now, and you're already way better than me at rootwork and all," he said. "You were able to do something for Mr. Benjamin, really help him. And I . . . I ain't done much at all for anyone."

"No, I don't think so. We're gonna be good at different things at different times. That's normal. It doesn't mean you're not getting better. We—"

I stopped myself. It was clear now that Jay didn't want us to get far apart like I thought he did when he wanted Tony to be his blood brother. I had been scared we were growing apart, and here he was, scared I was going to outgrow *him*.

"Well," I said, "since we're gonna have different things happen to us, then it means it's even more important we stay close."

He nodded, his lower lip puffed out a bit.

I threw my arm around his shoulders and gave him a quick squeeze. "Don't worry. I'm not gonna leave you."

He let me hug him for a minute before he pushed me away. But it meant he was back to himself. Tough on the edges, trying to hide his softness. "One thing I ain't worried about is you, Jezebel." But his smile was twitching the corners of his mouth as he ran down the path to our house.

"You better be," I yelled before racing after him.

Dinner was wonderful. A little sadness still curled inside me because this was the first time we'd ever had a Thanksgiving dinner without Gran. She loved to cook and she loved to take care of all of us, so she didn't let us do much work toward making the meal. But this year, everyone had a part in creating this food, and we were grateful for that.

By the time dinner was over, me and Jay both needed to lie down.

"You had a good day, Jez?" Jay asked me, yawning wide and long.

I smiled and hugged my pillow. "I did. I wasn't sure I would, because it's been a hard week in a lot of ways."

Jay sucked his teeth. "Been hard longer than that. Been a hard school year for you so far."

"And it's not even half over yet!" I rolled onto my back. "Don't remind me, Jay. Let's just enjoy what's left of this day."

He grinned at me. "It was a good day. And good pie." He rubbed his belly.

I swallowed a laugh when I felt a cold chill of intuition come over me. Something was happening. My head felt light, like it was lifting away from my body. That meant it was something bad.

Jay felt it too—I could see it on his face. He jumped out of bed and into his overalls and ran out of our room. I scrambled out of bed, threw my clothes and shoes on, and followed my brother.

Doc was at his worktable, surrounded by the bags of grave-yard dirt we collected for him. He also had a red brick in front of him on the table, broken into big chunks, and he was pounding them into powder when we arrived.

"What's wrong with you two?" he asked.

I sat down on one of the stools to catch my breath. "We . . . felt something bad was going to happen. I can't explain it."

Doc stopped what he was doing. "You feel it too, then?"

I nodded. "It was strong. I got really cold all of a sudden."

Doc hummed deep in his throat while he bit his lip. "Whatever it is, we need to be ready for it. Help me mix this up now."

We made two more pots of graveyard dirt mixed with brick dust and some rock salt; then we poured it in a wide circle all around the cabin. When we were done, me and Jay followed Doc up to the house to do the same there.

"You had already started making this when we came in. Do you know what's going to happen?" I whispered, keeping my bowl of protection powder close to my chest.

"I don't." He took a deep breath. "But there's something in the air, something off, and it concerns me."

"Intuition," I said.

He nodded.

"You always follow it?" Jay asked, his pot of dust almost empty. His lines of the mixture were thicker, wider than mine.

"Be generous with it, Jezebel," Doc said. Then he answered Jay. "Yes, most times. But sometimes, people forget to listen to it, that little voice that makes you stop and think. Makes the hairs on your arm stand up. Ever feel that?"

Jay nodded.

"Did you listen to it?"

"I did this time," he said.

I poured the last of the dirt, and the three lines of powder—Jay's, Doc's, and mine—came together in a broad oval around the house. "Now what do we do?"

"We go inside and wait."

At Doc's instruction, we carefully stepped over the

dust circle. Any smudging of the line would kill its protection, leaving us open to whatever was out there. When we got inside, Jay went to tell Mama what we'd done.

"I know how protection circles work, Jay. I watched you all. My question is," she said, squinting at her brother, "will it help if Deputy Collins shows up here? Or are you expecting some haints?"

Doc threw up his hands. "I don't know. Could be anything, Janey. Anyone. We just need to be prepared. This farm is all we have."

"Along with our lives."

"That goes without saying." Doc frowned. "But we're a family, and we can handle whatever is coming together, right?"

Mama pressed her lips together. Then she said, "Right." She looked at me and Jay. We threw our voices in as well.

"Right!"

I started to feel a little better.

And that was when Doc's cabin exploded.

22

Thick, black smoke poured out of what was left of the cabin and rose toward the sky. Flames crackled, adding the scent of burning pine to the overwhelming smells from all of Doc's potions and oils combined. As the wind blew, it shifted the smells: sweet spices to bitter moss to a plain funky, nasty stink.

Doc made like he was gonna run outside, but Mama grabbed his shirt. "Are you a fool? You don't know who or what is out there." She glanced at us. "You two get away from there."

But it was too late. We were already at the window, looking out at the burning cabin and farther, down the path into the marsh, now lit up by the flames coming from the fire. Jay saw it first, and he jerked back, away from the window.

"Mama," he yelled, pointing.

Then I saw it.

A slow-moving police car was coming up the path. No sirens, no lights, only the flames reflecting off the shiny black-and-white car.

"Edwards?" Doc asked, edging closer to the window.

"No," Mama said from the middle of the kitchen. "I don't think so."

The car stopped a good spitting distance from the porch, and the door eased open. We all held our breaths, not moving.

"Wrong time of year for a barbeque, ain't it, y'all?"

"Collins." Mama ground the name out from between her teeth.

We could hear his laughter through the closed window. A hush fell inside our house as we all looked at each other.

"Well, then," Mama said, and stomped off to her room. When she came back to the kitchen, she had a gun. It was so small, Mama's hand almost covered it completely. But I could see enough of the dark silver-gray metal to know it wasn't a toy. And it wasn't nothing to play with. Mama meant business.

Me and Jay each ran for opposite corners of the room while Doc stood there in shock. "Where on God's green earth did you get a pistol?" he asked. When Mama didn't answer, Doc kept at her. "What do you think you're gonna do with that? Shoot somebody? Then where are you gonna be?"

Mama's lips flattened out into a thin line that reminded me of Dinah's. "I will protect my family, John."

I had never heard Mama call Doc anything other than, well . . . Doc. Hearing his government name was more than a surprise. It made me look at him in a whole new way.

Jay tiptoed away from his corner, and I met him behind the big kitchen table. He slid his hand into mine, and Doc slowly stepped forward toward Mama. Her hands were shaking.

"I know you will," he said. "You always were the protector, even though I was born first. It's time to let me take on my responsibility, Janey. It's way past time."

Mama took in a deep, shuddering breath, as her fingers slid over the smooth metal of the gun. "I was never afraid of the ghosts, you know."

Doc nodded. "I've been knowing that." He brought Mama her favorite apron, the one with the palmetto trees on it. The one with the big pockets. "Put this on. Keep that with you if it makes you feel better." He nodded at the gun. "But I need you to trust me that this is all going to be okay."

She looked at Doc first, then at me and Jay standing together. Then she nodded once and slipped the small gun into her pocket.

"Evening to ya," the deputy yelled from the bottom of the steps. He looked like a ghost set against the darkening night. "Got a call there was a disturbance out here."

"You're not even wearing a uniform," I yelled back.

"Hush up," Jay said from the side of his mouth.

"True enough, girl." Deputy Collins grinned and pulled up his dungarees at the waist. "Thing is, as an officer of the law, don't matter what I got on when it comes to doing my job."

"Oh, I'm not doing this. I'm not dealing with this foolishness." Mama shoved her way past Doc and opened the door. The heat from the fire hit our faces and took the chill off the night. Once Mama was out on the porch, she folded her arms across her chest. "What do you want out here?" Her voice was hard.

"Nothing to do with you, Janey, so don't get all worked up. I'm here for your brother."

"Stay back." Mama's head tilted up, and I couldn't tell if she was talking to the deputy or me and Jay. She moved over to block the open door. "For what reason?"

Me and Jay crouched down under the window. What could we do? Jay looked at me for an answer and I didn't have one. Out of habit I reached in my pocket and froze.

Dinah wasn't there. She was in our room, and I didn't dare move to go back there and get her.

But I did have the coin, the one I got from my trip to Zar. I rubbed it, flipping it round and round in my fingers, thinking. Thinking that if I had stayed there in that place of joy and beauty, I wouldn't be here now. And I knew I was supposed to be. I had to find a way to help.

"That's between me and him," Deputy Collins continued. "A man-to-man discussion. Tell him to come on out. Or I got a lot more gasoline where that came from." He placed one hand near the gun on his side. "I know you must be in there, Doc. You shoulda just stepped in that trap—then I wouldn't be out here now."

"My brother ain't—"

"It's okay, Janey." Doc placed a hand on each of our shoulders and gave a gentle squeeze. Then he went to the door. "Here I am, Collins. Leave the rest of them be."

"Doc, don't you do this," Mama warned.

"I don't see another way. Do you?" Doc's voice carried over the sound of our breathing, loud in the kitchen and against the still-crackling fire burning the remains of the cabin. "He will burn this place to the ground, you know it as well as I do. And he won't serve a day of jail time for it."

Mama's mouth opened and closed without a sound. She knew he was right; the laws didn't protect us—they were apparently only there to protect whites from us. Finally, she nodded.

The moment Doc stepped through the door onto the porch, Collins drew his gun and aimed it right at him. Even in the dying light from the fire, I could see it was much bigger than the one Mama had in her pocket.

"Good boy," he said. "Let's go now."

Doc frowned at the insult. After a second passed, he stepped down off the porch. He walked to Collins, twisting his face away from the heat of the fire and smothering smoke. We watched as both men approached the deputy's car. Doc went toward the back door, but Collins yanked him away by the neck of his shirt. Doc stumbled and reached out his hands to stop his fall. Collins brought the bottom of his gun down on his head.

"No!" me and Mama and Jay said all at once.

Doc stumbled again, but didn't fall. Not until the deputy hit him two more times with the nightstick he pulled from the belt around his waist. Collins turned back to us where we stood in the doorway of the house, frozen in shock, and grinned.

"Your brother got a harder head than your husband did, Janey. His split open the first time I hit him. Made such a mess, I threw him into Charleston Harbor for the ocean to bury."

Jay looked at me, and I knew he was thinking the same

thing as I was. Did what Collins said mean he . . . killed Daddy?

Mama blinked for a second. Then she screamed.

She tried pulling out her own gun, but it caught in the seams of her apron pocket. She yanked at it until I heard the fabric rip, but I was already running. Out of the kitchen and out the front door.

"Jezebel!" Jay's voice joined Mama's. I heard them, loud and scared, cutting through the sound of the fire. But there was no time for me to stop.

Outside, the smells were even stronger, burning wood and sweat and fear and hate. I ran down the steps out to the circle we'd laid earlier to protect us. Thumps came from behind the police car, where Collins had dragged Doc after he brought him to the ground.

A gunshot rang out, but I didn't know which direction it came from. I threw myself down to the dusty ground.

"Get back in here, Jez!" Mama's voice was going hoarse.

"I have to open the circle!" I yelled back.

"Jez, no!" Jay yelled. "What are you doing?"

I knew exactly what I was doing. Still, I worried it might not be enough. Through all the commotion and fire and the gunshot, would anything hear me? And even if they heard, would they come to help?

When I opened my mouth, the sharp smell from the gun firing mixed with the smoke coming from the cabin, and I swallowed it. It tasted like burnt toast dipped in motor oil and made me want to throw up. Instead I coughed, trying to get the smoke choking me to come out. On my belly I crawled, pulling myself along, to the edge of the dust ring. I smudged it with my hand until I'd made a wide opening.

Then I crawled though.

I turned toward the cabin, the wood burning lower now but still too high for me to get close enough to rub away the other circle. I sighed in frustration and beat my fists against the dirt, hot on top from the close fire, but cold underneath.

What could I do? I was eleven years old. And Collins was no haint that you could keep away with paint or dust. He was a grown man, an angry, violent one at that. I couldn't punch and kick and fight him to save Doc.

But maybe I could do something.

I sucked in a mouthful of thick air and held it in while I lay on the ground. Somewhere in all of that smoke were the potions and herbs Doc, Jay, and I had created together. It was full of our family's magic, made by our own hands with love and intent. Protection magic. Root magic. My lungs full of rootwork-rich air, I relaxed every part of me. Slowly, I felt myself lifting up, up away from my body.

The sounds of fear fell away as I lifted into the air. Looking down, I saw my uncle. Collins had him on the ground and was hitting him with his nightstick. The blood on Doc's skin was shiny under the firelight. Doc was trying to turn over and cover his face, but Collins kicked him in the side. Neither one of them noticed me above them. Or noticed my body on the ground where it lay not far from the car. Drizzling rain started to fall. I couldn't feel it, but I could see the drops plink off my body. Now was the moment I had to do something.

I couldn't do anything to make him stop, not from where I was. So, fast as I could, I flew down our path to the marsh. Through the cool night I flew, deep into the woods and away from the stink of smoke and hate.

As I went, I cried out for help. I remembered my root bag, still hidden under the house, full of my own breath that brought it to life. I concentrated on that little orange bag, and I hoped it had worked. I hoped I had a friend, somewhere, that would answer my cries.

Under my floating body, I heard a bush rustle. I heard the scrabbling of feet on dirt and dried leaves. Then I heard another sound, one I'd been hoping for.

Wow-oo-wow, wow-oo-wow.

Will you come? I asked. *I need your help.*

The big red wolf I'd saved stood up from a thick bed of leaves, pawed the ground. The smaller red wolf I'd seen with the first did the same. Soon, five wolves stood in a circle under me, yipping softly and prancing around.

Thank you, I said. *Thank you so much. Follow me!*

I flew back through the trees, edging around the marsh and back toward home. The wolves followed, used to traveling quietly to catch their food. I lost sight of them as I returned to my body with a hard jolt.

I opened my eyes and they stung with smoke. I shook my head to clear out the dizziness. Then I got to my hands and knees and crawled along the ground, around to the back of the police car, where Collins had Doc.

"There!" I yelled, standing up and pointing to the deputy. "He's the one!"

Collins looked around at me. His eyes had an angry fire in them and his lips pulled back from his teeth. He glanced at Doc, then back at me.

He pulled his gun from the holster at his waist. I froze, unable to move. My heart jumped in my chest, then it felt like it fell down into my stomach and lay there like a huge weight.

Thunder boomed as a fork of lightning shattered the night. Rain poured down, soaking me to the skin in an instant. I saw a glimpse of evil as Collins grinned at me. His finger moved, white against the dark of the gun.

I closed my eyes and put all my effort into thinking about that root bag. *Help. Please. Someone.*

As I spoke, a wind blew up, a sulfur-scented hurricane. But this was no normal storm. It had come up too fast, and it smelled like the marsh, full of life and the promise of freedom. The wind brought the rest of the burning cabin down to ashes, soaking it with icy rain.

It raged on, and I thought I could hear the call of a

screech bird—an owl or a hawk—within it.

A furious growl sounded behind the deputy. There was a gasp that reached my ears even over the wind, then a wail unlike any other sound I'd ever heard. When the wind died down, I finally opened my eyes. A blue-skinned creature was kneeling in front of me, and Collins was on the ground moaning in pain.

"Hello, Jezebel."

"Susie?" I asked.

When the creature nodded, I gasped. She was bigger than last time, and her fingers were longer than any I'd ever seen. Her nails were sharp like claws. In the firelight, the claws looked dark and wet.

My legs almost gave out, I was so relieved to see her. "You came!"

"Of course," she said. "We're lunch buddies, remember?"

There was a scrabbling that came from the ground, and I looked over to where Collins lay.

Or used to lay. He was now standing, leaning one injured hand against his car. The other hand still had his gun trained on both me and my friend.

"I don't know what kinda monster you are, but I'm pretty sure you ain't bulletproof."

Bushes rustled as streaks of red-brown fur bolted toward Collins. He didn't have time to face the attack. Before I could draw breath again, he fell to the ground with a loud grunt. His gun slid out of his hand and spun across the hard dirt to land at my feet.

The largest wolf had Collins pinned to the ground, its huge fangs bared. The other four wolves snarled and moved in closer, making a tighter circle to make sure he couldn't escape.

"Good babies," I said.

Collins turned to look at me, and his eyes were wide and full of fear. "Get . . . get it offa me. Get this dog offa me!"

"It's actually a wolf," I said, smiling.

One wolf grabbed Collins's ankle in its teeth, and the deputy howled with pain. Another wolf snapped its teeth around his wrist, and they dragged him off, away from the fire, until I couldn't see them anymore.

Doc groaned, and I rushed over to him.

"Can you walk?" I asked, taking his arm. He tried to turn over, but he was so weak and hurt, he collapsed in my arms. I pulled, trying to lift him up, but he was too heavy. I couldn't move him at all.

"Come on, Doc! Please get up!"

"Do you need my help, Jezebel?"

I nodded. "Yes, please."

Susie lifted Doc's limp body in her long, thin arms as her patent-leather black eyes searched my face. "Are you all right?"

"I'm fine."

I scrambled to my feet and headed for the house, with Susie carrying Doc behind me.

On the way, I carefully picked up the gun by its handle, using my dress. We went up to the house, where Mama stood on the porch. I gave her the gun, and she went inside and wrapped it in one of her old aprons. Even in the dim light from our lamp, I could see the blood on Doc. I went inside, but Susie stayed where she was on the porch.

"Your house is blue, Jezebel. I can't enter on my own. You have to bring me in."

Even though Susie looked different, I wasn't scared. I took her arm and led her inside. Her skin was warm to touch and it slid around on her bones a little, which was strange, but I didn't let her know I thought so.

The blue-skinned hag laid Doc down on my bed. He was in bad shape, with bruises and cuts all over his face and neck. He was bleeding from somewhere on top of his head too; I could see the red trickling down from his salt-and-pepper gray hair.

Mama looked at Susie. Her eyes widened, but she didn't say anything. Instead, she checked Doc over, then wet a few rags with cool water and a little dish soap. She gave one to Jay, then plopped down on Jay's bed. "Help me clean your uncle up, please."

"Is he dead?" Jay asked.

"No, thank the Lord," Mama said. "I'll have no more

ghosts in this house. Bad enough beating, but he'll live. He'd better."

"What about you?" Jay asked me.

"Now that everyone is home, I'm okay." I hated to ask the question, but I felt like I needed to know if I ever wanted to sleep safe again. "What about Collins?"

"It's a good thing you opened that circle, Jezebel," Susie said. "Circles hide you from beings like me. I wouldn't have been able to help if you hadn't."

I opened my mouth to say that wasn't an answer, but Susie wasn't finished. "He won't be bothering you again, if those wolves have anything to say about it." Susie put her hand on my shoulder. "That was some impressive magic, there."

"Thanks," I whispered. I ran my teeth over my lip. "I need to take care of Mom and Doc."

Susie gave me a soft smile with her blue lips closed. Then she turned to go.

"How can I repay you?" I asked to her back.

She made it to the porch, then turned around. "I'm repaying *you*. You saved my life. Let's call it even."

"Does that mean we won't see each other anymore?"

"I said I consider you a friend and I meant that. Do you still consider me your friend?" She looked a little worried about my answer, but I smiled.

"Yeah, I do. You're my best friend." I ran out to the

porch and hugged her. Her dress was too thin for this type of weather, but she didn't seem to be cold. "Except for Doc and Mama and Jay."

"You're my best friend too, you know." She hugged me back. "Remember that, okay?"

"Okay," I said as she leaped from the porch into the night sky.

Doc woke up as Jay and Mama washed his wounds, then covered them with a healing oil we'd made. He drank a little medicine, then went back to sleep. Mama stayed up to watch Doc, sitting in the chair in our room. Me and Jay lay on Mama's bed in opposite directions: his head near my feet and mine near his head.

"I knew Daddy didn't leave us," I said, holding Dinah while she nestled in the crook of my arm.

"Yeah," Jay said. "He wasn't that kinda person. He wanted to stay with us."

"But Collins . . ." I couldn't say the words, but I thought them. *Collins killed our dad.*

"I know."

The look in Jay's eyes told me he really did know how I felt. He wasn't just saying it. Sick inside, hurt, and maybe a little tiny bit of relief that we now knew for sure what happened to our dad.

"Do you feel better?" I asked him. "Now that you know?"

He thought about it a long time before he answered.

"I don't know when I'm gonna feel better. I imagine it's gonna hurt for a long time."

Dinah's hair wrapped around my fingers and her hums turned into a lullaby I remembered Gran singing to us. The ache squeezing my heart eased up a little, and somehow, I was able to fall asleep.

First thing in the morning, when the sky was lightening up, I heard a sharp knock on the front door. When I answered it, Sheriff Edwards stood there, hat in hand.

I didn't feel afraid of him the way I had been of Collins. I led him to the room I shared with Jay, where Mama had fallen asleep in the chair beside Doc. He kneeled down next to her. Slowly, Mama woke up, frowning and rubbing her eyes. When she saw the sheriff there, she jumped up out of the chair with a gasp, looking around the room.

"Everybody okay?" he asked her.

Mama nodded. "I'm fine, and so are the kids. Doc'll be fine after a while. Collins did a number on him."

"Speaking of," Sheriff said, "I need to deal with Collins. What happened to him?"

Mama stared him straight in the eye and said, "Justice." She walked over to where she had the gun Collins used in her apron and gave it to the sheriff.

Sheriff Edwards looked right back at her like he was searching for something. Then he took it carefully and nodded. "All right, then. So are the rumors true?" he asked, a half smile on his face. "Have I got myself a family of witches within my jurisdiction?"

I tapped him on the shoulder and he turned to me. "A family of rootworkers," I said, proud to admit it for the first time. "Or witch doctors is fine too."

"So we haven't scared you away?" Mama whispered so she wouldn't wake Doc up.

"I want to help make things better, Mrs. Turner." He sighed. "It might take some time, but I'm here to stay."

They both focused on me—Mama standing in front of the rocking chair and Sheriff kneeling on the floor at her feet. Mama took my hands in hers when she told me, "You know this can't get out to anybody, Jez. If it does, we could all be in real big trouble."

A little worry still lived inside me, but I knew we could handle anything that came our way. We were Turners, and Turners don't run from anybody. I touched the Devil's Shoestrings bracelet on my wrist. It no longer scratched my skin when I wore it. The bracelet had become part of me, just as rootwork was a part of who I was. Who my family was.

"That's okay." I smiled, full of hope and promise. "I know how to keep a secret."

23

When Gullah people die, babies in the family are passed over the coffin so the dead person won't come back from the beyond to take them away. No one did that today with me and Jay. Not because we were too old, but because Daddy didn't have a coffin. We didn't have to dig a big rectangle for him to be buried in. There was no way to find where his body was to bury because the water would have taken him away long ago.

Even so, we as a community on this island still came together to say goodbye to one of our people. Me and Jay had learned enough rootwork to add our own handmade powder to the line of protection surrounding the marsh as people walked in, carefully stepping over the line we made to get to the water's edge. Some of the kids at the funeral service were girls from school, who had laughed when Lettie told me how stupid and backward rootworking was. But they lifted their feet and stepped over my line of protection powder just like everyone else. I looked at them until they turned away and kept their eyes on the ground. Today, not even they would dare to say anything nasty. Another death in this community was a reason for all of us to come together, not tear each other apart. I shook my head and poured out the rest of my powder, then tucked the bag into my pocket.

Me and Jay were old enough to share stories of the man we remembered our daddy to be when the pastor asked. We were old enough to add our voices to the songs of mourning and rejoicing that he was in a better place.

Dinah wriggled in the pocket of my best dress. The same black-and-gray one that I'd worn to Gran's funeral. Mama had to let the seams out for me to fit into it. Under Dinah's headscarf, the little patch of hag skin was gone, leaving a paler brown piece of cloth. But I had stitched her crepe wool hair back down and tied the bright scarf back in place, and she was good as new. I smoothed her hair and she calmed after squeezing my finger with one of her tight curls.

Turns out Gran didn't need the hag skin to make Dinah alive. She was so powerful that her blowing her breath into the doll was enough to make her move, and smile, and make me feel connected to my grandmother even though she was gone. One day, if I studied hard and learned everything I needed to, I might be just as powerful as she was, and make as much of a difference in the lives of our people.

Finally, we all gathered around the water's edge to have a homegoing service for Daddy. Mama wore her black dress without her hat this time, and the breeze, mild for early December, ruffled her pressed hair. Her eyes looked shimmery, like they were brimming with tears, but instead she turned her face into the wind and breathed deep. She kept her eyes open, and when she looked back down at me, they were dry and calm, like some kind of peace had been returned to her. She walked through the bulrushes and cordgrass to the very edge of the marsh's waterline. She mouthed a few words I couldn't hear, then threw a rose made of woven palmetto leaves into the water. Doc followed and did the same. Then Jay.

Mama turned to look at me, but she didn't have to tell me it was my turn this time. I walked up to the marsh, a place that had held such fascination and fun and fear for me, and placed my feet at the edge of the water. Here was where I had almost lost everything, even my life, but it was also the place where I found that I was connected to the people who loved me. And it didn't matter that some of them might be gone for now. I was here, and I would remember them, always.

"I love you, Daddy. I miss you so much. Good luck on your journey to Zar." I threw my own rose—the first one I'd made that held together the way it should—into the water.

After I did, one of the older women from the church began to sing, and soon the rest of the people's voices joined in as we stood on the bank and watched the water ebb away, taking the Gullah roses out into the sea.

I didn't feel alone anymore. Things will always change. People grow up, move away, or even pass on, but I now knew it didn't mean they'd left me alone. I'd made friends, ones I didn't expect. I'd found my connection to my family, my people, and my magic.

I reached out and took Mama's hand, then Jay's, and watched as he reached for Doc's. We stood together as a family, and finally, I added my voice to the song.

Author's Note

I wrote *Root Magic* because of two Helens: my grandmother and my great-aunt.

Big Helen was my grandfather's sister, born and raised on one of Charleston's Sea Islands. She was a rootworker who always told the best stories, punctuated by her table-slapping laugh. Clients came to her for helpful spells: to find jobs, do well on a test, or address a health condition if they couldn't afford a doctor.

My grandfather married a woman named Helen, who was the daughter of a pig-and-tobacco farmer. My grandmother wasn't a fan of rootworking. She wanted me to stay away from it and focus on education, so I could get a good job and take care of myself.

Because of the two Helens in my life, I wanted to write a book that showed some of the challenges of living in a family with very different views on rootwork. I also wanted to feature the two worlds many Gullah-Geechee people live in: the one they were born into and the one they learn as they grow older and enter school, meet friends, and encounter people not familiar with our way of life.

Speaking of rootwork, it is not a religion. It's a spiritual and magical practice whose traditions have been passed down either in families or to apprentices who have sought training. Rootwork, along with many of our food traditions, is one of the connections Gullah-Geechee people share with the African continent. Some say that Black people don't have our own culture, folklore, and traditions, but that's far from the truth. We have a cultural link to the African continent, inseparable from the American part of our culture where we survived chattel slavery by making a way where there was none.

Rootwork exists in many variations wherever African-Americans are. (Although it's sometimes called hoodoo or conjure or a host of other names.) Its original purpose was to make life better for the rootworker and those around them. In the earliest examples of this magic in the United States, protection spells took precedence. As time went on, additional spells—luring love, luck, and financial success—increased in popularity.

I've seen a great deal about conjure magic in books and movies. Many of them portray conjure magic and those who use it as an evil that must be destroyed. In reality, rootworkers are regular people who hold jobs, pay taxes, raise families, and are compensated for their knowledge and talents.

Both of the Helens in my life are gone now, off to that place beyond far. I set the story back in the 1960s, a troubled and terrifying time in South Carolina. It was a time when both Helens lived and dealt with many of the things described in this book. In fact, much of this book is based on their stories (and my mother's too!). *Root Magic* is my way of remembering both women, their work, and their sacrifices to educate me and bring me up with the best of both worlds.

Acknowledgments

My sincerest gratitude and appreciation go out to my family—both here and gone—for all you've sacrificed and all you've taught me. Especially to my mama: thanks for giving me you. To my husband for being the most amazing, loving, supportive, and patient man I've ever known.

There are so many others I'd like to thank, but I'd have another book if I named them all. But I'd be remiss if I didn't mention:

Justina Ireland and Saundra Mitchell for reading early versions of *Root Magic* and encouraging me along this path. Sara Makeba Daise for your knowledge, your work, your love of our people and your continued support. To those who've read and loved my short stories and asked me about writing a novel.

Last but not least, to my fellow Gullah-Geechees for being resilient and connected people who have always made a way when there was no way.